THE HARDY BOYS

Undercover Brothers®

PAPERCUTZ™

THE HARDY BOYS GRAPHIC NOVELS FROM PAPERCUTZ

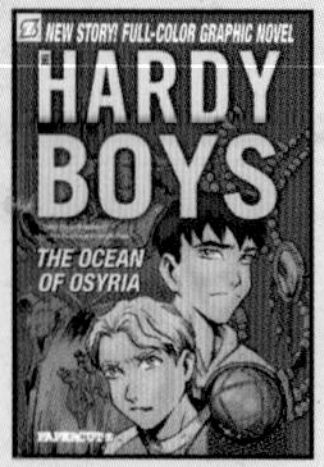
NEW STORY! FULL-COLOR GRAPHIC NOVEL
HARDY
BOYS
THE OCEAN OF OSYRIA
PAPERCUTZ

#1 "The Ocean of Osyria"

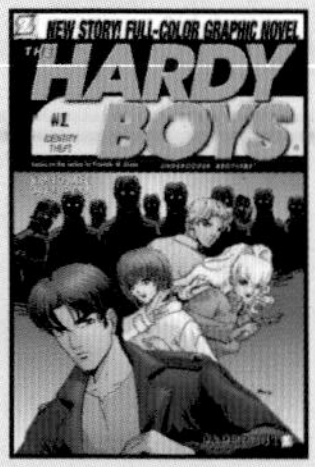
NEW STORY! FULL-COLOR GRAPHIC NOVEL
HARDY
BOYS

#2 "Identity Theft"

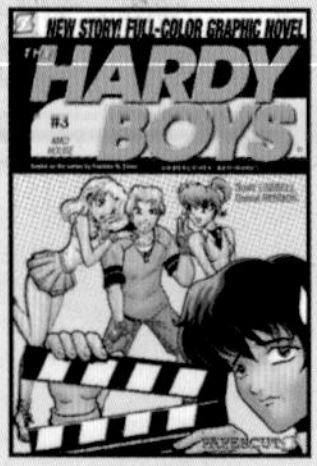
NEW STORY! FULL-COLOR GRAPHIC NOVEL
HARDY
BOYS
PAPERCUTZ

#3 "Mad House"

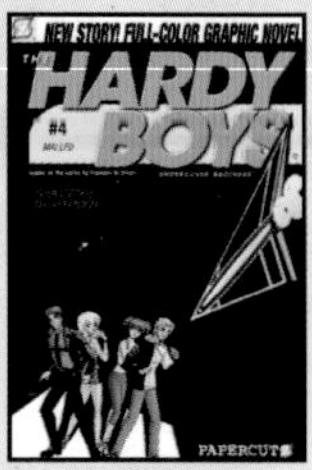
NEW STORY! FULL-COLOR GRAPHIC NOVEL
HARDY
BOYS
PAPERCUTZ

#4 "Malled"

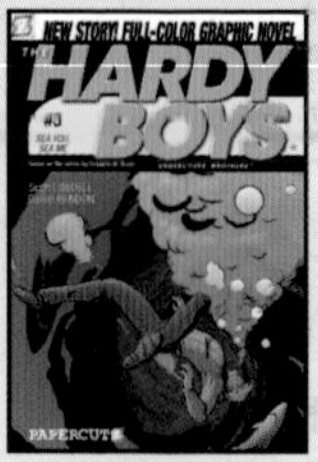
NEW STORY! FULL-COLOR GRAPHIC NOVEL
HARDY
BOYS
PAPERCUTZ

#5 "Sea You, Sea Me!"

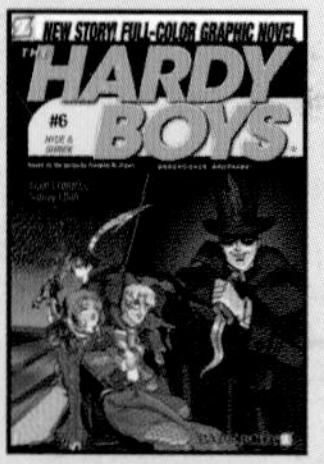
NEW STORY! FULL-COLOR GRAPHIC NOVEL
HARDY
BOYS
PAPERCUTZ

#6 "Hyde & Shriek"

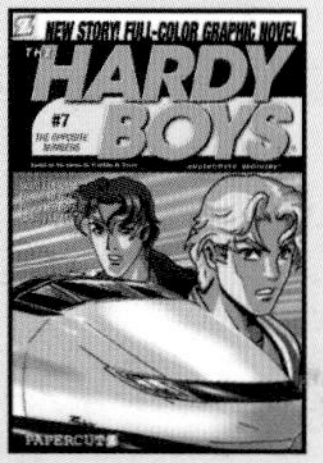
NEW STORY! FULL-COLOR GRAPHIC NOVEL
HARDY
BOYS
PAPERCUTZ

#7 "The Opposite Numbers"

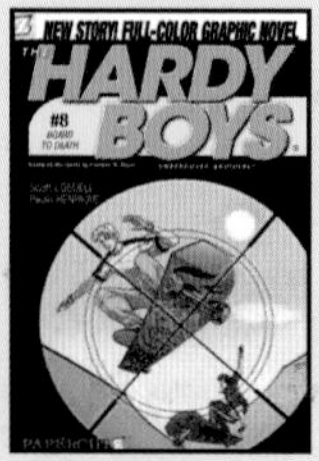
NEW STORY! FULL-COLOR GRAPHIC NOVEL
HARDY
BOYS
PAPERCUTZ

#8 "Board To Death"

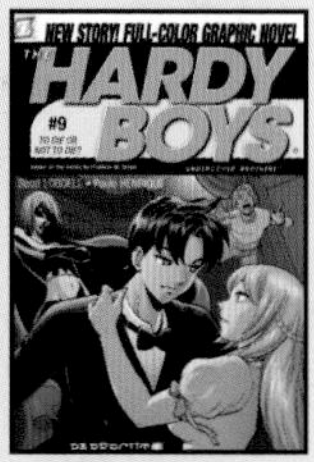
NEW STORY! FULL-COLOR GRAPHIC NOVEL
HARDY
BOYS

#9 "To Die Or Not To Die?"

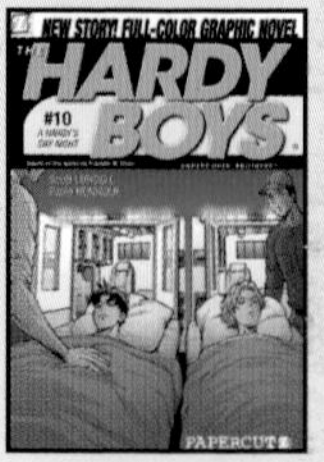
NEW STORY! FULL-COLOR GRAPHIC NOVEL
HARDY
BOYS
PAPERCUTZ

#10 "A Hardy Day's Night"

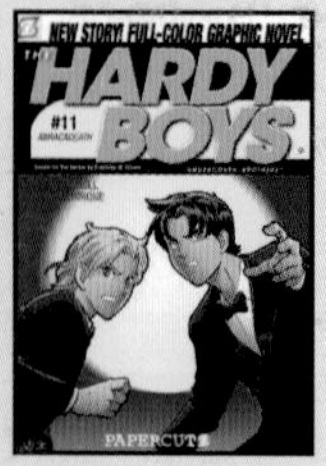
NEW STORY! FULL-COLOR GRAPHIC NOVEL
HARDY
BOYS
PAPERCUTZ

#11 "Abracadeath"

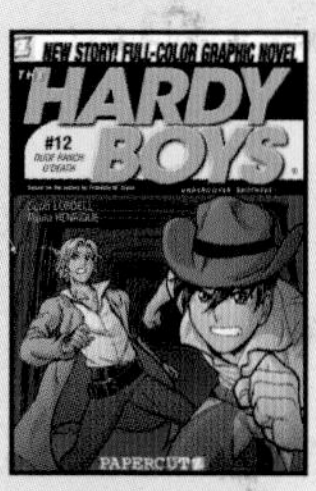
NEW STORY! FULL-COLOR GRAPHIC NOVEL
HARDY
BOYS
PAPERCUTZ

#12 "Dude Ranch O' Death!"

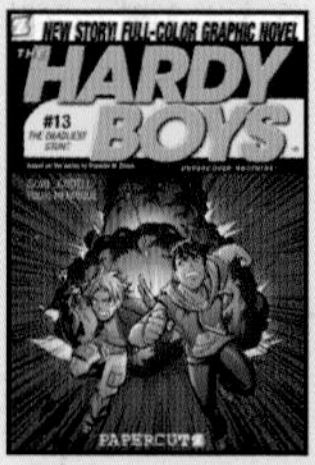
NEW STORY! FULL-COLOR GRAPHIC NOVEL
HARDY
BOYS
PAPERCUTZ

#13 "The Deadliest Stunt"

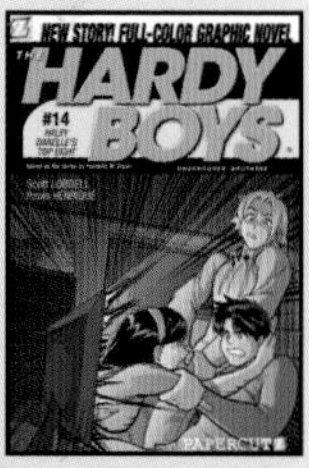
NEW STORY! FULL-COLOR GRAPHIC NOVEL
HARDY
BOYS
PAPERCUTZ

#14 "Haley Danielle's Top Eight!"

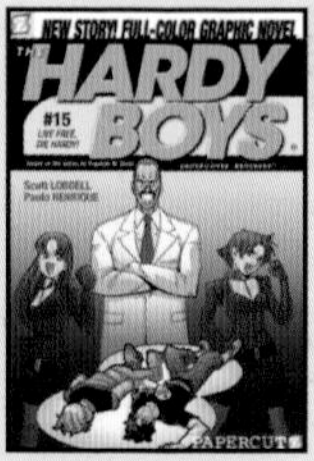
NEW STORY! FULL-COLOR GRAPHIC NOVEL
HARDY
BOYS
PAPERCUTZ

#15 "Live Free, Die Hardy!"

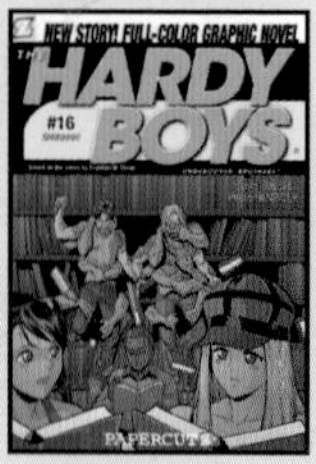
NEW STORY! FULL-COLOR GRAPHIC NOVEL
HARDY
BOYS
PAPERCUTZ

#16 "Shhhhhh!"

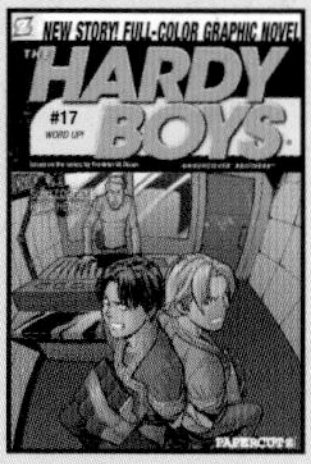
NEW STORY! FULL-COLOR GRAPHIC NOVEL
HARDY
BOYS
PAPERCUTZ

#17 "Word Up!"

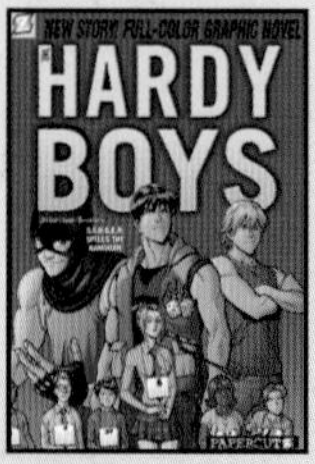
NEW STORY! FULL-COLOR GRAPHIC NOVEL
HARDY
BOYS
PAPERCUTZ

#18 "D.A.N.G.E.R Spells the Hangman"

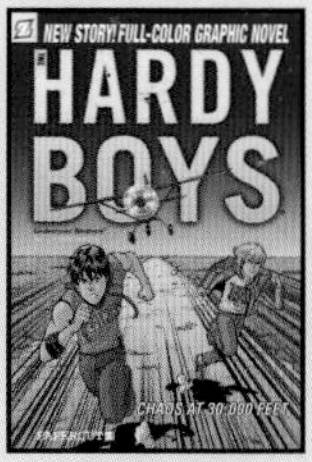
NEW STORY! FULL-COLOR GRAPHIC NOVEL
HARDY
BOYS
CHAOS AT 30,000 FEET
PAPERCUTZ

#19 "Chaos at 30,000 Feet"

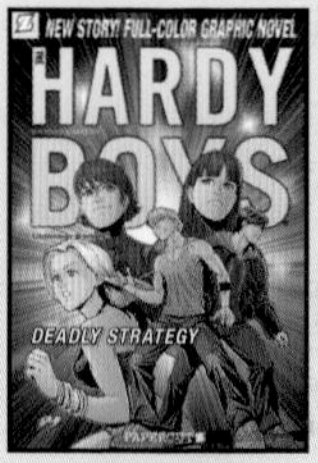
NEW STORY! FULL-COLOR GRAPHIC NOVEL
HARDY
BOYS
DEADLY STRATEGY
PAPERCUTZ

#20 "Deadly Strategy"

$7.95 each in paperback, $12.95 each in hardcover except #20, $8.99 pb/$13.99 hc. Please add $4.00 for postage and handling for the first book, add $1.00 for each additional book. Please make check payable to NBM Publishing. Send to: **Papercutz, 40 Exchange Place, Suite 1308, New York, NY 10005 • 1-800-886-1223 • www.papercutz.com**

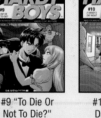

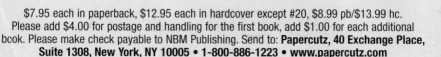

THE **HARDY BOYS**

Undercover Brothers®

#20 *Deadly Strategy*

SCOTT LOBDELL • Writer

PAULO HENRIQUE MARCONDES • Artist

Based on the series by
FRANKLIN W. DIXON

PAPERCUT**Z**™

New York

Deadly Strategy
SCOTT LOBDELL — Writer
PAULO HENRIQUE MARCONDES — Artist
LAURIE E. SMITH — Colorist
MARK LERER — Letterer
CHRIS NELSON & CAITLIN HINRICHS — Production
MICHAEL PETRANEK — Editorial Assistant
JIM SALICRUP
Editor-in-Chief

ISBN: 978-1-59707-182-6 paperback edition
ISBN: 978-1-59707-183-3 hardcover edition

Printed in Korea
May 2010 by Tara TPS
192-1 Sangjisuk-ri, Kyoha-eub,
Paju-Si, Kyunggi-do 413-836

Distributed by Macmillan.

10   9   8   7   6   5   4   3   2   1

CHAPTER ONE: "DEATH... IN BLACK AND WHITE!"

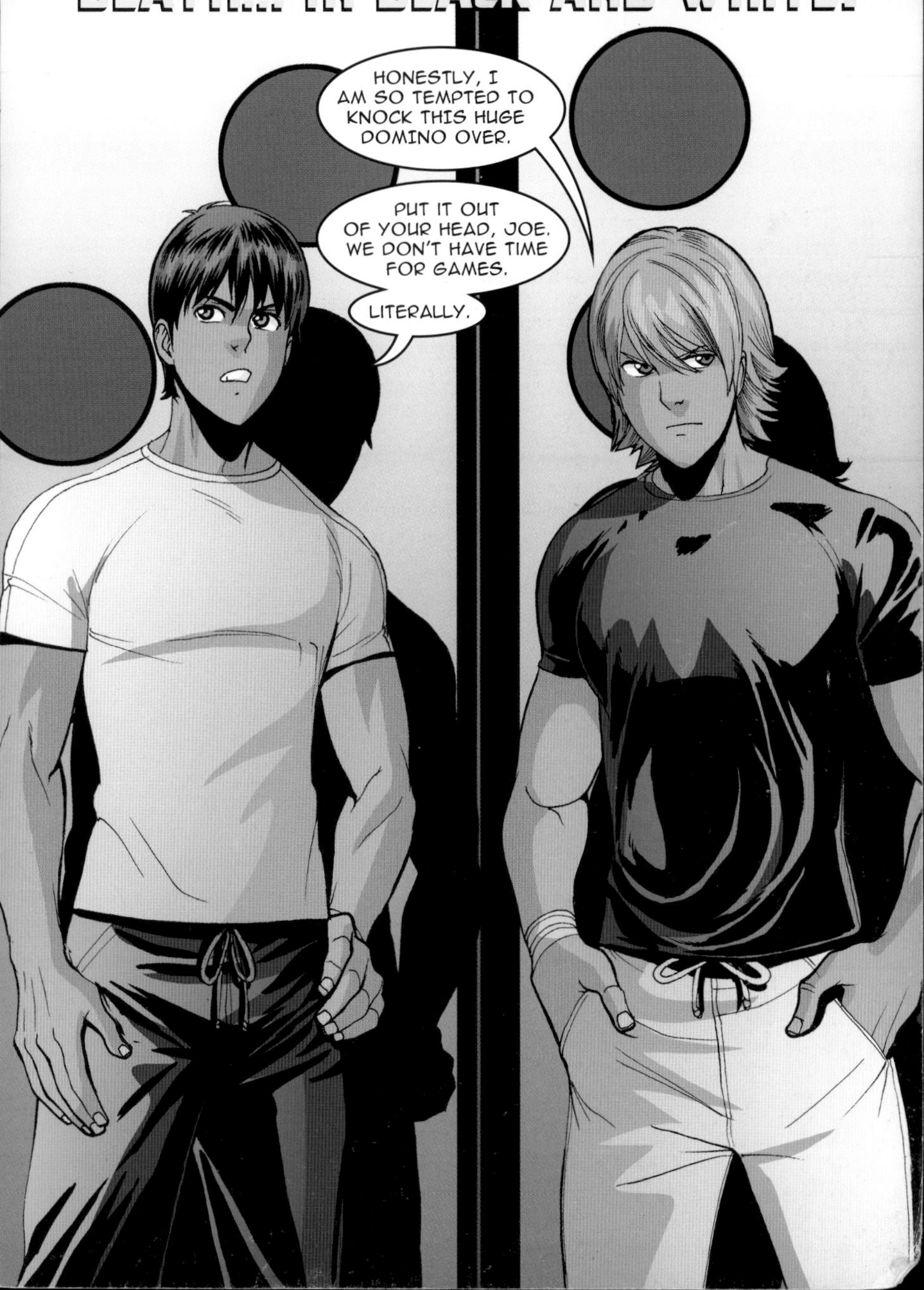

HONESTLY, I AM SO TEMPTED TO KNOCK THIS HUGE DOMINO OVER.
PUT IT OUT OF YOUR HEAD, JOE. WE DON'T HAVE TIME FOR GAMES.
LITERALLY.

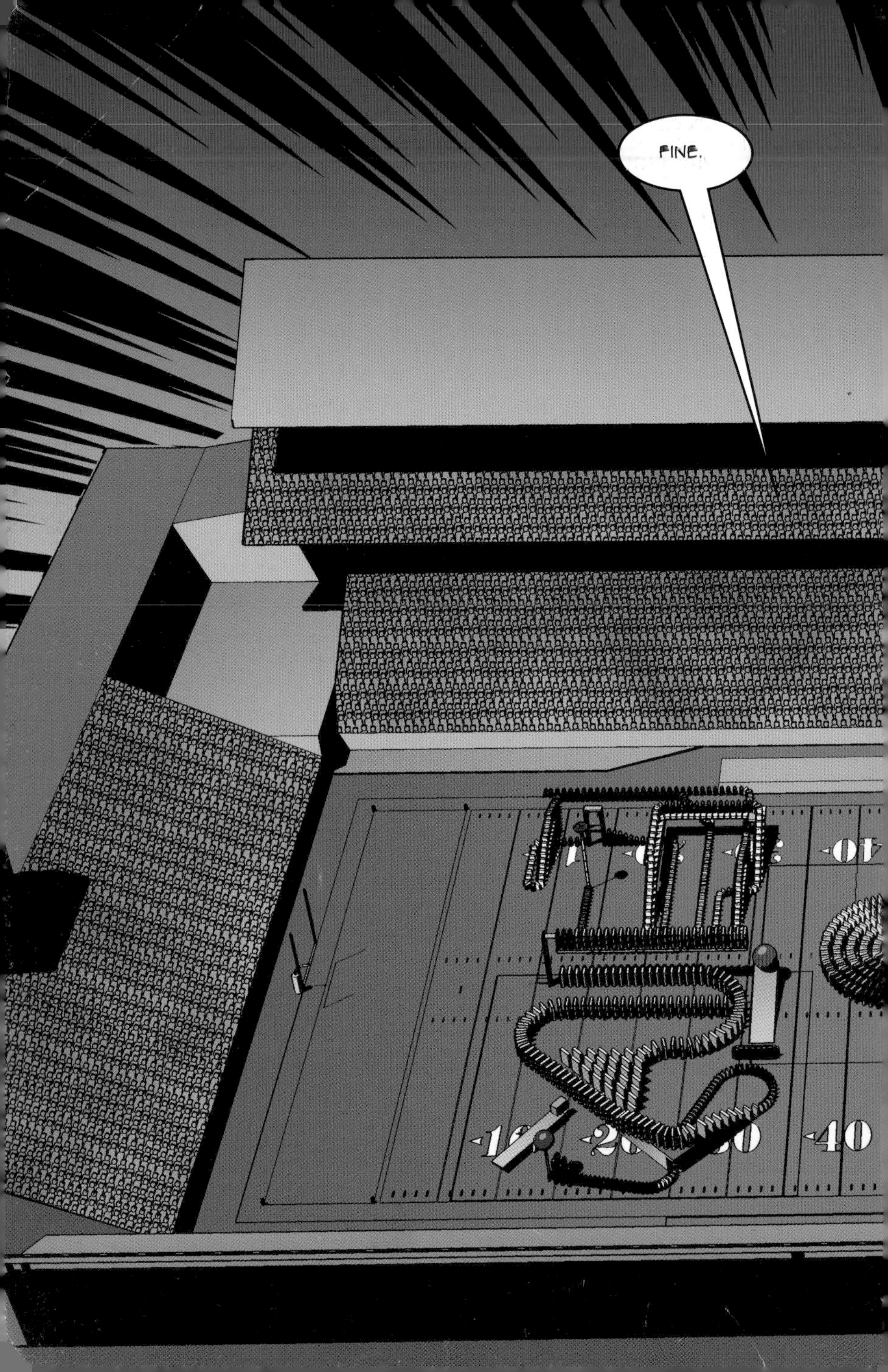
FINE.

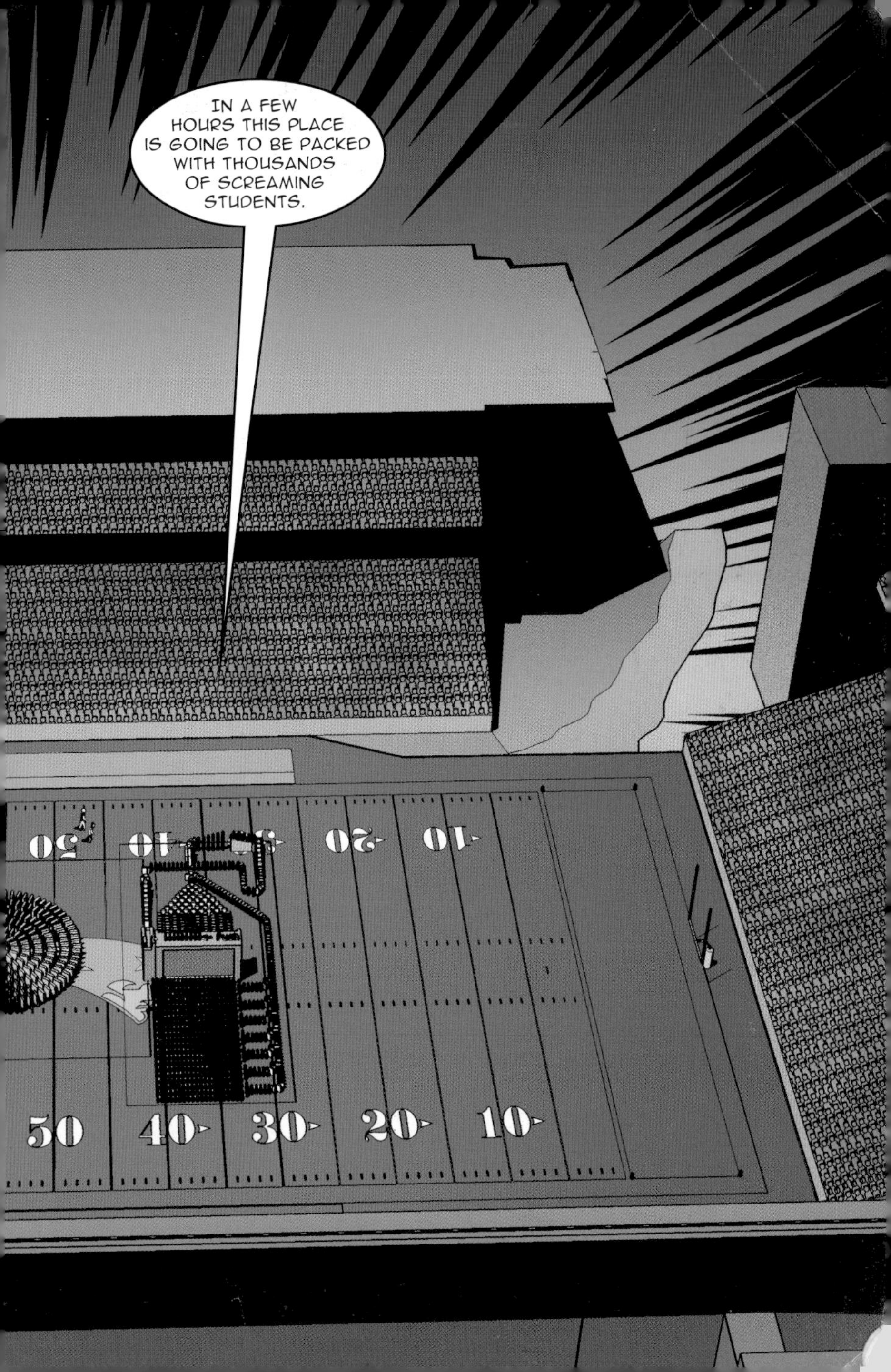
IN A FEW HOURS THIS PLACE IS GOING TO BE PACKED WITH THOUSANDS OF SCREAMING STUDENTS.
50 40 30 20 10
50 40 30 20 10

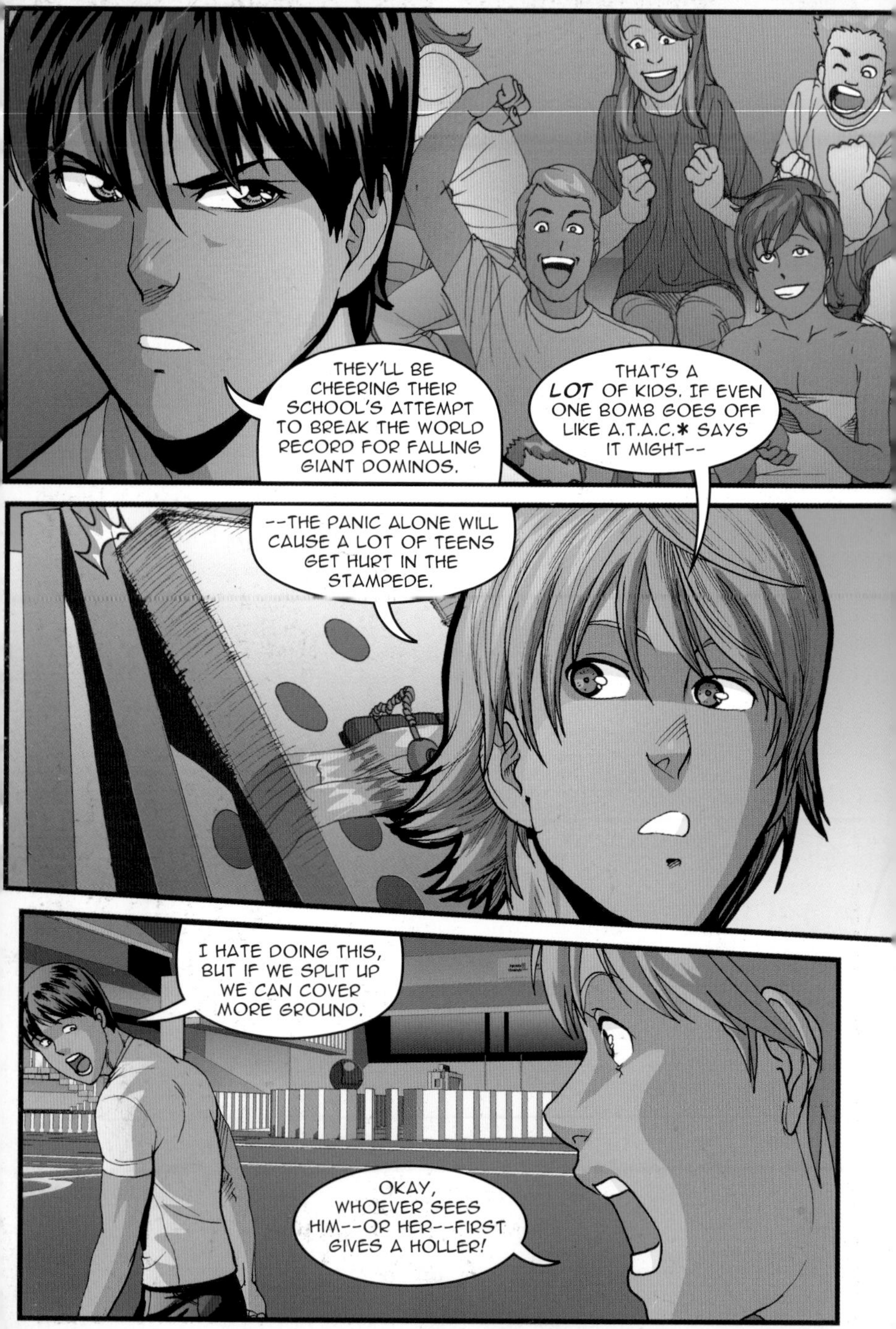
THEY'LL BE CHEERING THEIR SCHOOL'S ATTEMPT TO BREAK THE WORLD RECORD FOR FALLING GIANT DOMINOS.
THAT'S A *LOT* OF KIDS. IF EVEN ONE BOMB GOES OFF LIKE A.T.A.C.* SAYS IT MIGHT--
--THE PANIC ALONE WILL CAUSE A LOT OF TEENS GET HURT IN THE STAMPEDE.
I HATE DOING THIS, BUT IF WE SPLIT UP WE CAN COVER MORE GROUND.
OKAY, WHOEVER SEES HIM--OR HER--FIRST GIVES A HOLLER!

***A.T.A.C.: AMERICAN TEENS AGAINST CRIME.**

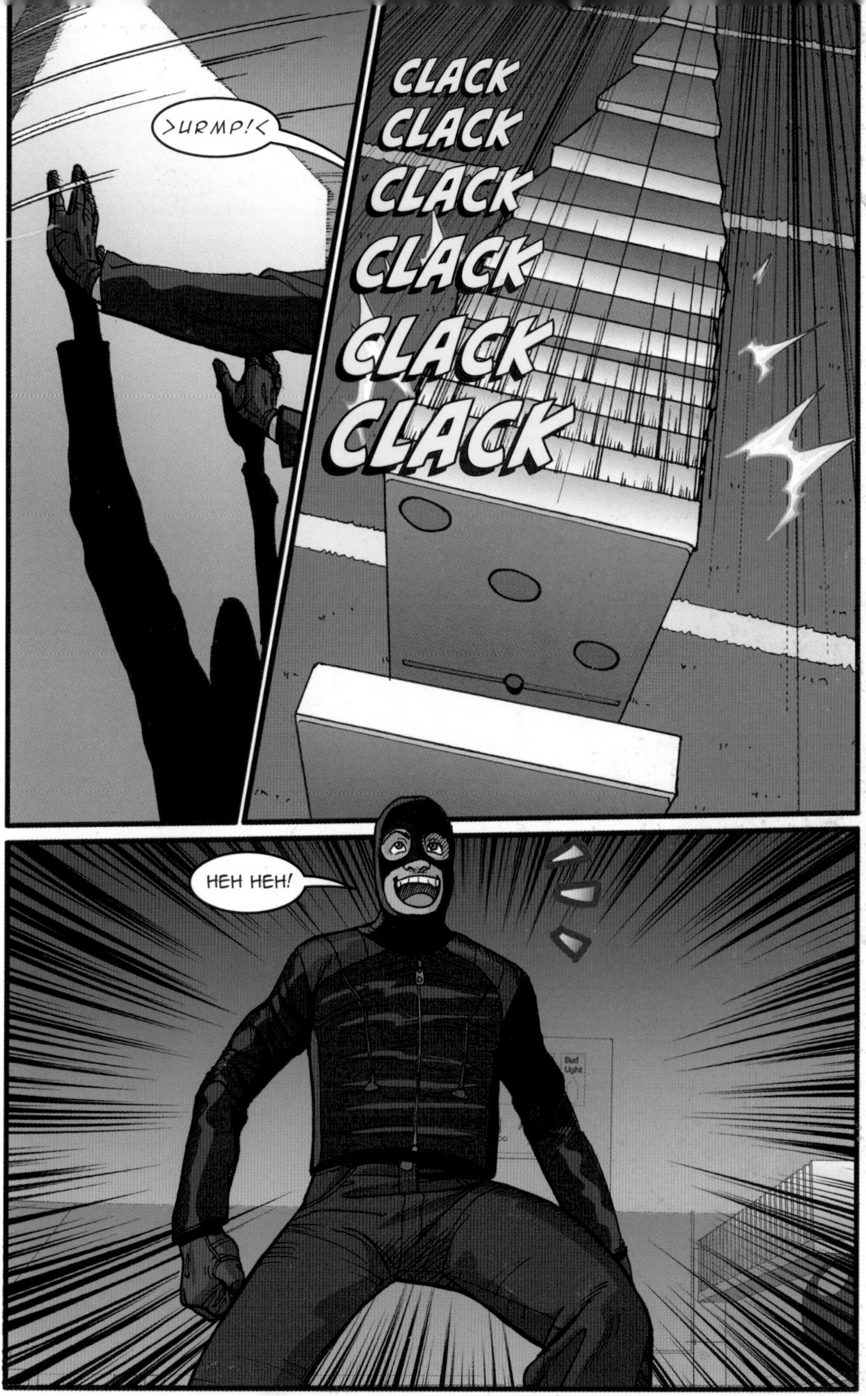
>URMP!<
CLACK
CLACK
CLACK
CLACK
CLACK
CLACK
HEH HEH!
Bud Light

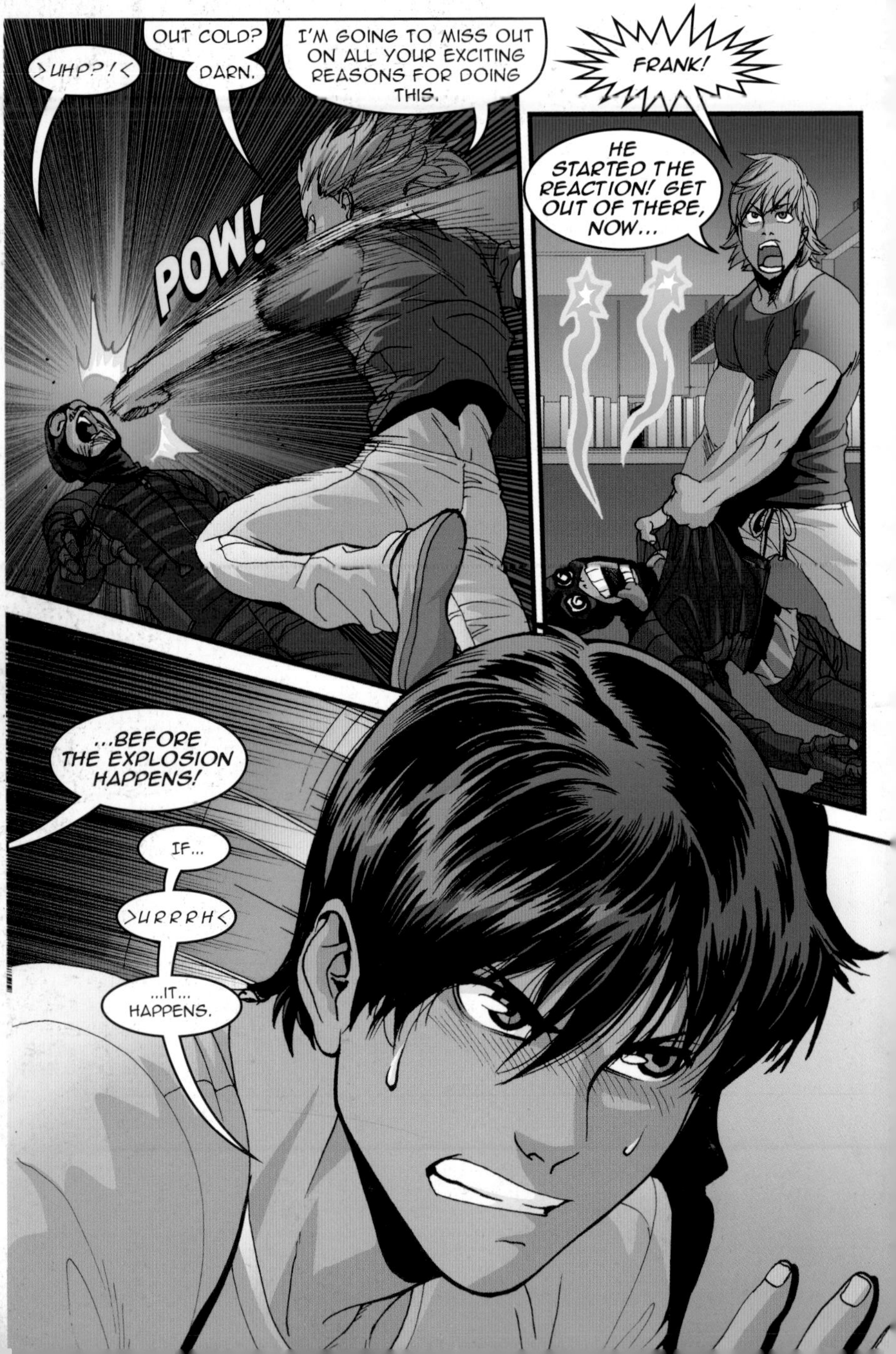

>UHP?!<
OUT COLD?
DARN.
I'M GOING TO MISS OUT ON ALL YOUR EXCITING REASONS FOR DOING THIS.
POW!
FRANK!
HE STARTED THE REACTION! GET OUT OF THERE, NOW...
...BEFORE THE EXPLOSION HAPPENS!
IF...
>URRRH<
...IT... HAPPENS.

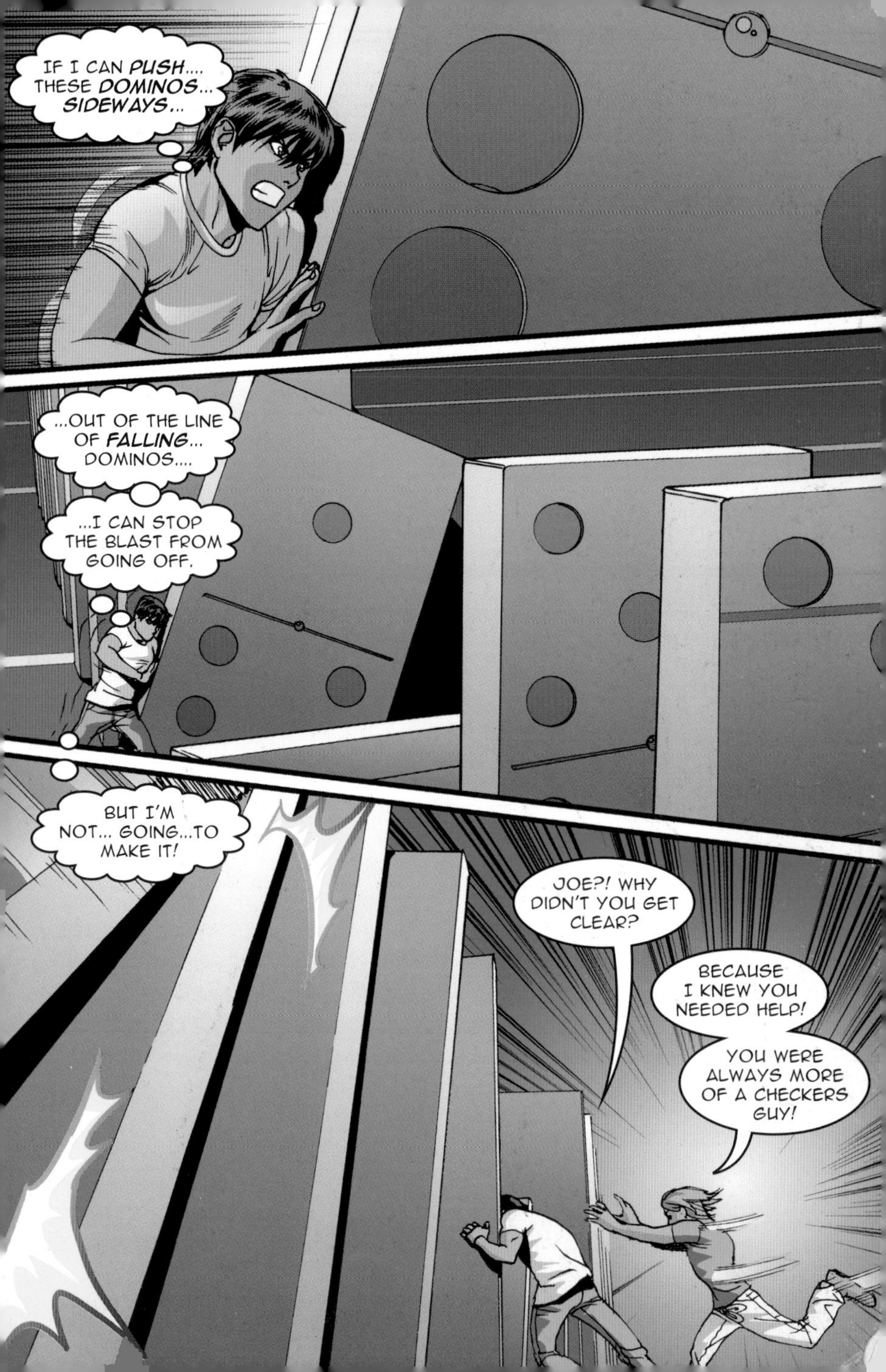
IF I CAN PUSH.... THESE DOMINOS... SIDEWAYS...
...OUT OF THE LINE OF FALLING... DOMINOS....
...I CAN STOP THE BLAST FROM GOING OFF.
BUT I'M NOT... GOING...TO MAKE IT!
JOE?! WHY DIDN'T YOU GET CLEAR?
BECAUSE I KNEW YOU NEEDED HELP!
YOU WERE ALWAYS MORE OF A CHECKERS GUY!

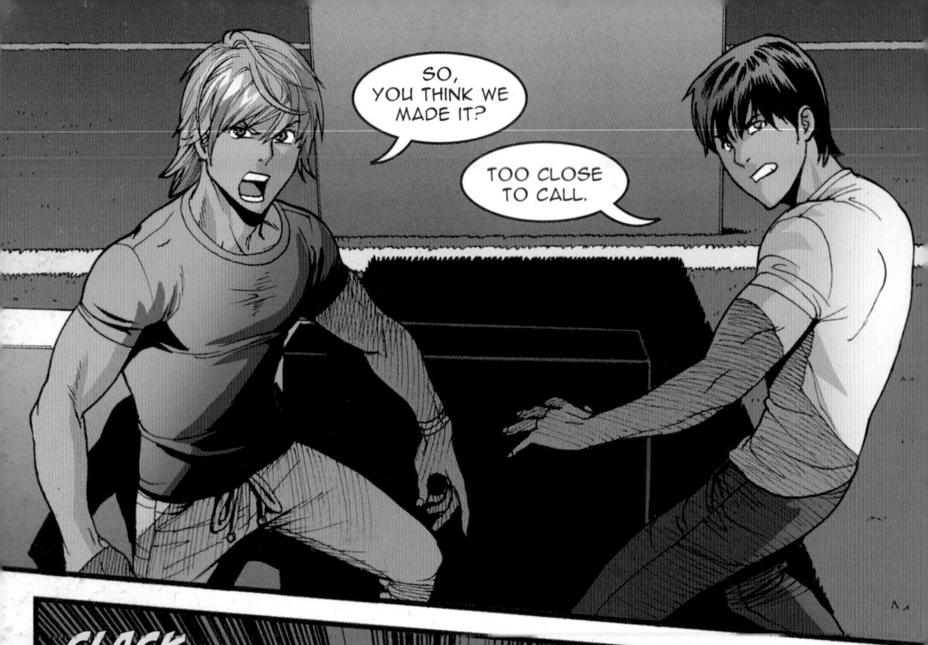
SO, YOU THINK WE MADE IT?
TOO CLOSE TO CALL.

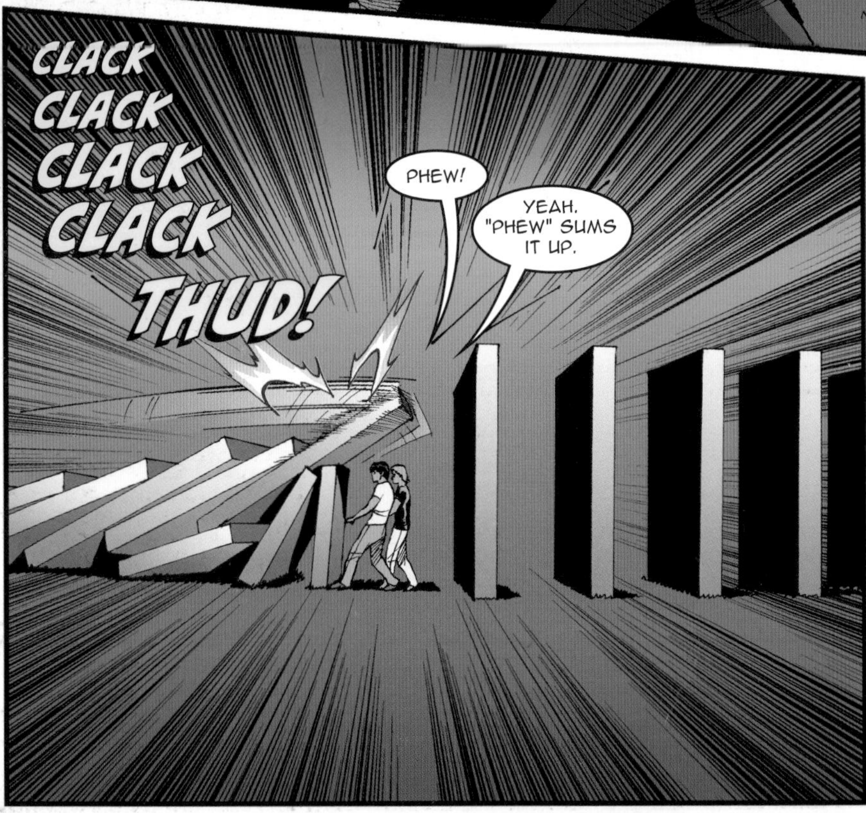
CLACK
CLACK
CLACK
CLACK
THUD!
PHEW!
YEAH. "PHEW" SUMS IT UP.

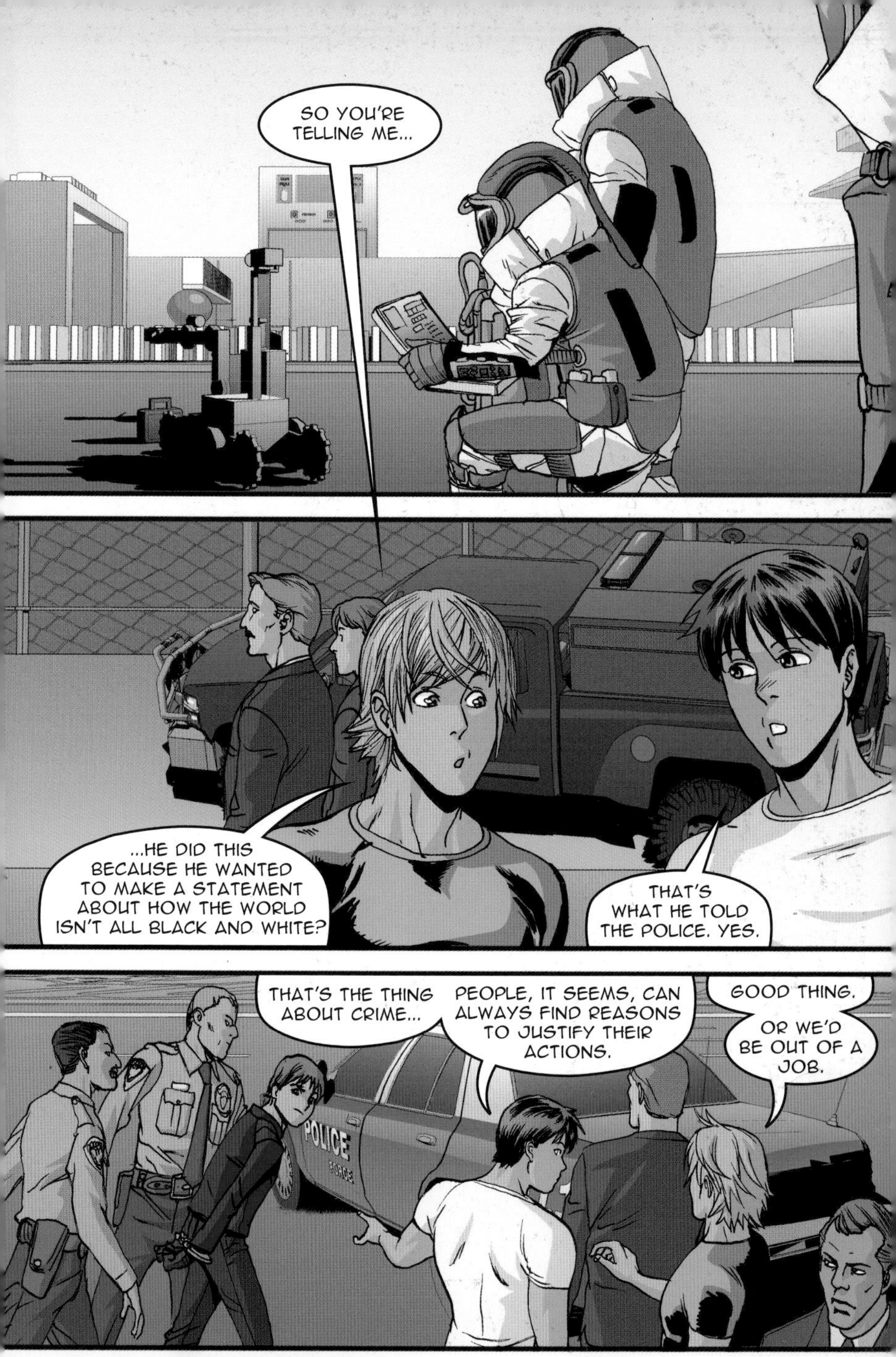
SO YOU'RE TELLING ME...
...HE DID THIS BECAUSE HE WANTED TO MAKE A STATEMENT ABOUT HOW THE WORLD ISN'T ALL BLACK AND WHITE?
THAT'S WHAT HE TOLD THE POLICE. YES.
THAT'S THE THING ABOUT CRIME...
PEOPLE, IT SEEMS, CAN ALWAYS FIND REASONS TO JUSTIFY THEIR ACTIONS.
GOOD THING.
OR WE'D BE OUT OF A JOB.
POLICE
FORCE

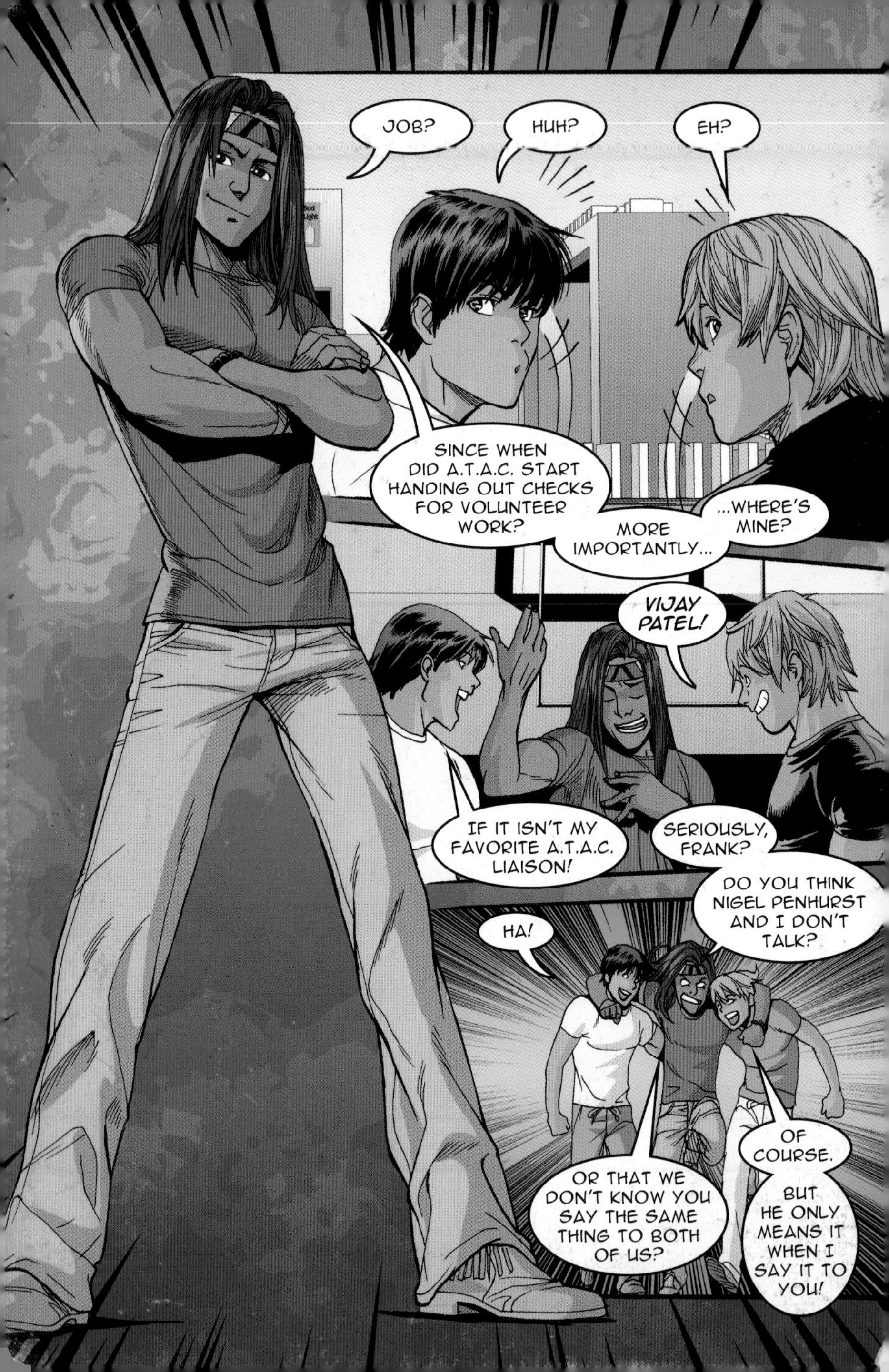
JOB?
HUH?
EH?
SINCE WHEN DID A.T.A.C. START HANDING OUT CHECKS FOR VOLUNTEER WORK?
MORE IMPORTANTLY...
...WHERE'S MINE?
VIJAY PATEL!
IF IT ISN'T MY FAVORITE A.T.A.C. LIAISON!
SERIOUSLY, FRANK?
DO YOU THINK NIGEL PENHURST AND I DON'T TALK?
HA!
OR THAT WE DON'T KNOW YOU SAY THE SAME THING TO BOTH OF US?
OF COURSE.
BUT HE ONLY MEANS IT WHEN I SAY IT TO YOU!

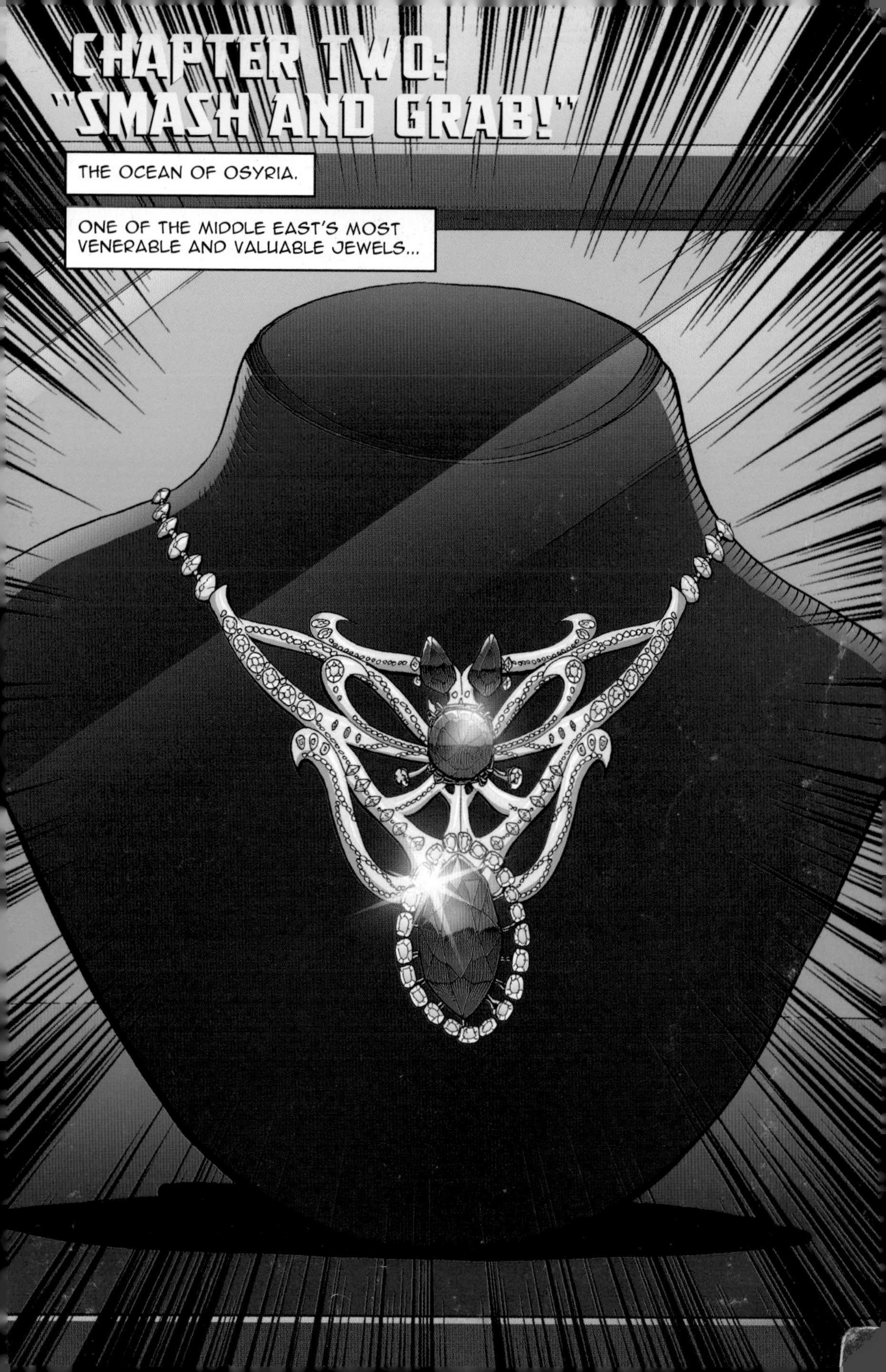
CHAPTER TWO:
"SMASH AND GRAB!"
THE OCEAN OF OSYRIA.
ONE OF THE MIDDLE EAST'S MOST VENERABLE AND VALUABLE JEWELS...

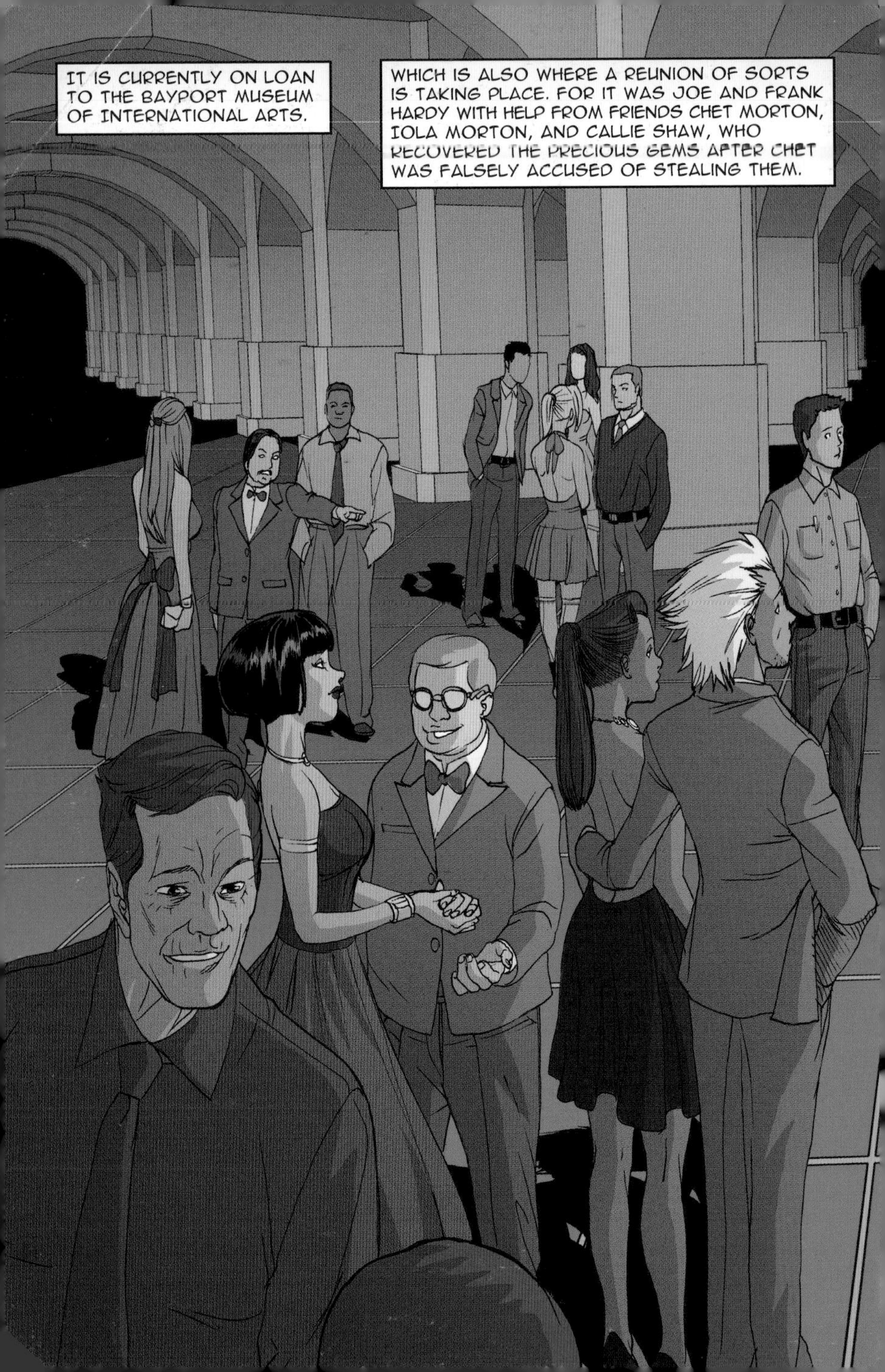
IT IS CURRENTLY ON LOAN TO THE BAYPORT MUSEUM OF INTERNATIONAL ARTS.
WHICH IS ALSO WHERE A REUNION OF SORTS IS TAKING PLACE. FOR IT WAS JOE AND FRANK HARDY WITH HELP FROM FRIENDS CHET MORTON, IOLA MORTON, AND CALLIE SHAW, WHO RECOVERED THE PRECIOUS GEMS AFTER CHET WAS FALSELY ACCUSED OF STEALING THEM.

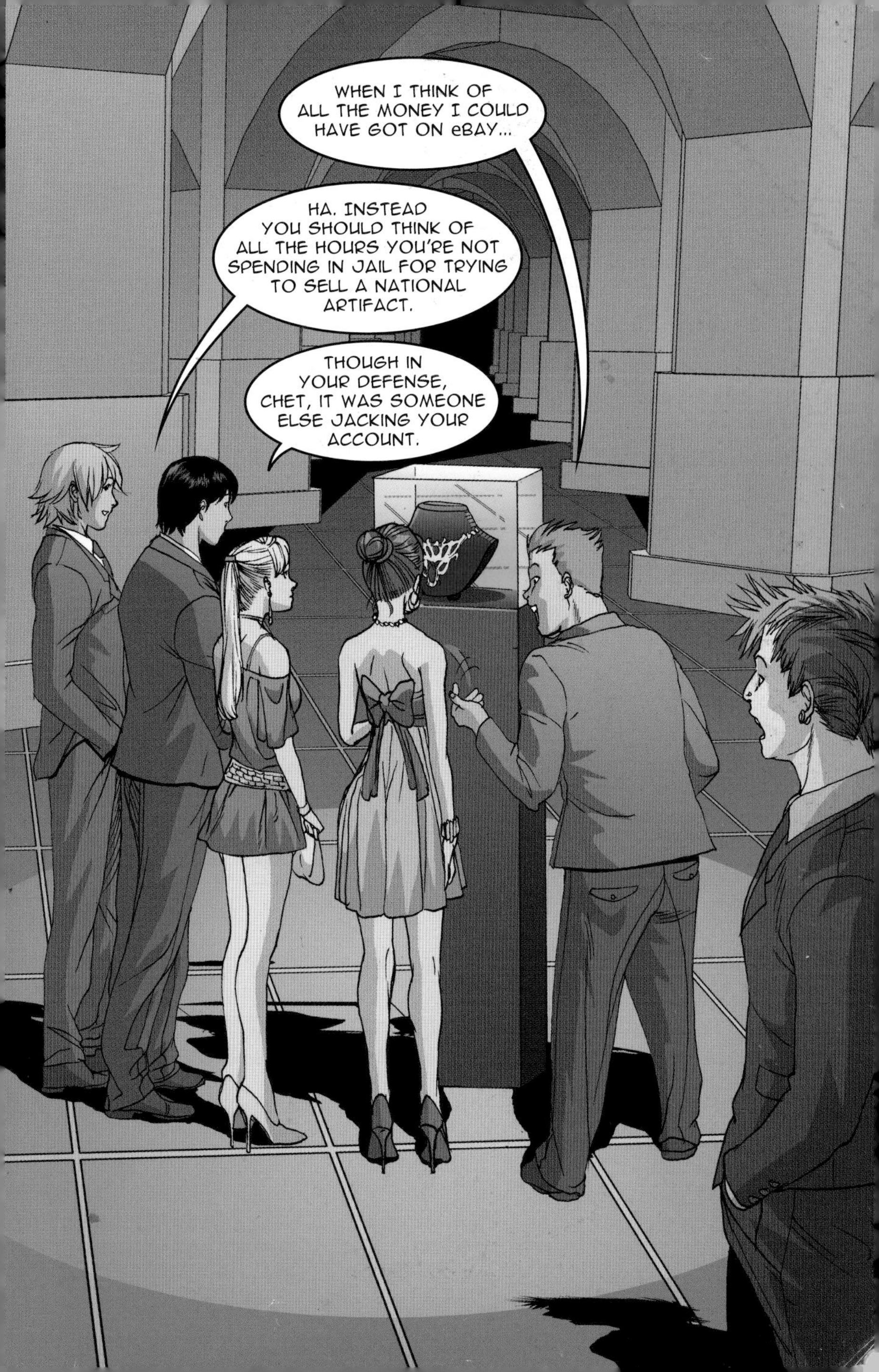
WHEN I THINK OF ALL THE MONEY I COULD HAVE GOT ON eBAY...
HA. INSTEAD YOU SHOULD THINK OF ALL THE HOURS YOU'RE NOT SPENDING IN JAIL FOR TRYING TO SELL A NATIONAL ARTIFACT.
THOUGH IN YOUR DEFENSE, CHET, IT WAS SOMEONE ELSE JACKING YOUR ACCOUNT.

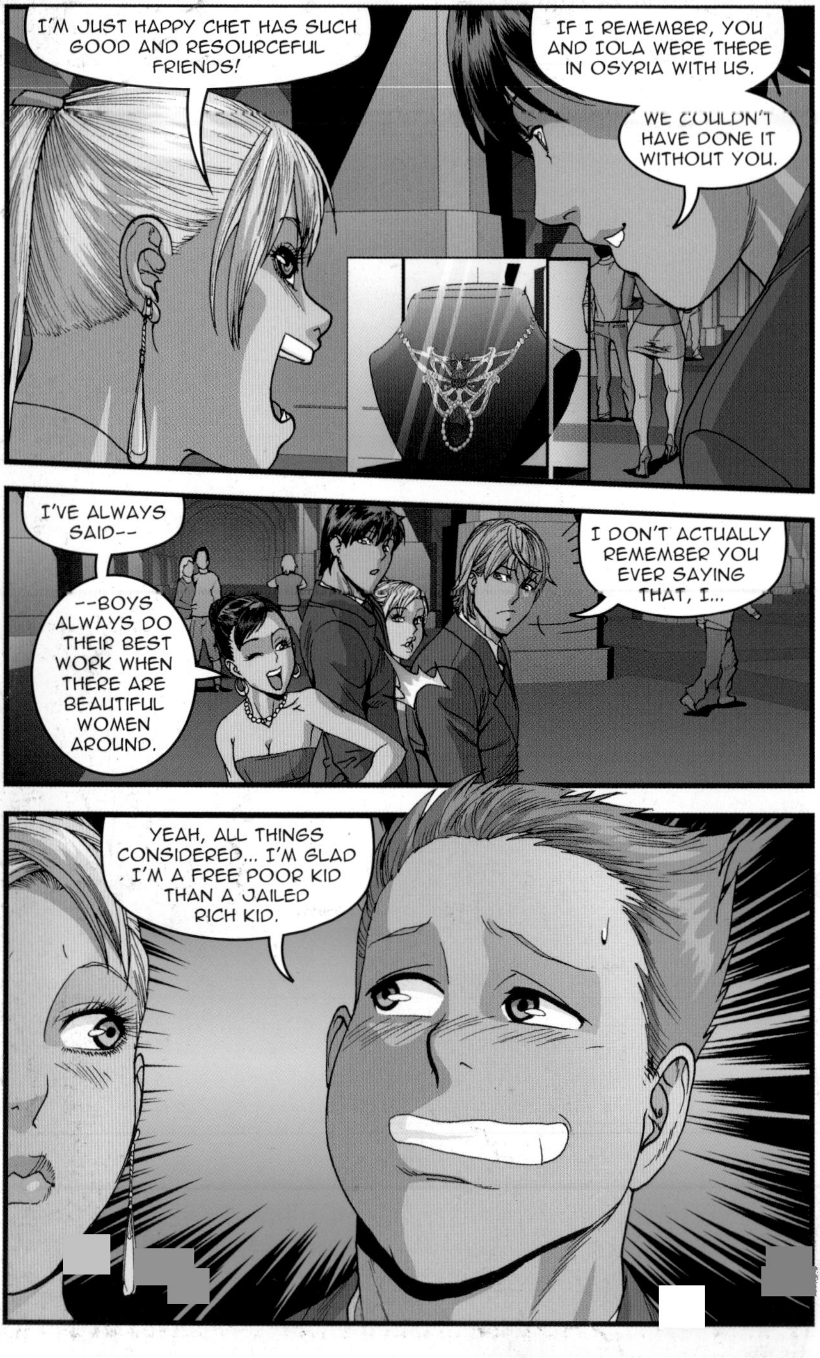
I'M JUST HAPPY CHET HAS SUCH GOOD AND RESOURCEFUL FRIENDS!
IF I REMEMBER, YOU AND IOLA WERE THERE IN OSYRIA WITH US.
WE COULDN'T HAVE DONE IT WITHOUT YOU.
I'VE ALWAYS SAID--
--BOYS ALWAYS DO THEIR BEST WORK WHEN THERE ARE BEAUTIFUL WOMEN AROUND.
I DON'T ACTUALLY REMEMBER YOU EVER SAYING THAT, I...
YEAH, ALL THINGS CONSIDERED... I'M GLAD I'M A FREE POOR KID THAN A JAILED RICH KID.

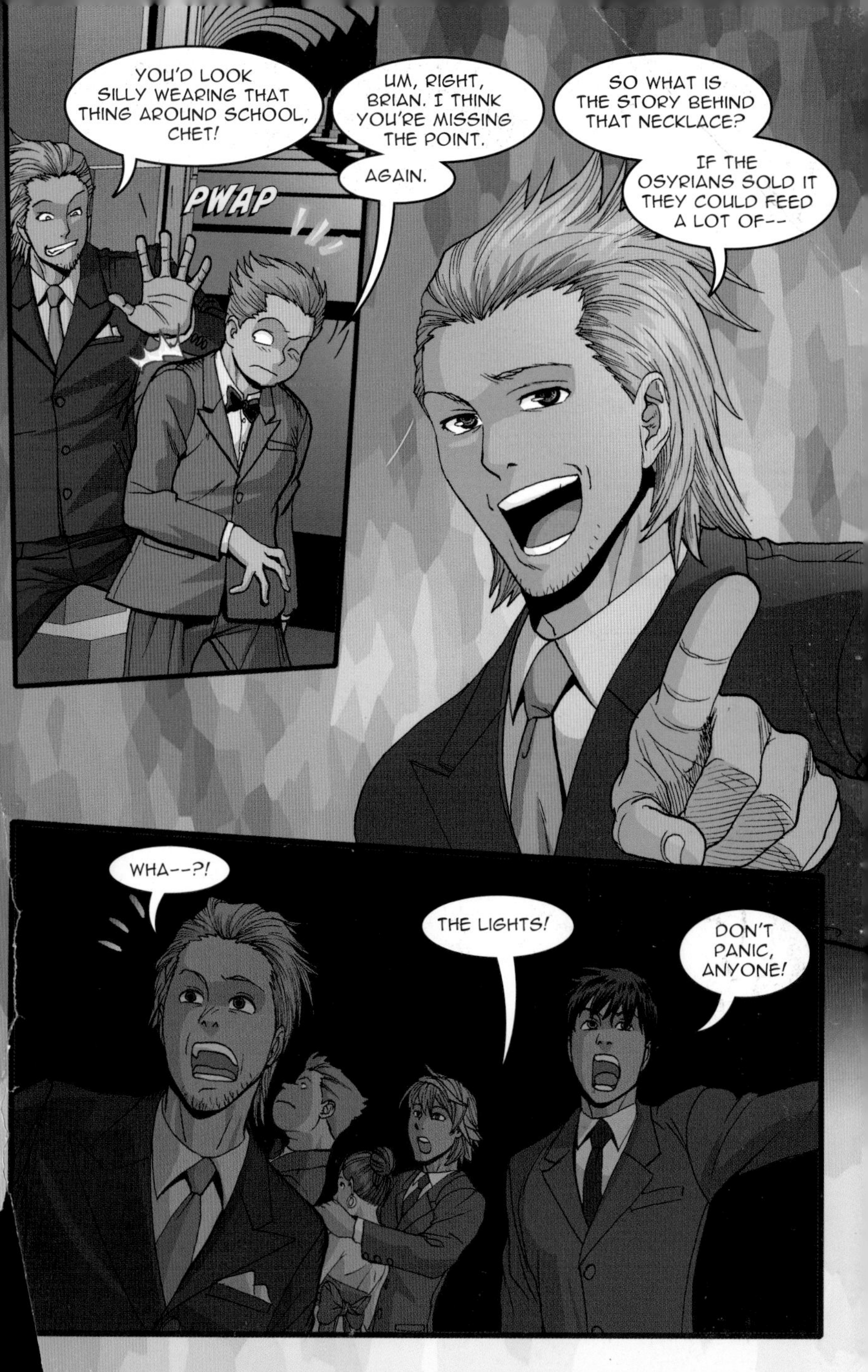
YOU'D LOOK SILLY WEARING THAT THING AROUND SCHOOL, CHET!
UM, RIGHT, BRIAN. I THINK YOU'RE MISSING THE POINT.
AGAIN.
PWAP
SO WHAT IS THE STORY BEHIND THAT NECKLACE?
IF THE OSYRIANS SOLD IT THEY COULD FEED A LOT OF--
WHA--?!
THE LIGHTS!
DON'T PANIC, ANYONE!

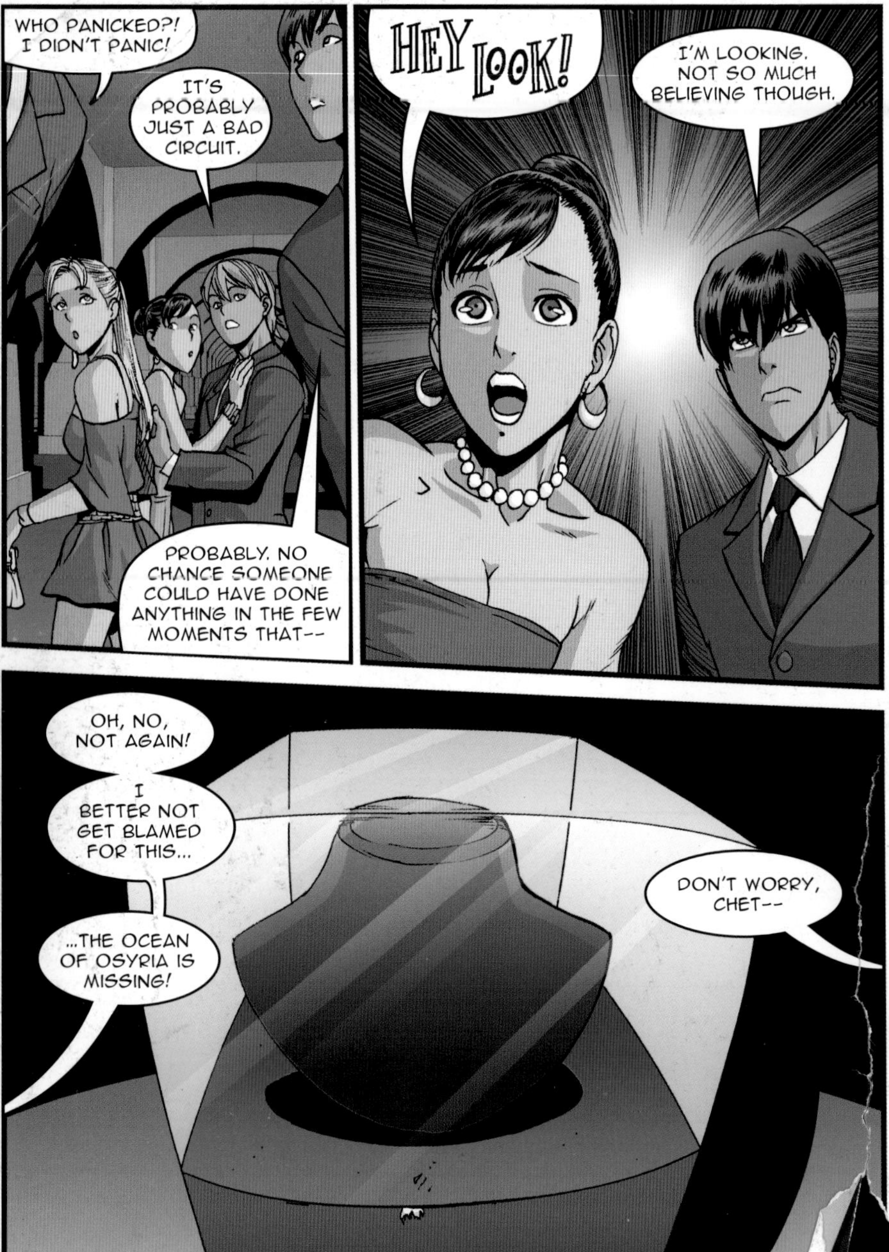
WHO PANICKED?! I DIDN'T PANIC!
IT'S PROBABLY JUST A BAD CIRCUIT.
PROBABLY. NO CHANCE SOMEONE COULD HAVE DONE ANYTHING IN THE FEW MOMENTS THAT--
HEY LOOK!
I'M LOOKING. NOT SO MUCH BELIEVING THOUGH.
OH, NO, NOT AGAIN!
I BETTER NOT GET BLAMED FOR THIS...
...THE OCEAN OF OSYRIA IS MISSING!
DON'T WORRY, CHET--

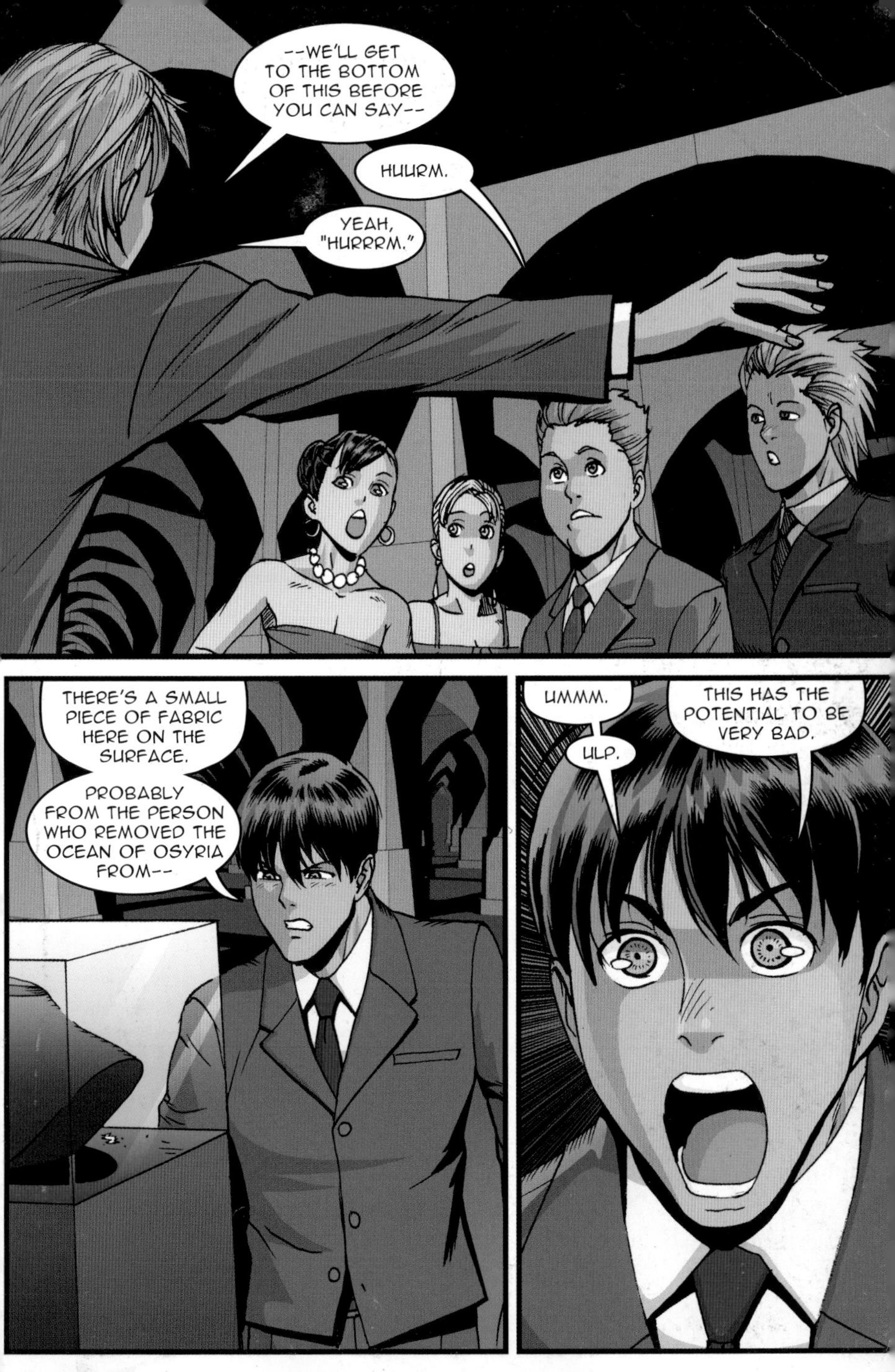
--WE'LL GET TO THE BOTTOM OF THIS BEFORE YOU CAN SAY--
HUURM.
YEAH, "HURRRM."
THERE'S A SMALL PIECE OF FABRIC HERE ON THE SURFACE.
PROBABLY FROM THE PERSON WHO REMOVED THE OCEAN OF OSYRIA FROM--
UMMM.
ULP.
THIS HAS THE POTENTIAL TO BE VERY BAD.

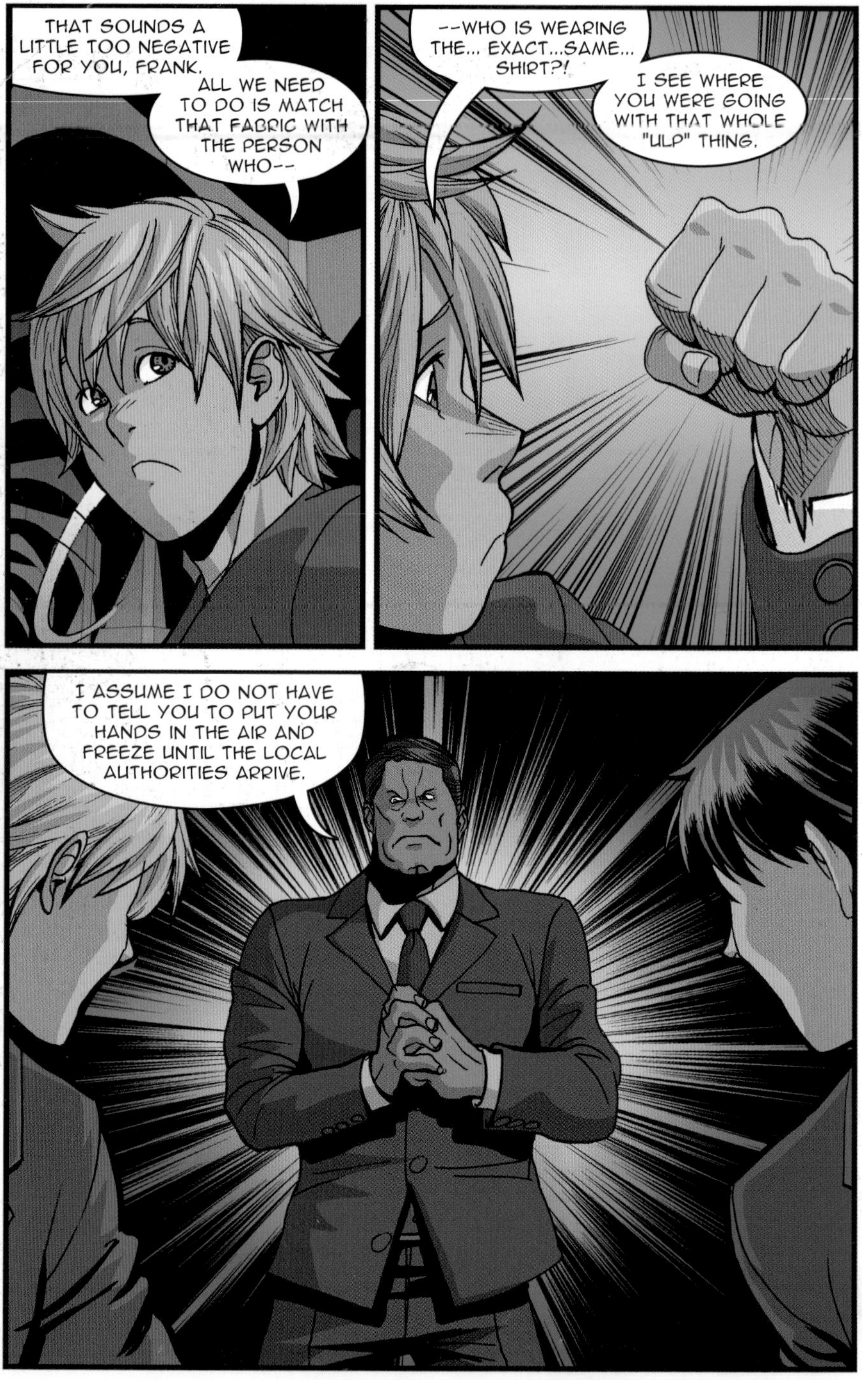
THAT SOUNDS A LITTLE TOO NEGATIVE FOR YOU, FRANK.
ALL WE NEED TO DO IS MATCH THAT FABRIC WITH THE PERSON WHO--
--WHO IS WEARING THE... EXACT...SAME... SHIRT?!
I SEE WHERE YOU WERE GOING WITH THAT WHOLE "ULP" THING.
I ASSUME I DO NOT HAVE TO TELL YOU TO PUT YOUR HANDS IN THE AIR AND FREEZE UNTIL THE LOCAL AUTHORITIES ARRIVE.

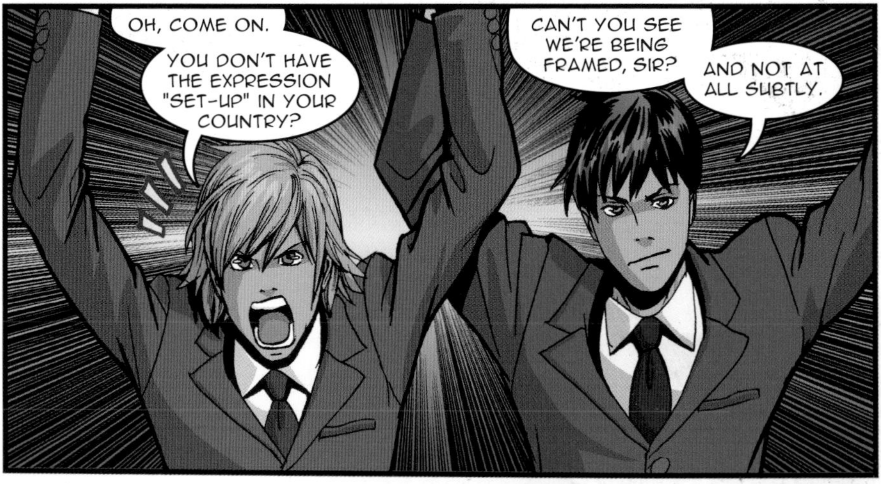
OH, COME ON.
YOU DON'T HAVE THE EXPRESSION "SET-UP" IN YOUR COUNTRY?
CAN'T YOU SEE WE'RE BEING FRAMED, SIR?
AND NOT AT ALL SUBTLY.

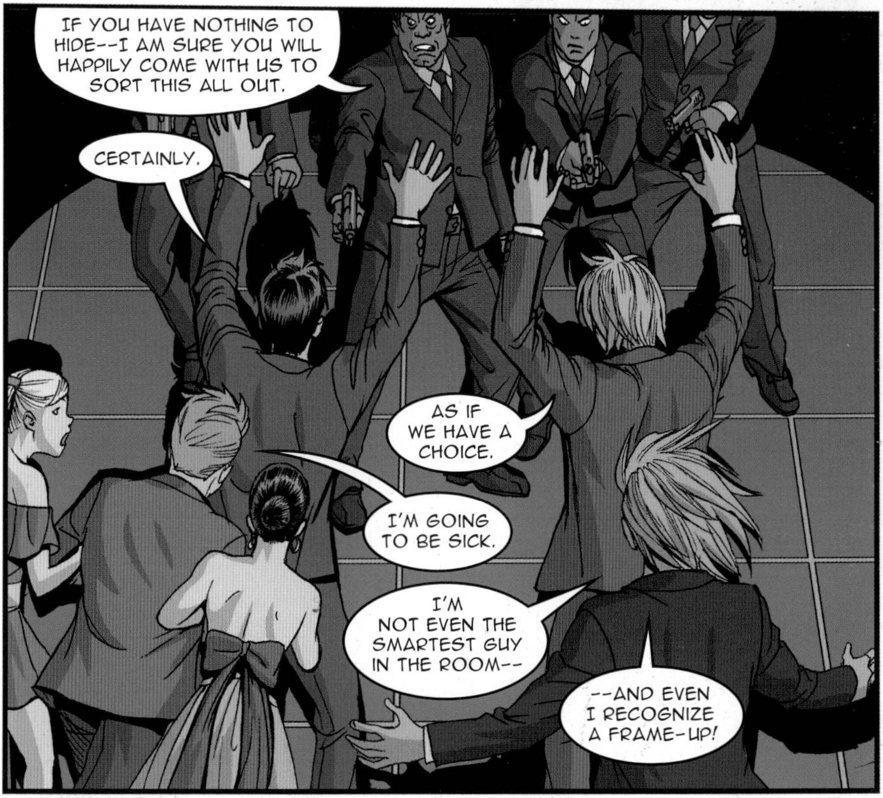
IF YOU HAVE NOTHING TO HIDE--I AM SURE YOU WILL HAPPILY COME WITH US TO SORT THIS ALL OUT.
CERTAINLY.
AS IF WE HAVE A CHOICE.
I'M GOING TO BE SICK.
I'M NOT EVEN THE SMARTEST GUY IN THE ROOM--
--AND EVEN I RECOGNIZE A FRAME-UP!

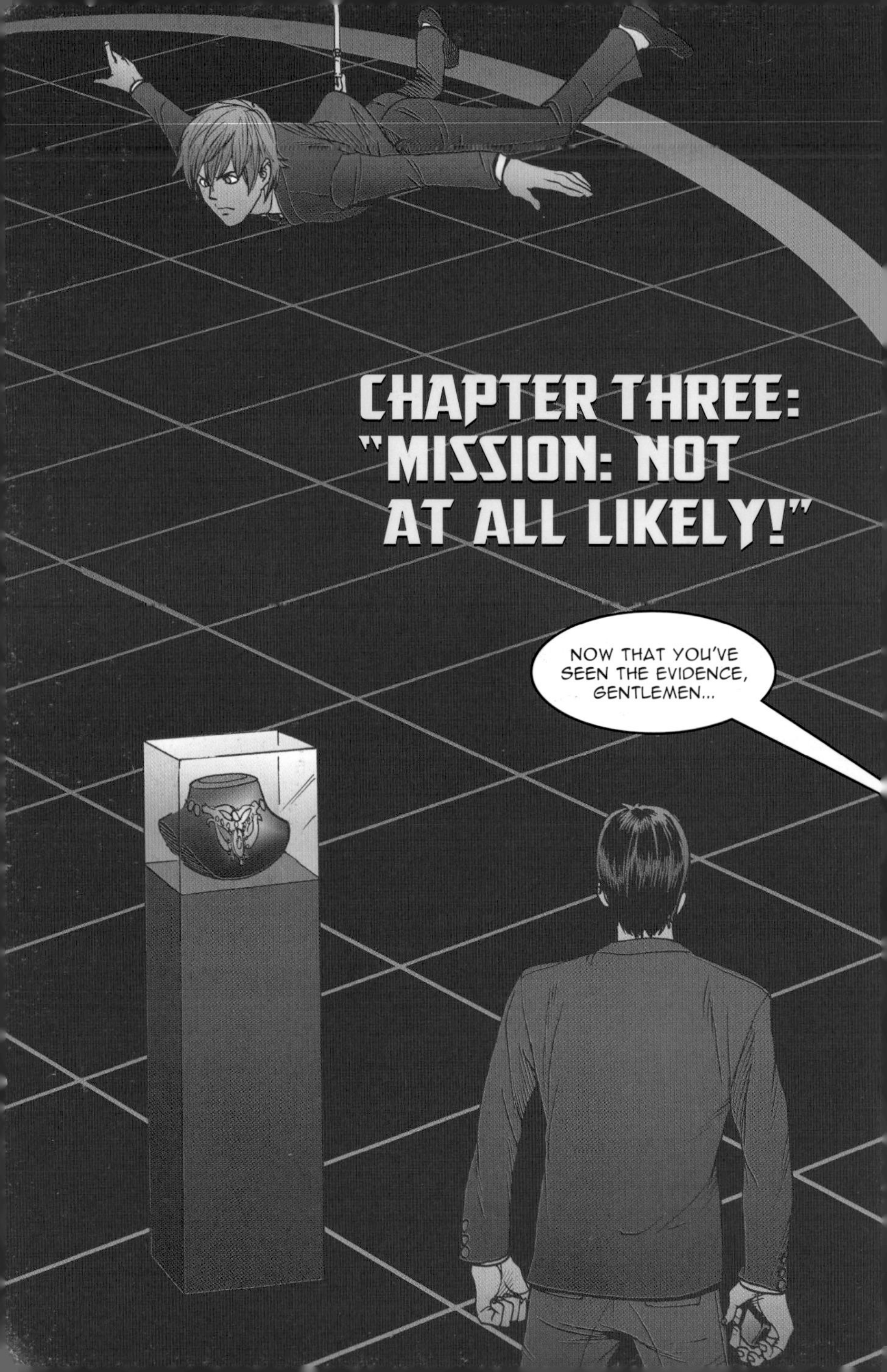
CHAPTER THREE:
"MISSION: NOT AT ALL LIKELY!"
NOW THAT YOU'VE SEEN THE EVIDENCE, GENTLEMEN...

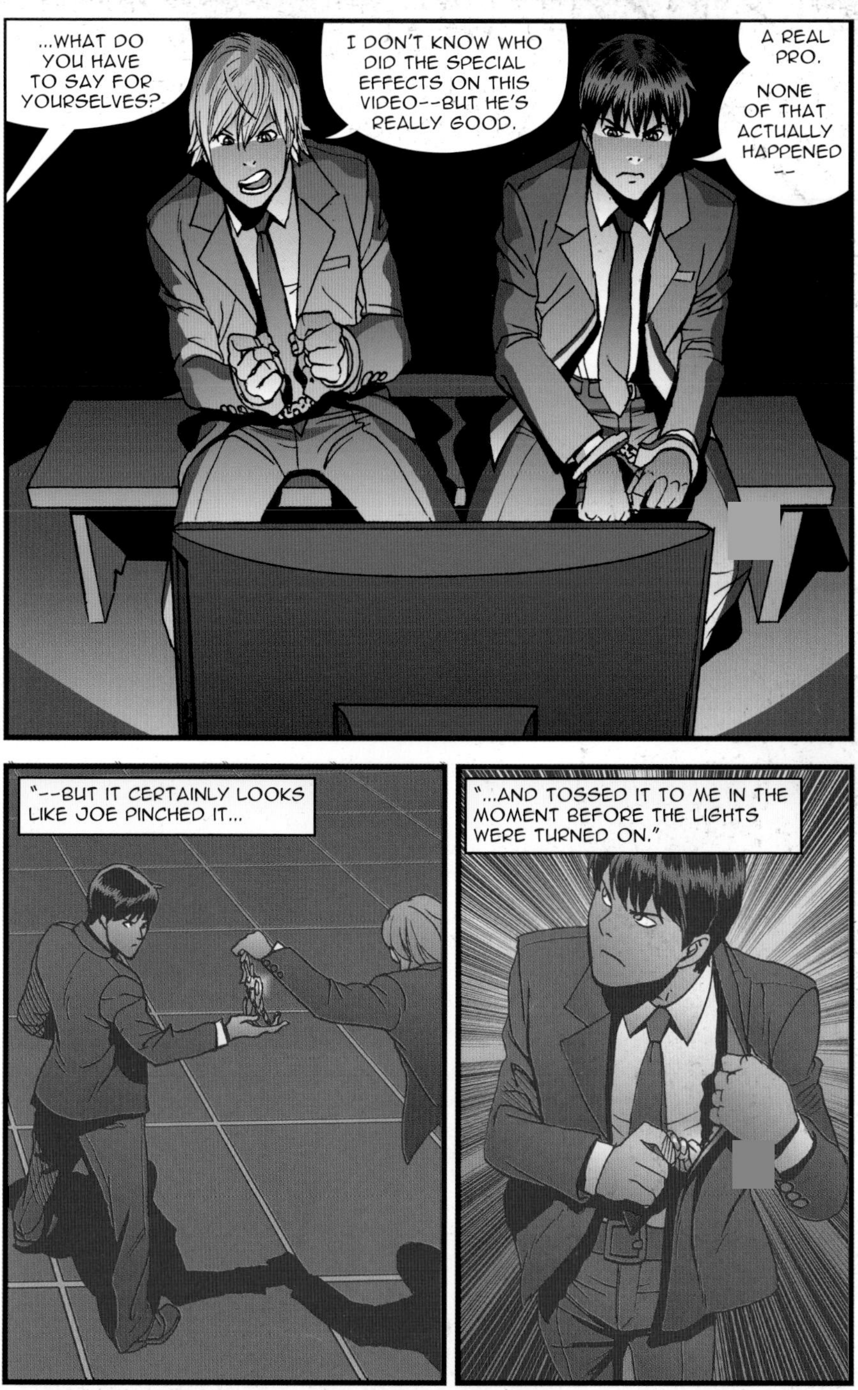
...WHAT DO YOU HAVE TO SAY FOR YOURSELVES?
I DON'T KNOW WHO DID THE SPECIAL EFFECTS ON THIS VIDEO--BUT HE'S REALLY GOOD.
A REAL PRO.
NONE OF THAT ACTUALLY HAPPENED --
"--BUT IT CERTAINLY LOOKS LIKE JOE PINCHED IT...
"...AND TOSSED IT TO ME IN THE MOMENT BEFORE THE LIGHTS WERE TURNED ON."

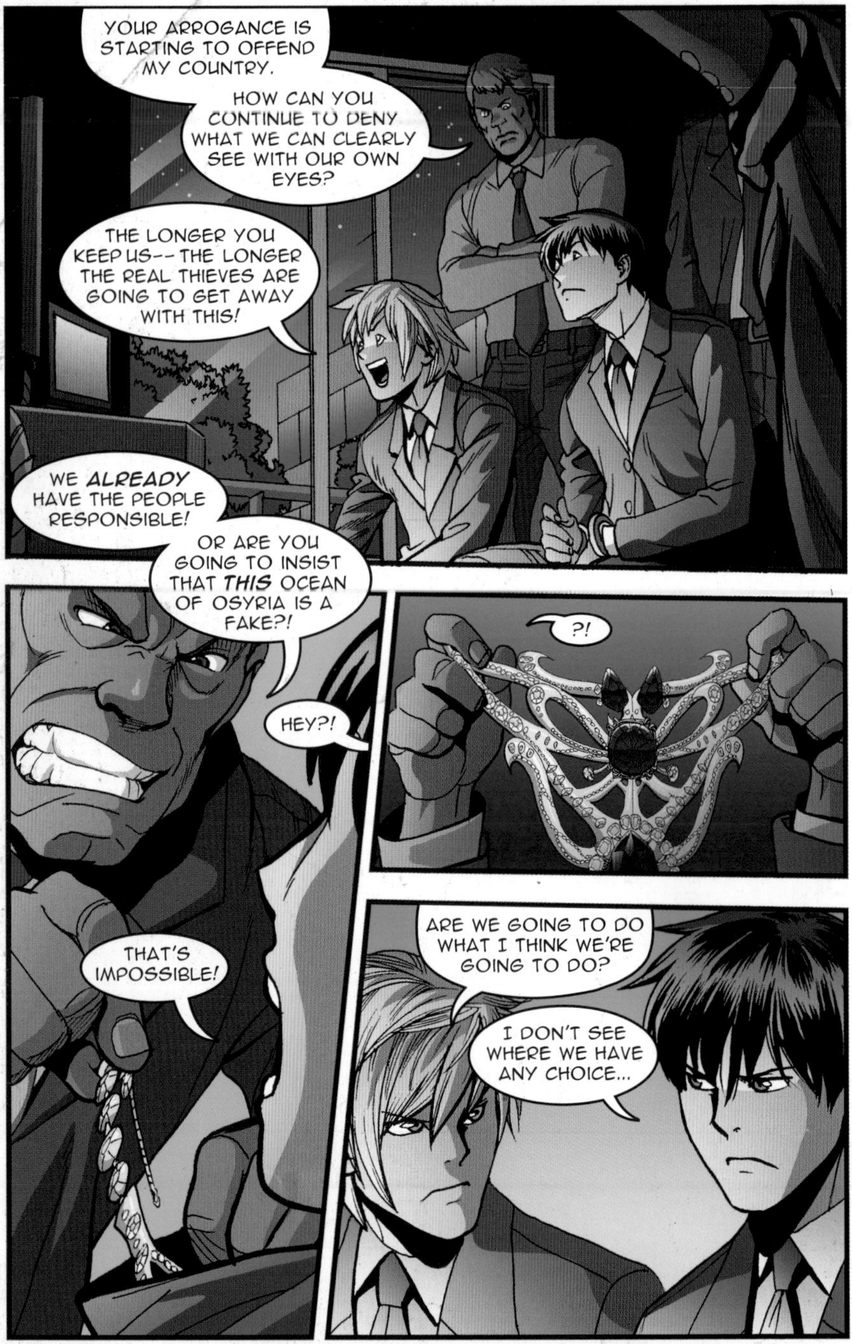
YOUR ARROGANCE IS STARTING TO OFFEND MY COUNTRY.
HOW CAN YOU CONTINUE TO DENY WHAT WE CAN CLEARLY SEE WITH OUR OWN EYES?
THE LONGER YOU KEEP US-- THE LONGER THE REAL THIEVES ARE GOING TO GET AWAY WITH THIS!
WE ALREADY HAVE THE PEOPLE RESPONSIBLE!
OR ARE YOU GOING TO INSIST THAT THIS OCEAN OF OSYRIA IS A FAKE?!
HEY?!
?!
THAT'S IMPOSSIBLE!
ARE WE GOING TO DO WHAT I THINK WE'RE GOING TO DO?
I DON'T SEE WHERE WE HAVE ANY CHOICE...

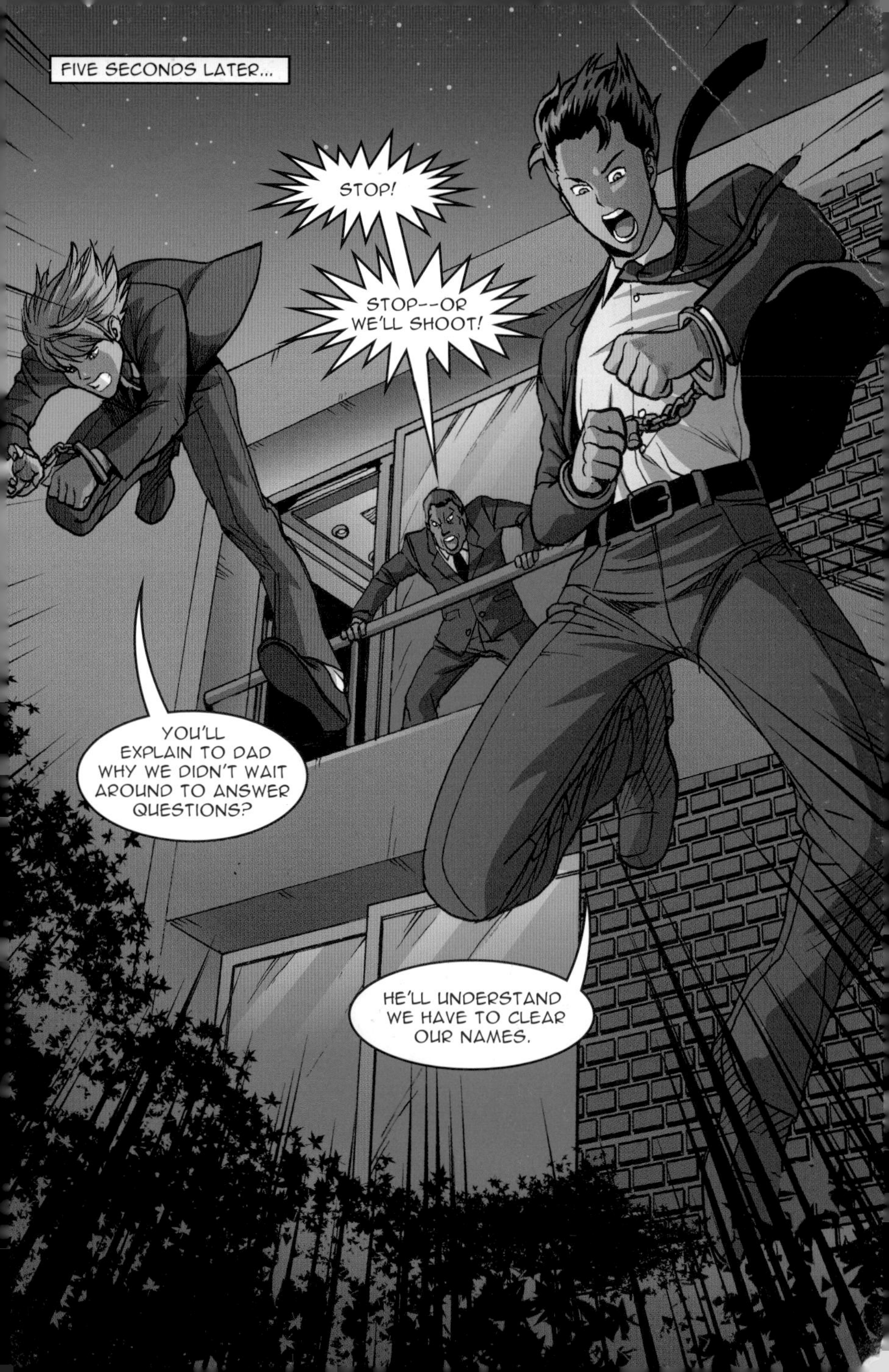
FIVE SECONDS LATER...
STOP!
STOP--OR WE'LL SHOOT!
YOU'LL EXPLAIN TO DAD WHY WE DIDN'T WAIT AROUND TO ANSWER QUESTIONS?
HE'LL UNDERSTAND WE HAVE TO CLEAR OUR NAMES.

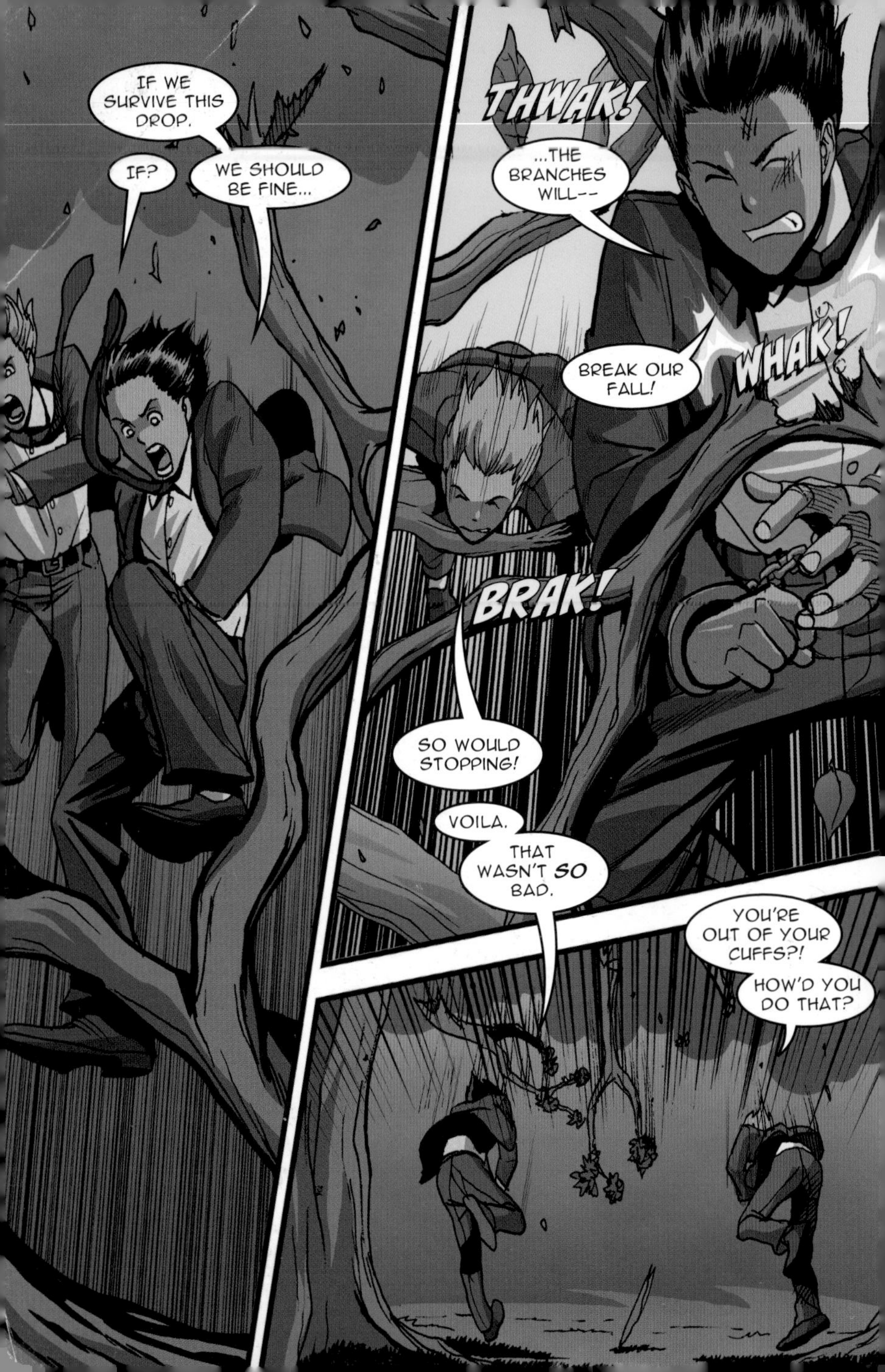
IF WE SURVIVE THIS DROP,
IF?
WE SHOULD BE FINE...
THWAK!
...THE BRANCHES WILL--
BREAK OUR FALL!
WHAK!
BRAK!
SO WOULD STOPPING!
VOILA.
THAT WASN'T SO BAD.
YOU'RE OUT OF YOUR CUFFS?!
HOW'D YOU DO THAT?

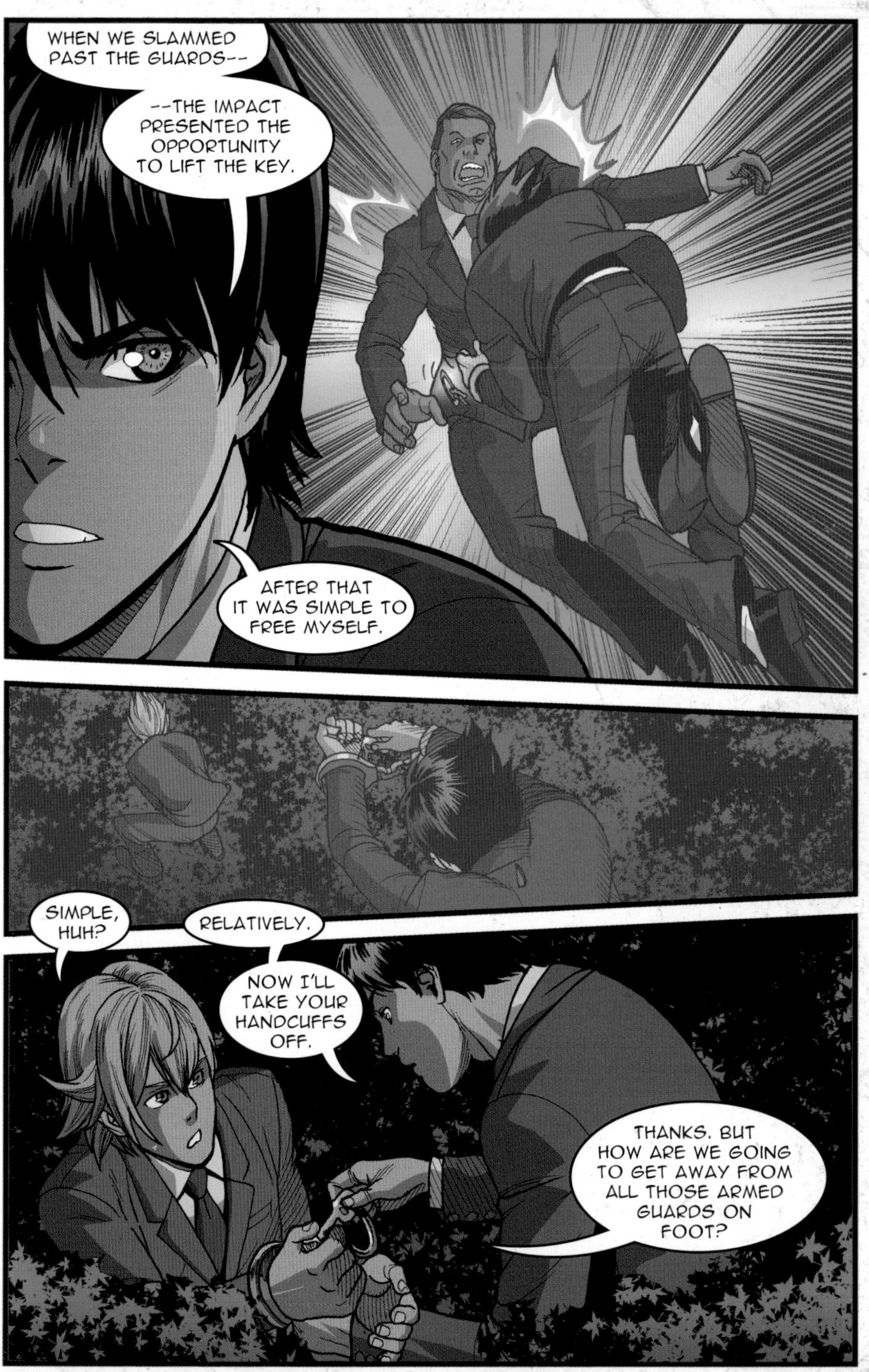
WHEN WE SLAMMED PAST THE GUARDS--
--THE IMPACT PRESENTED THE OPPORTUNITY TO LIFT THE KEY.
AFTER THAT IT WAS SIMPLE TO FREE MYSELF.
SIMPLE, HUH?
RELATIVELY.
NOW I'LL TAKE YOUR HANDCUFFS OFF.
THANKS. BUT HOW ARE WE GOING TO GET AWAY FROM ALL THOSE ARMED GUARDS ON FOOT?

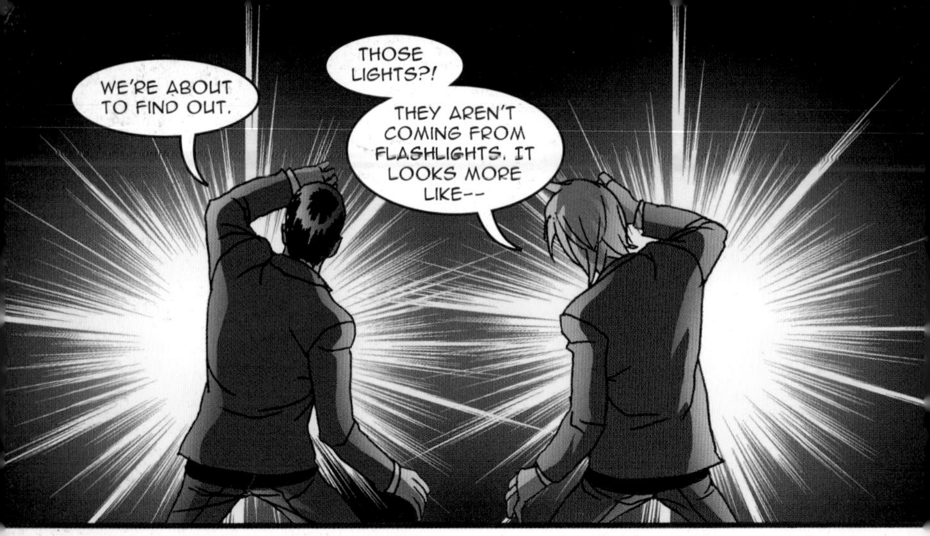
WE'RE ABOUT TO FIND OUT.
THOSE LIGHTS?!
THEY AREN'T COMING FROM FLASHLIGHTS. IT LOOKS MORE LIKE--

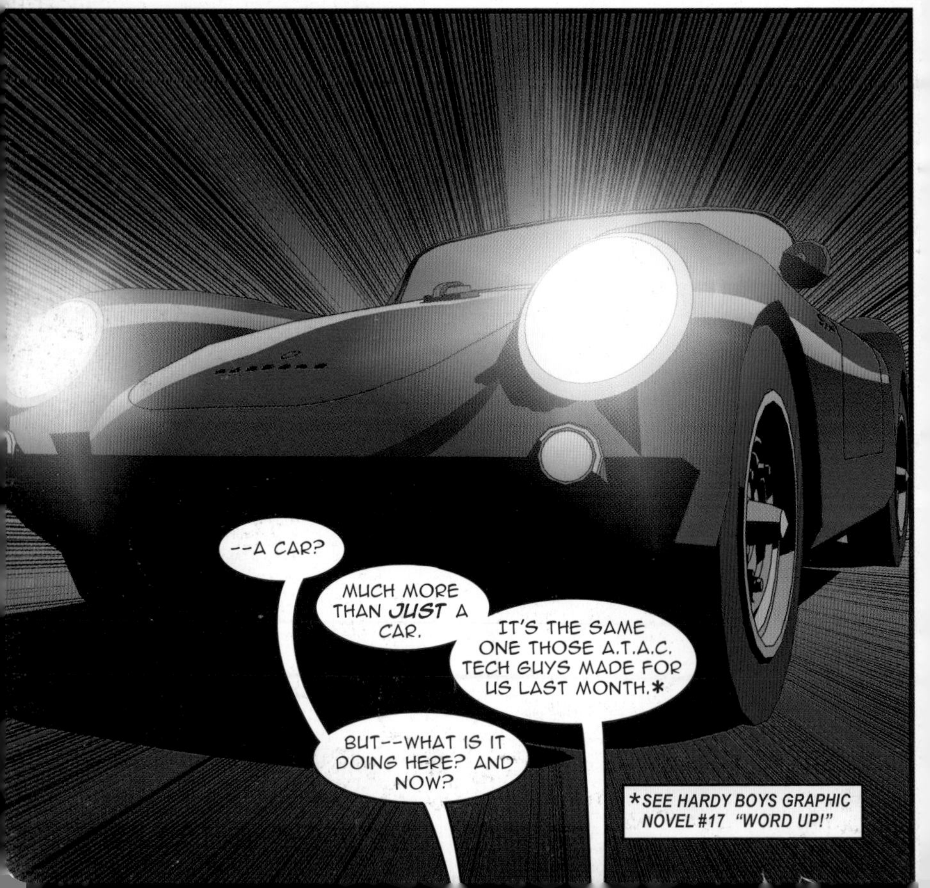
--A CAR?
MUCH MORE THAN JUST A CAR.
IT'S THE SAME ONE THOSE A.T.A.C. TECH GUYS MADE FOR US LAST MONTH.*
BUT--WHAT IS IT DOING HERE? AND NOW?
*SEE HARDY BOYS GRAPHIC NOVEL #17 "WORD UP!"

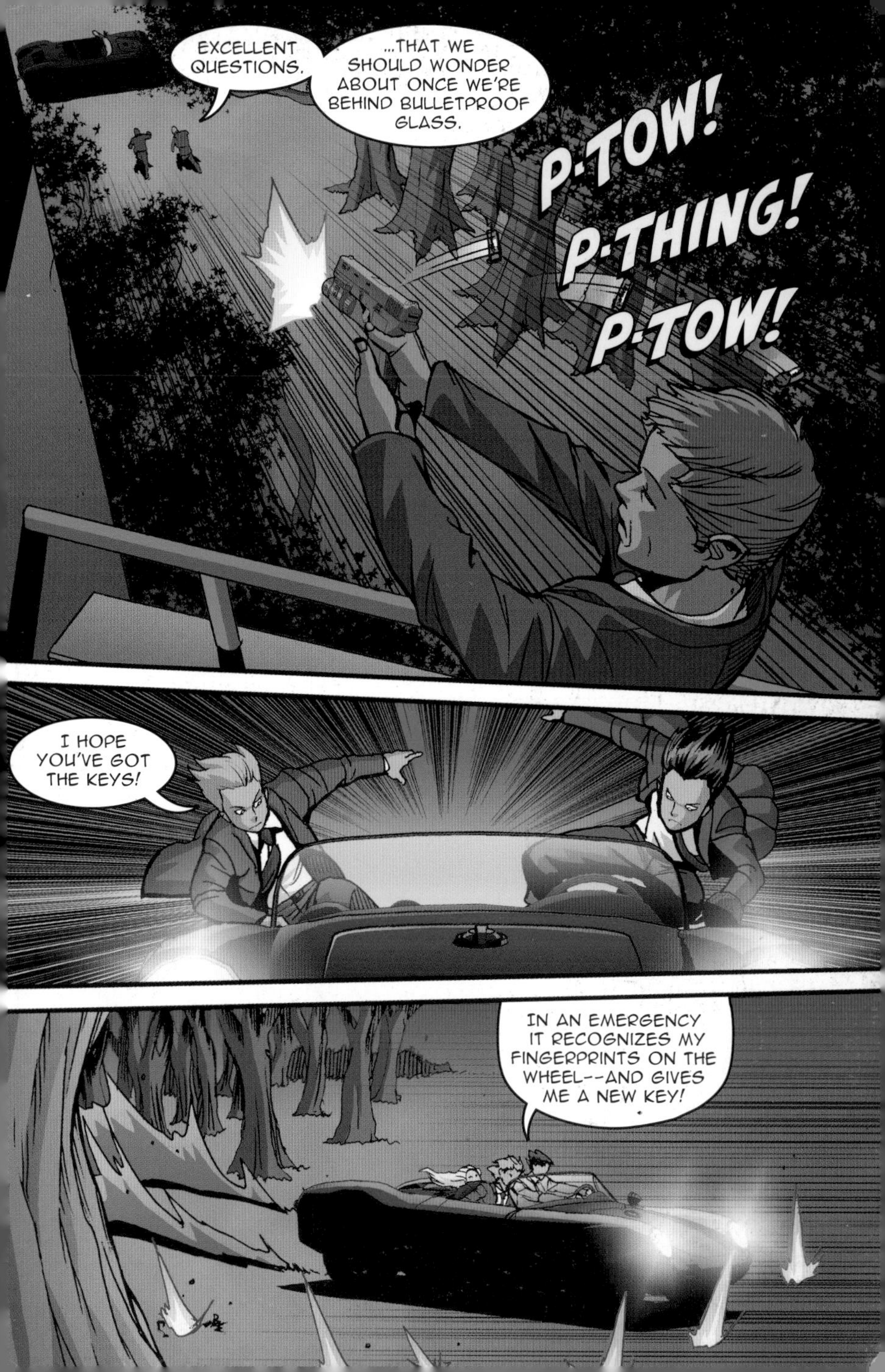
EXCELLENT QUESTIONS.
...THAT WE SHOULD WONDER ABOUT ONCE WE'RE BEHIND BULLETPROOF GLASS.
P·TOW!
P·THING!
P·TOW!
I HOPE YOU'VE GOT THE KEYS!
IN AN EMERGENCY IT RECOGNIZES MY FINGERPRINTS ON THE WHEEL--AND GIVES ME A NEW KEY!

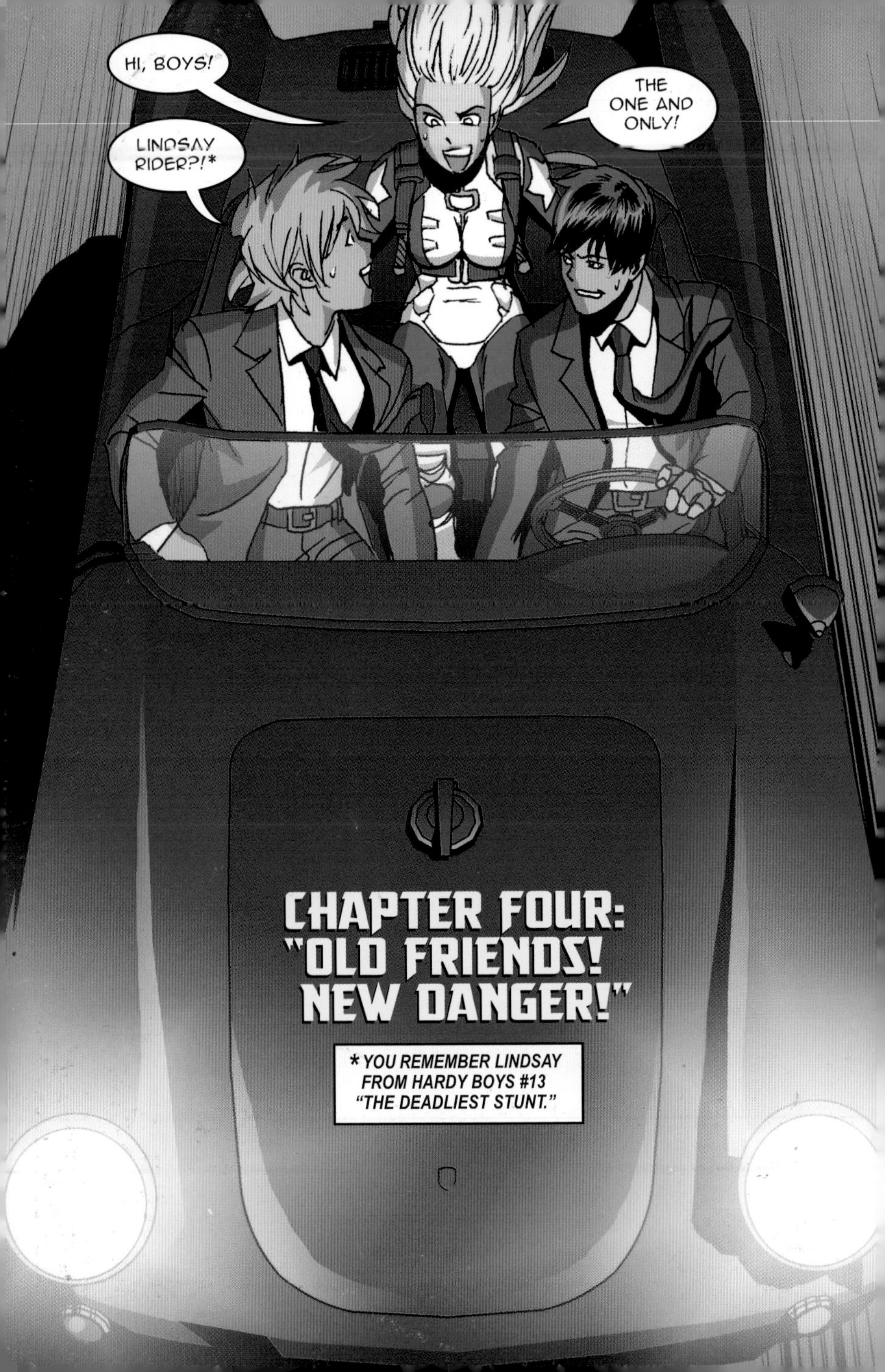
HI, BOYS!
LINDSAY RIDER?!*
THE ONE AND ONLY!
CHAPTER FOUR: "OLD FRIENDS! NEW DANGER!"
* YOU REMEMBER LINDSAY FROM HARDY BOYS #13 "THE DEADLIEST STUNT."

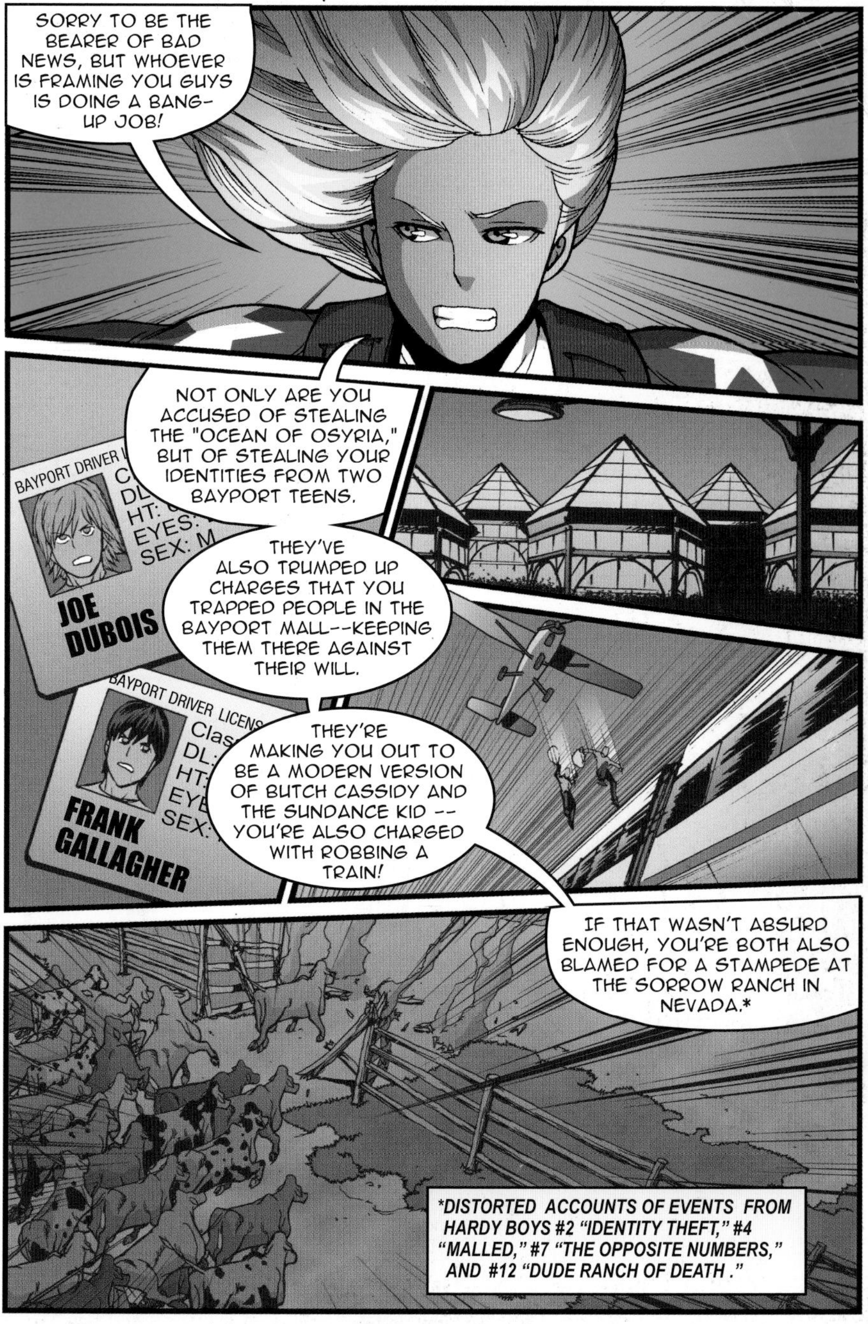
SORRY TO BE THE BEARER OF BAD NEWS, BUT WHOEVER IS FRAMING YOU GUYS IS DOING A BANG-UP JOB!
NOT ONLY ARE YOU ACCUSED OF STEALING THE "OCEAN OF OSYRIA," BUT OF STEALING YOUR IDENTITIES FROM TWO BAYPORT TEENS.
BAYPORT DRIVER
HT:
EYES:
SEX: M
JOE DUBOIS
THEY'VE ALSO TRUMPED UP CHARGES THAT YOU TRAPPED PEOPLE IN THE BAYPORT MALL--KEEPING THEM THERE AGAINST THEIR WILL.
BAYPORT DRIVER LICENS
FRANK GALLAGHER
THEY'RE MAKING YOU OUT TO BE A MODERN VERSION OF BUTCH CASSIDY AND THE SUNDANCE KID -- YOU'RE ALSO CHARGED WITH ROBBING A TRAIN!
IF THAT WASN'T ABSURD ENOUGH, YOU'RE BOTH ALSO BLAMED FOR A STAMPEDE AT THE SORROW RANCH IN NEVADA.*
*DISTORTED ACCOUNTS OF EVENTS FROM HARDY BOYS #2 "IDENTITY THEFT," #4 "MALLED," #7 "THE OPPOSITE NUMBERS," AND #12 "DUDE RANCH OF DEATH ."

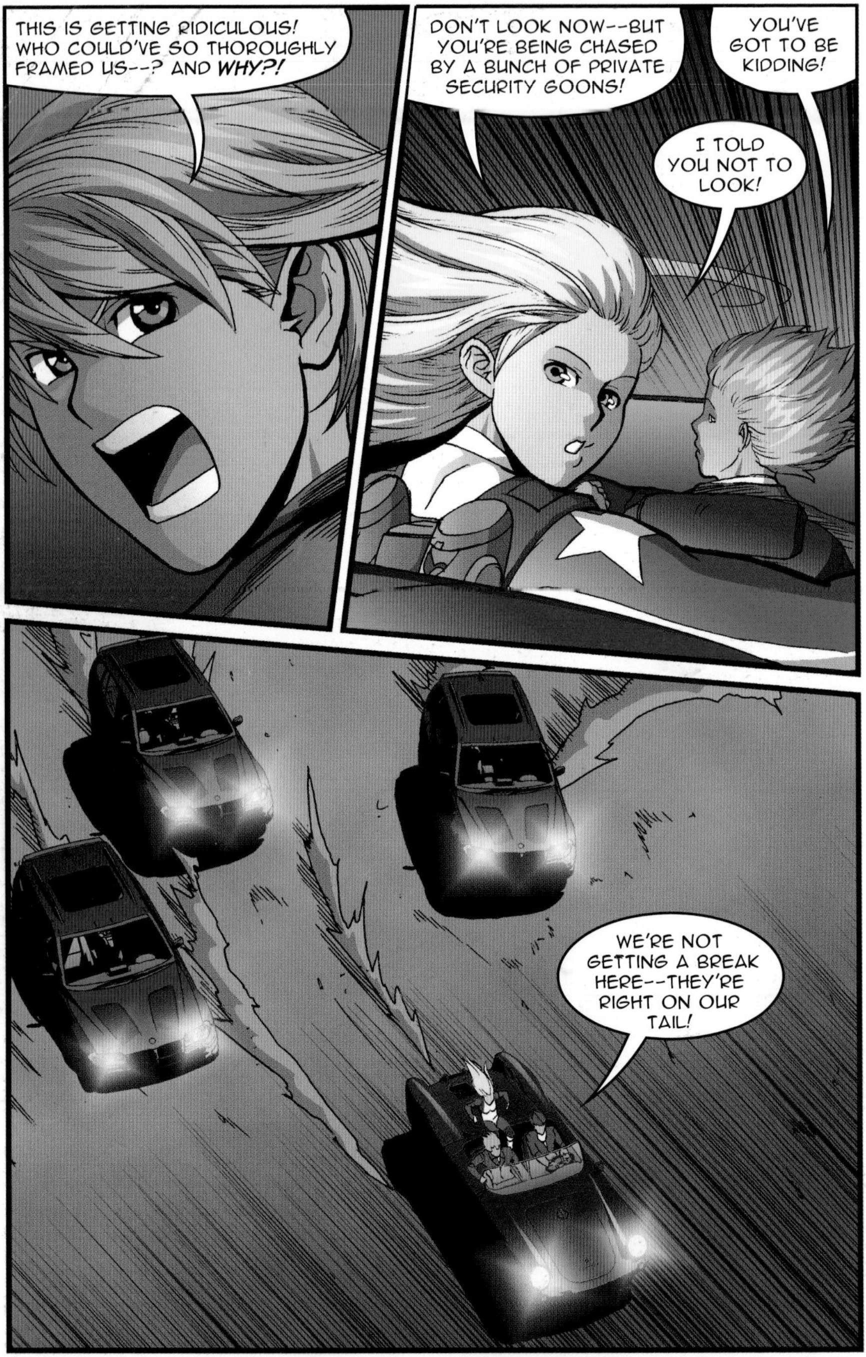
THIS IS GETTING RIDICULOUS! WHO COULD'VE SO THOROUGHLY FRAMED US--? AND WHY?!
DON'T LOOK NOW--BUT YOU'RE BEING CHASED BY A BUNCH OF PRIVATE SECURITY GOONS!
YOU'VE GOT TO BE KIDDING!
I TOLD YOU NOT TO LOOK!
WE'RE NOT GETTING A BREAK HERE--THEY'RE RIGHT ON OUR TAIL!

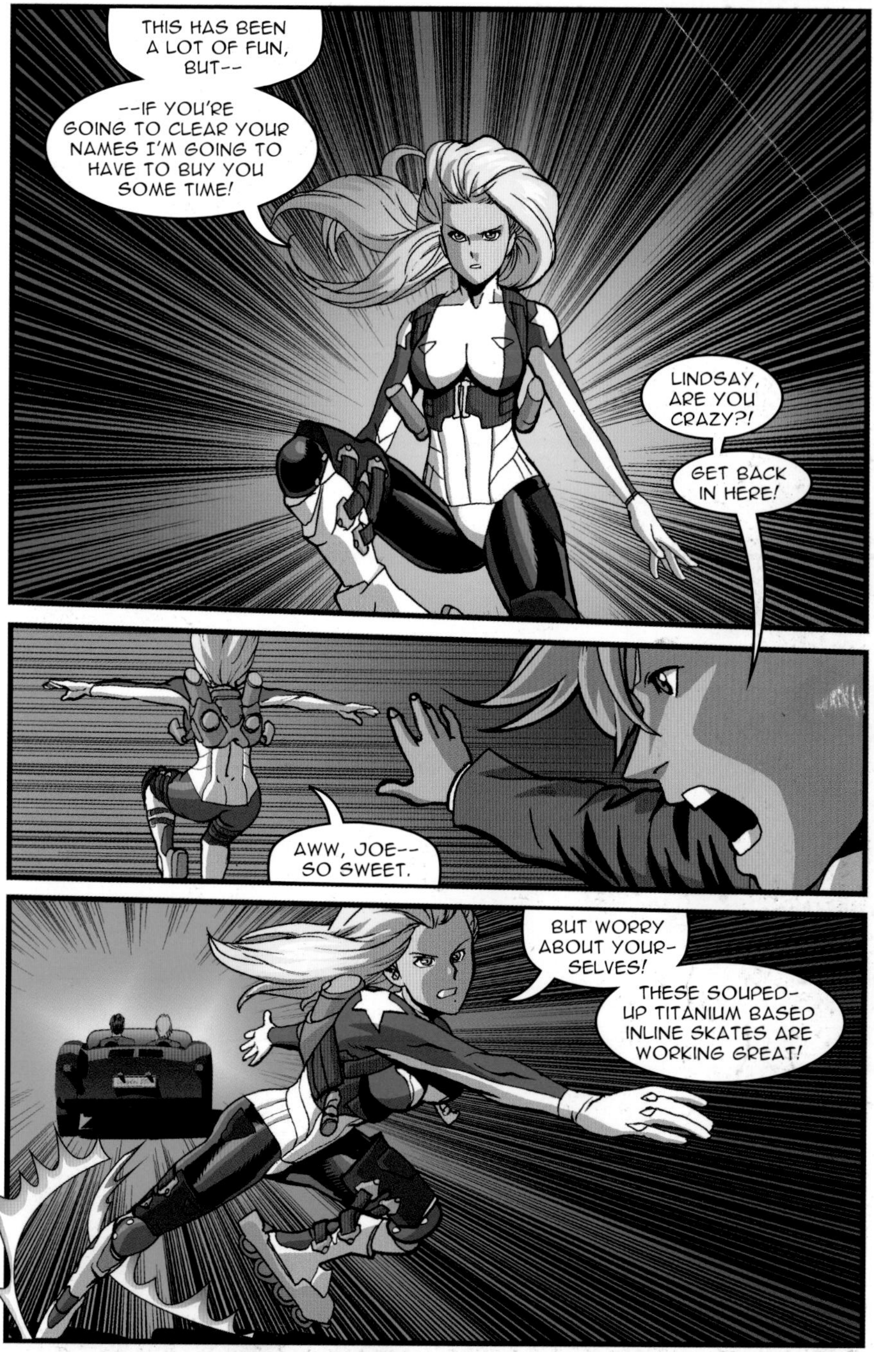
THIS HAS BEEN A LOT OF FUN, BUT--
--IF YOU'RE GOING TO CLEAR YOUR NAMES I'M GOING TO HAVE TO BUY YOU SOME TIME!
LINDSAY, ARE YOU CRAZY?!
GET BACK IN HERE!
AWW, JOE-- SO SWEET.
BUT WORRY ABOUT YOUR-SELVES!
THESE SOUPED-UP TITANIUM BASED INLINE SKATES ARE WORKING GREAT!

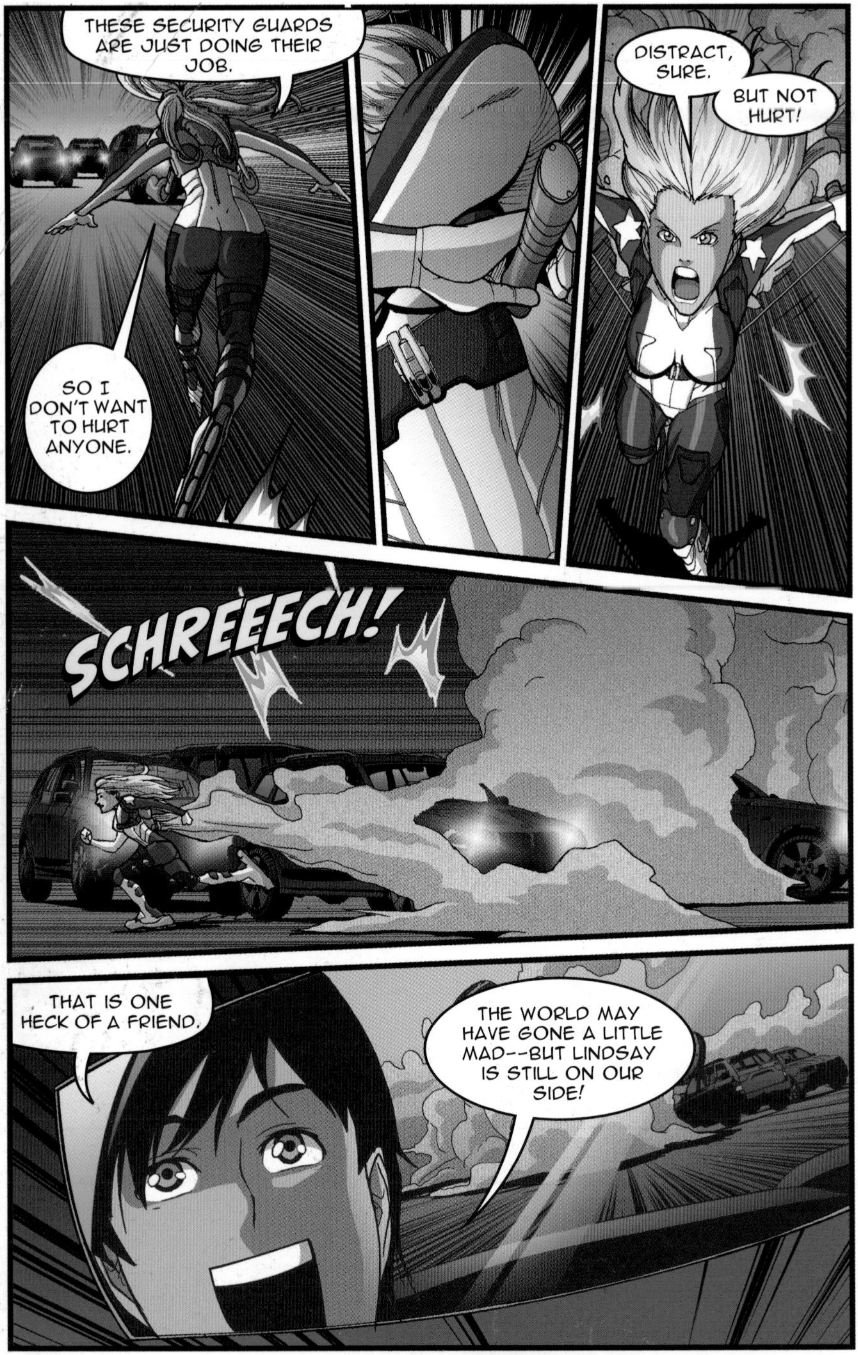
THESE SECURITY GUARDS ARE JUST DOING THEIR JOB.
SO I DON'T WANT TO HURT ANYONE.
DISTRACT, SURE.
BUT NOT HURT!
SCHREEECH!
THAT IS ONE HECK OF A FRIEND.
THE WORLD MAY HAVE GONE A LITTLE MAD--BUT LINDSAY IS STILL ON OUR SIDE!

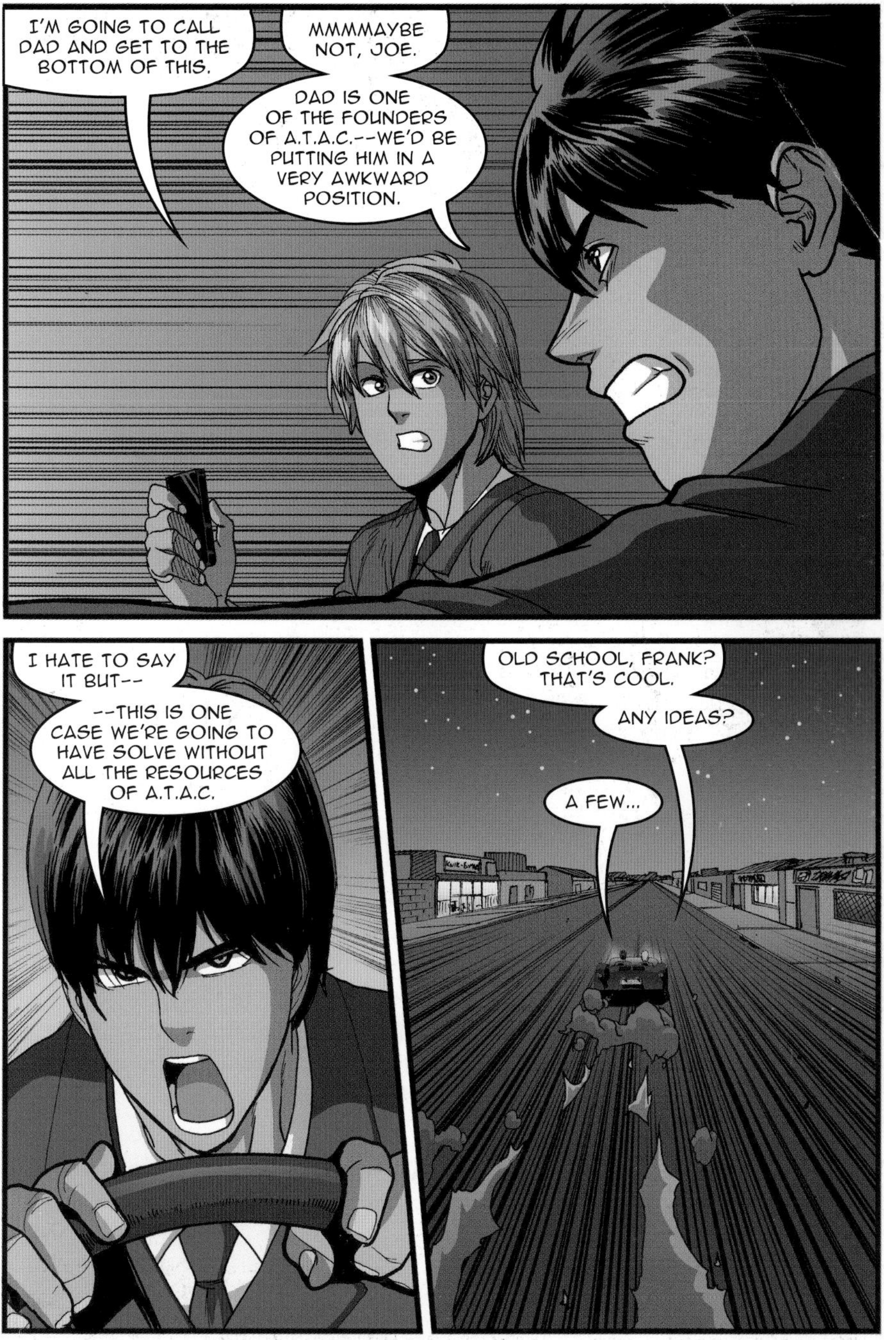
I'M GOING TO CALL DAD AND GET TO THE BOTTOM OF THIS.
MMMMAYBE NOT, JOE.
DAD IS ONE OF THE FOUNDERS OF A.T.A.C.--WE'D BE PUTTING HIM IN A VERY AWKWARD POSITION.
I HATE TO SAY IT BUT--
--THIS IS ONE CASE WE'RE GOING TO HAVE SOLVE WITHOUT ALL THE RESOURCES OF A.T.A.C.
OLD SCHOOL, FRANK? THAT'S COOL.
ANY IDEAS?
A FEW...

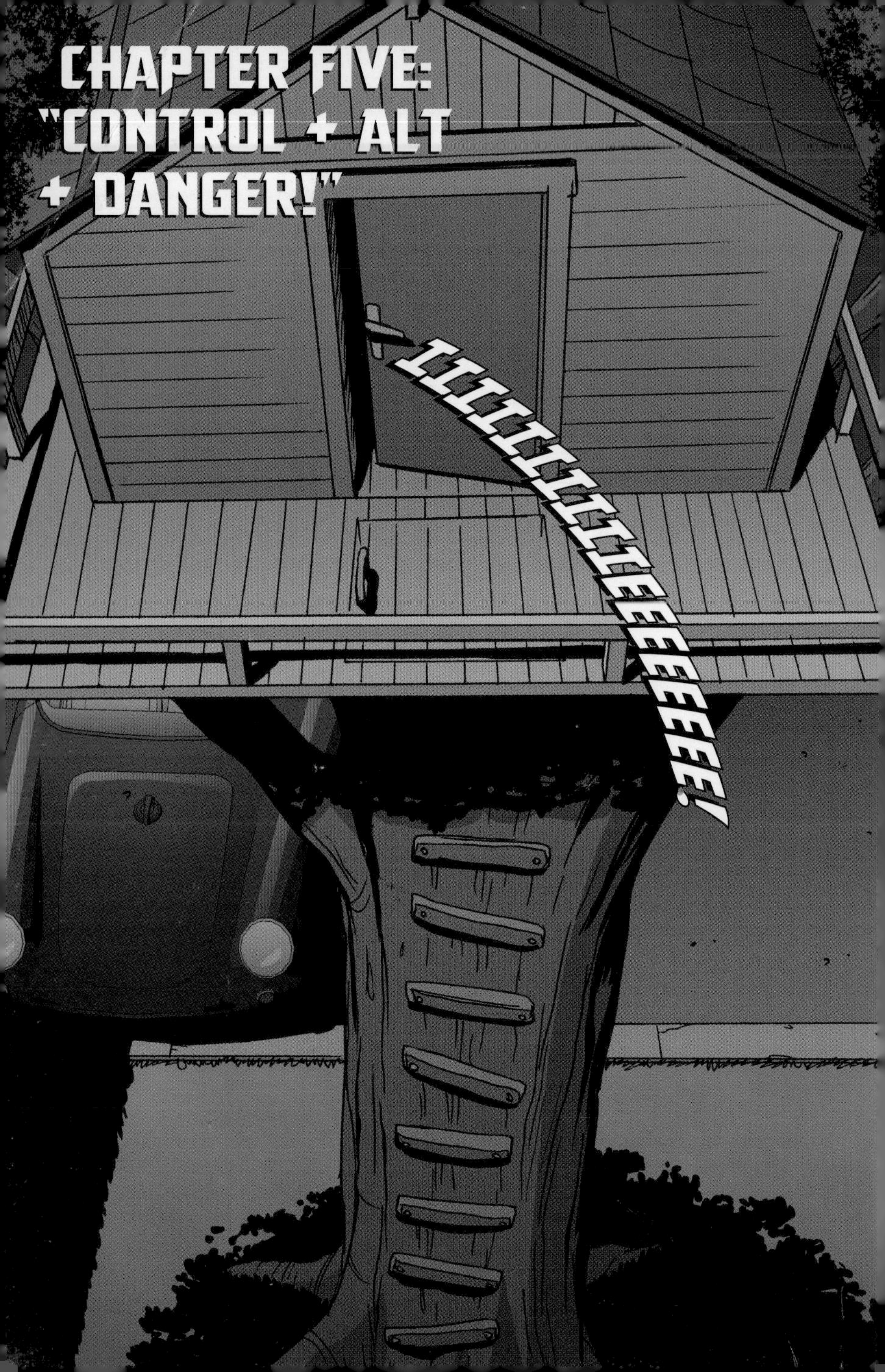
CHAPTER FIVE:
"CONTROL + ALT
+ DANGER!"
IIIIIIIIIIIEEEEEEEEE!

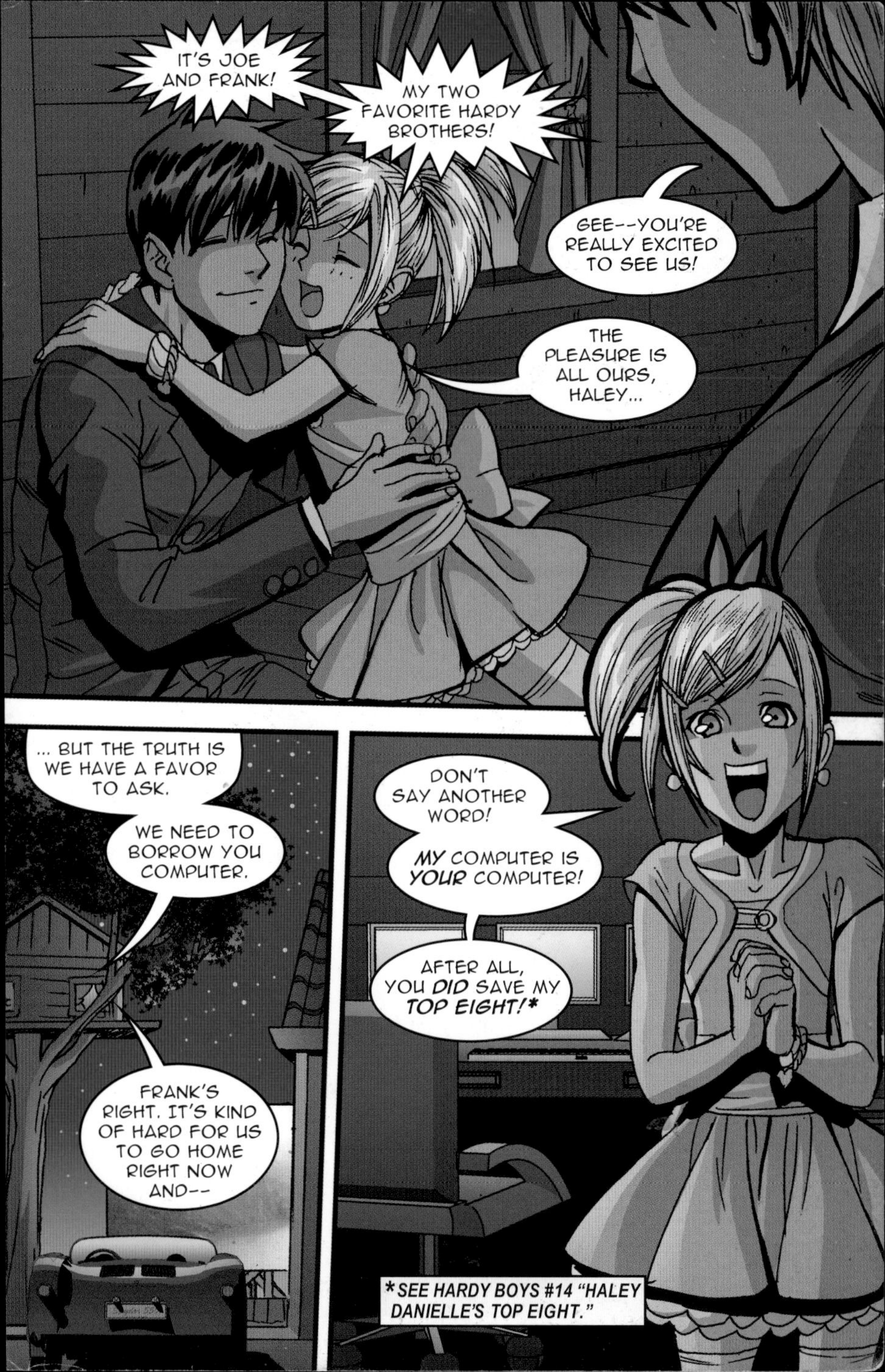
IT'S JOE AND FRANK!
MY TWO FAVORITE HARDY BROTHERS!
GEE--YOU'RE REALLY EXCITED TO SEE US!
THE PLEASURE IS ALL OURS, HALEY...
... BUT THE TRUTH IS WE HAVE A FAVOR TO ASK.
WE NEED TO BORROW YOU COMPUTER.
FRANK'S RIGHT. IT'S KIND OF HARD FOR US TO GO HOME RIGHT NOW AND--
DON'T SAY ANOTHER WORD!
MY COMPUTER IS *YOUR* COMPUTER!
AFTER ALL, YOU *DID* SAVE MY *TOP EIGHT!**
*SEE HARDY BOYS #14 "HALEY DANIELLE'S TOP EIGHT."

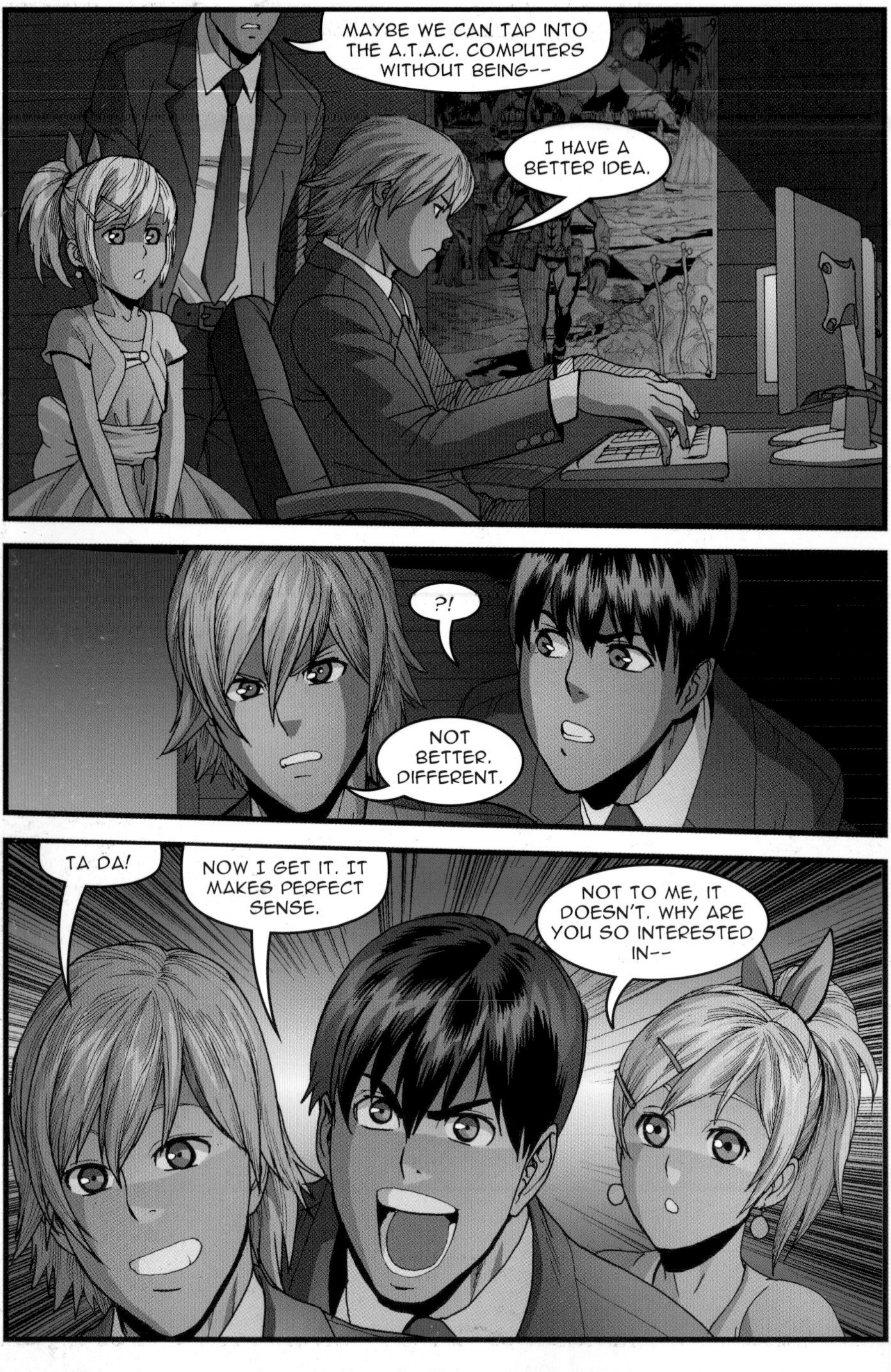

MAYBE WE CAN TAP INTO THE A.T.A.C. COMPUTERS WITHOUT BEING--
I HAVE A BETTER IDEA.
?!
NOT BETTER. DIFFERENT.
TA DA!
NOW I GET IT. IT MAKES PERFECT SENSE.
NOT TO ME, IT DOESN'T. WHY ARE YOU SO INTERESTED IN--

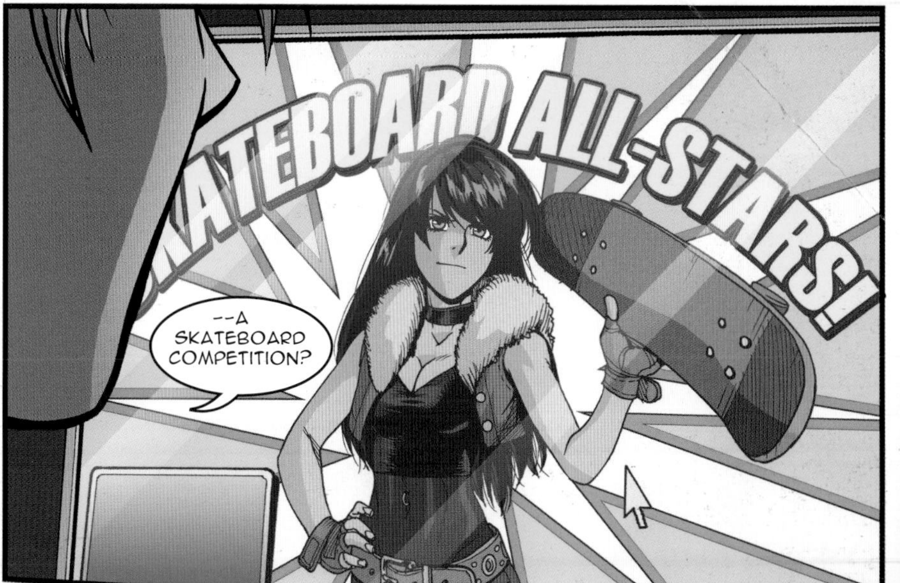
SKATEBOARD ALL-STARS!
--A SKATEBOARD COMPETITION?

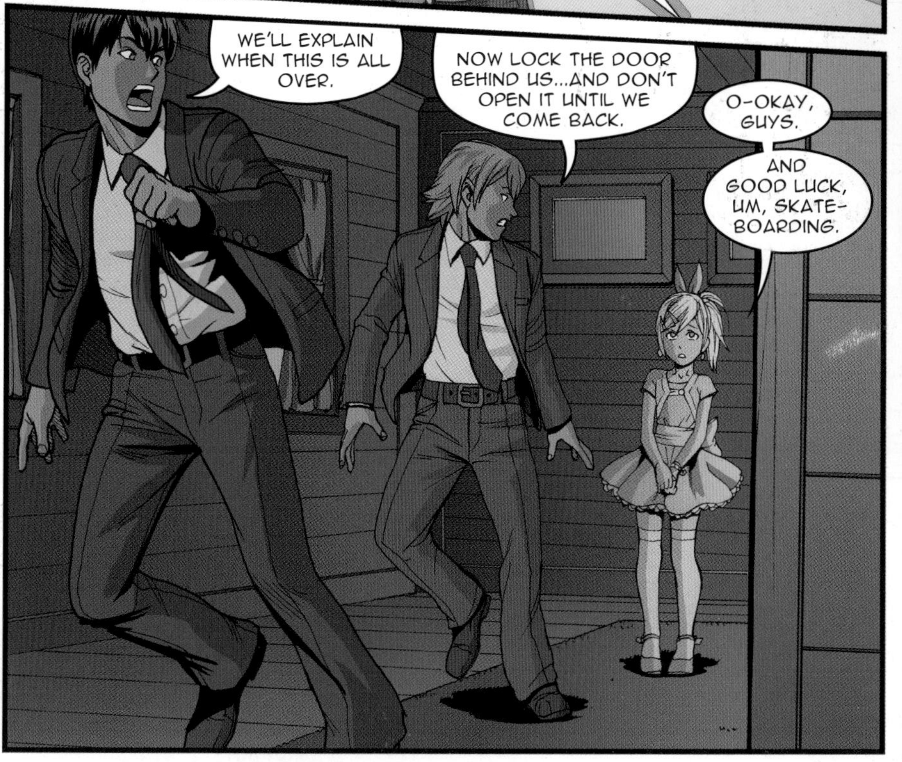
WE'LL EXPLAIN WHEN THIS IS ALL OVER.
NOW LOCK THE DOOR BEHIND US...AND DON'T OPEN IT UNTIL WE COME BACK.
O-OKAY, GUYS.
AND GOOD LUCK, UM, SKATE-BOARDING.

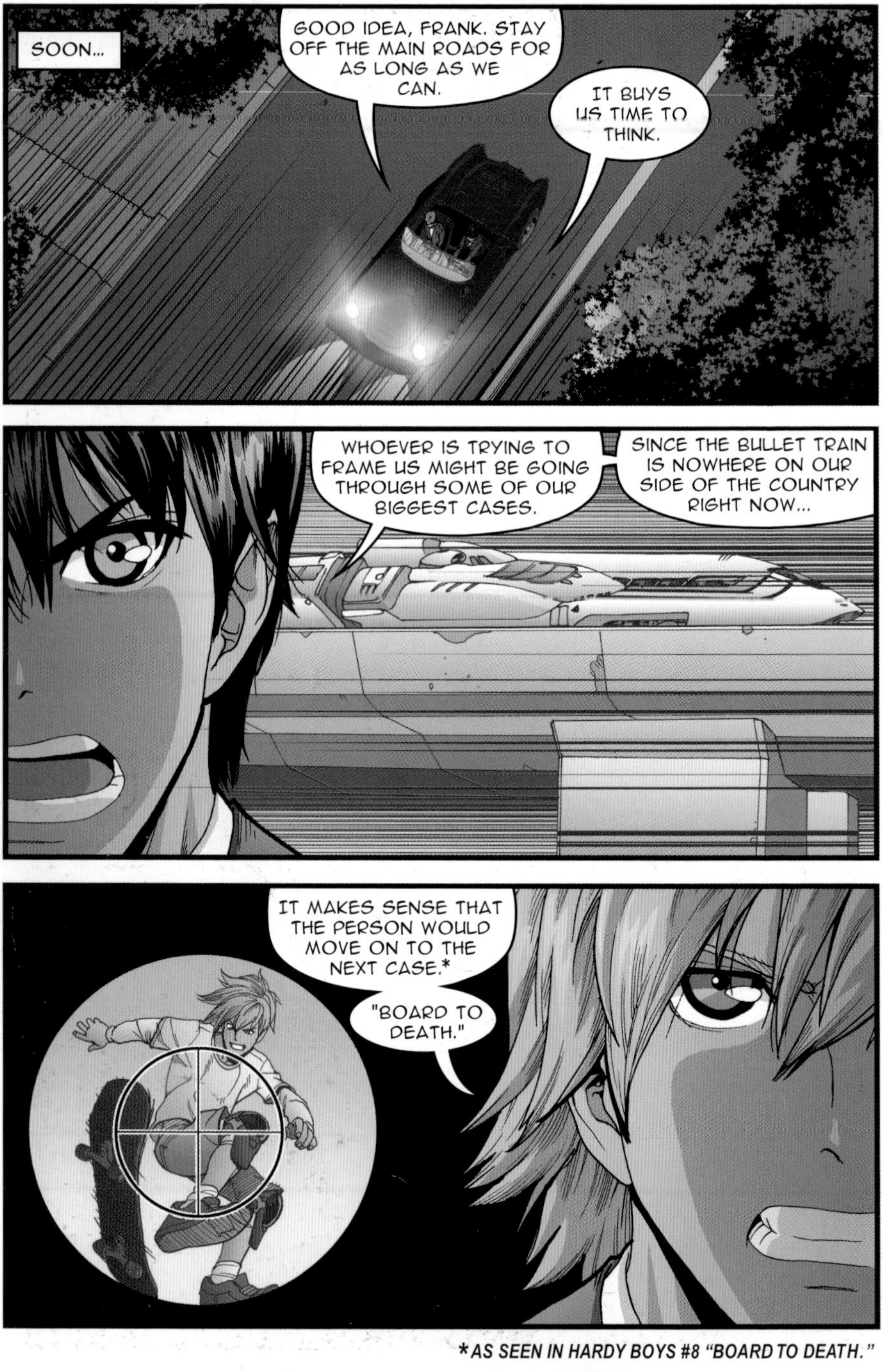
SOON...
GOOD IDEA, FRANK. STAY OFF THE MAIN ROADS FOR AS LONG AS WE CAN.
IT BUYS US TIME TO THINK.
WHOEVER IS TRYING TO FRAME US MIGHT BE GOING THROUGH SOME OF OUR BIGGEST CASES.
SINCE THE BULLET TRAIN IS NOWHERE ON OUR SIDE OF THE COUNTRY RIGHT NOW...
IT MAKES SENSE THAT THE PERSON WOULD MOVE ON TO THE NEXT CASE.*
"BOARD TO DEATH."

*AS SEEN IN HARDY BOYS #8 "BOARD TO DEATH."

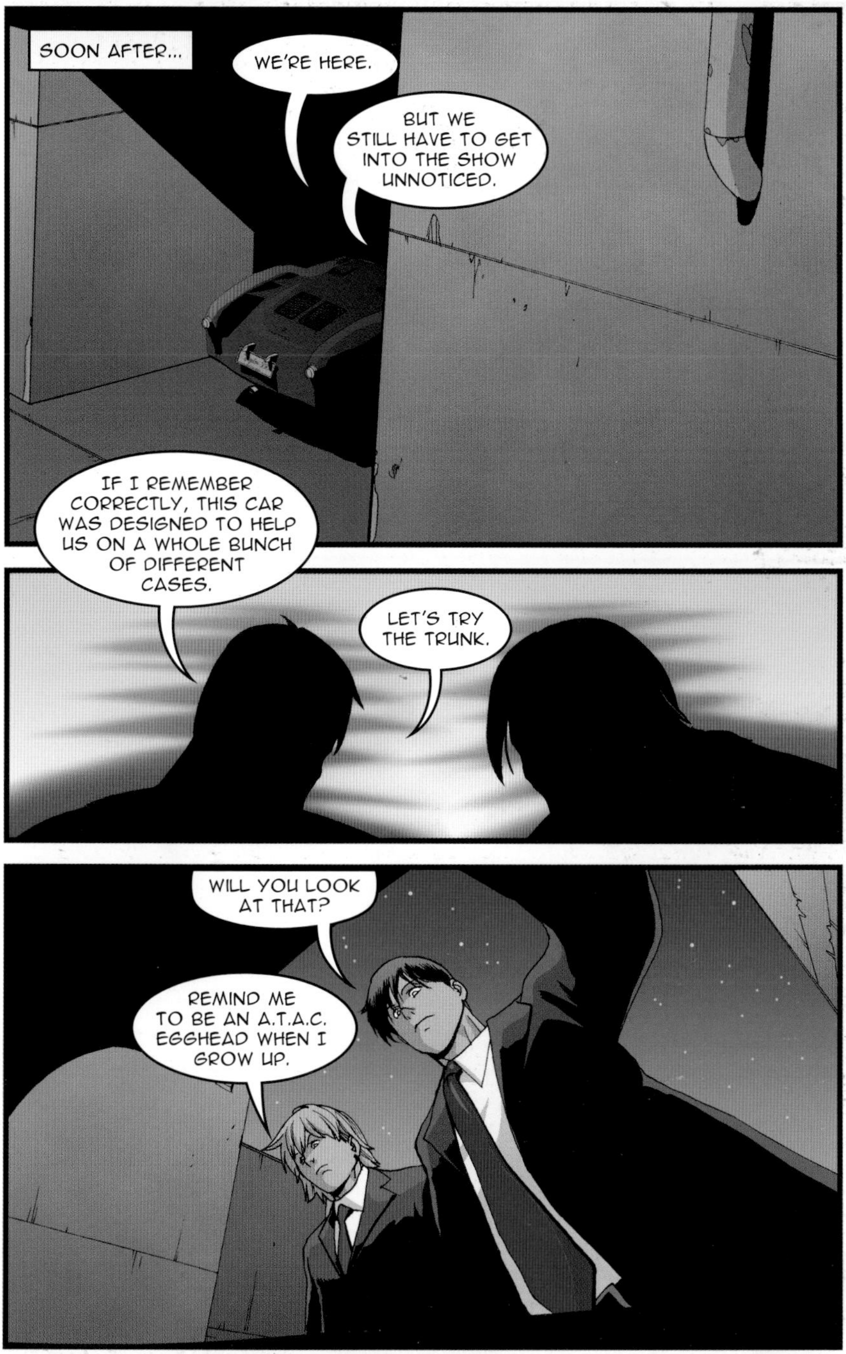
SOON AFTER...
WE'RE HERE.
BUT WE STILL HAVE TO GET INTO THE SHOW UNNOTICED.
IF I REMEMBER CORRECTLY, THIS CAR WAS DESIGNED TO HELP US ON A WHOLE BUNCH OF DIFFERENT CASES.
LET'S TRY THE TRUNK.
WILL YOU LOOK AT THAT?
REMIND ME TO BE AN A.T.A.C. EGGHEAD WHEN I GROW UP.

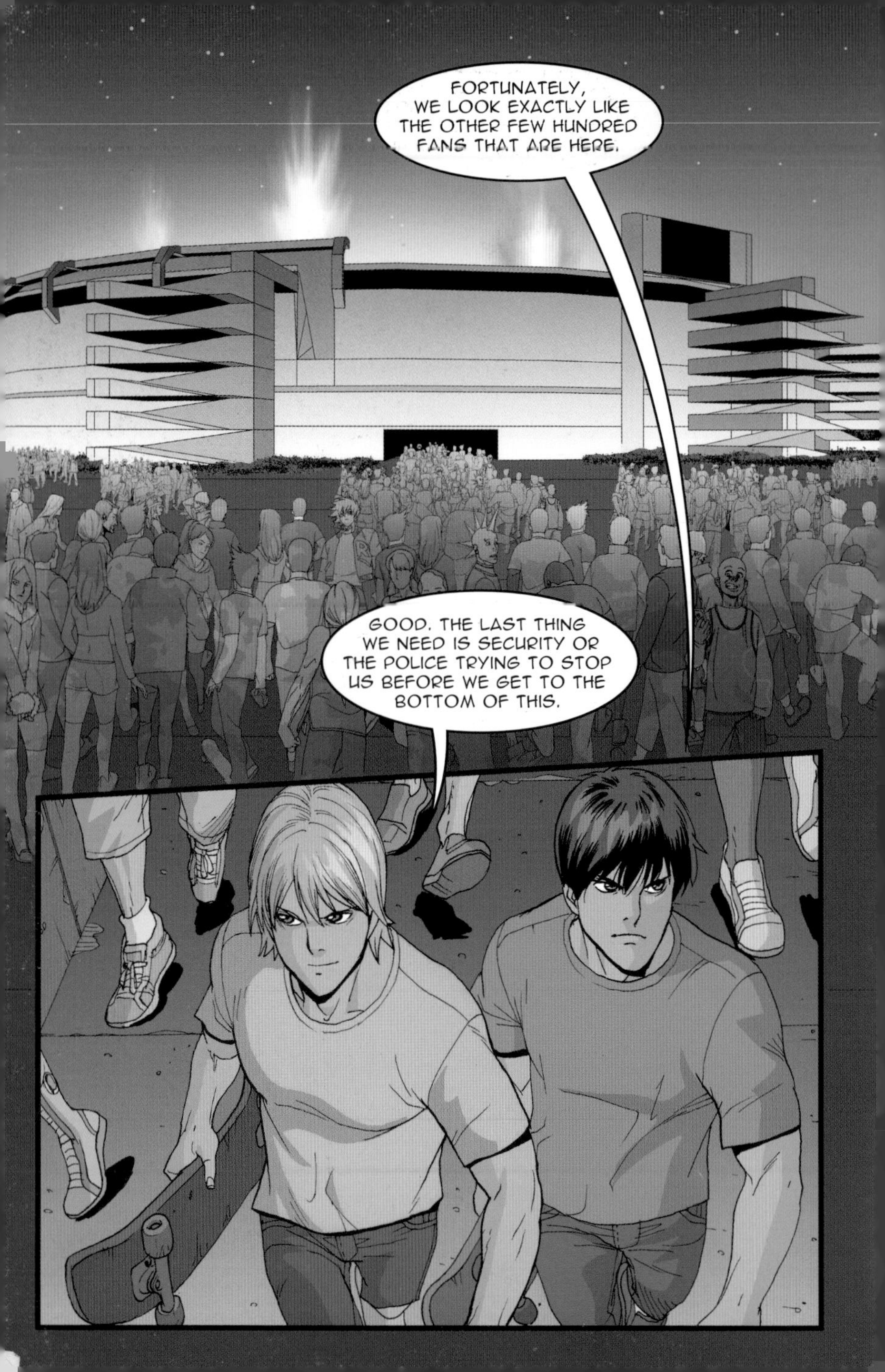
FORTUNATELY, WE LOOK EXACTLY LIKE THE OTHER FEW HUNDRED FANS THAT ARE HERE.
GOOD. THE LAST THING WE NEED IS SECURITY OR THE POLICE TRYING TO STOP US BEFORE WE GET TO THE BOTTOM OF THIS.

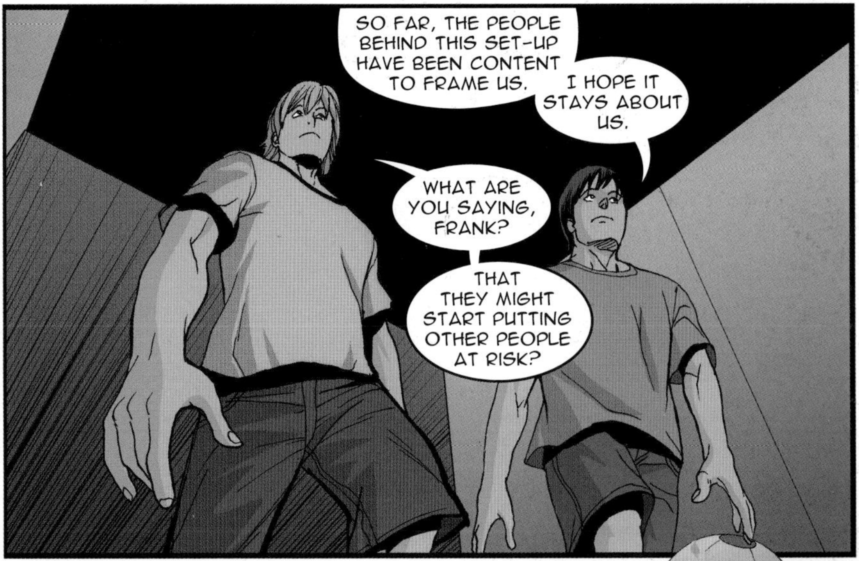
SO FAR, THE PEOPLE BEHIND THIS SET-UP HAVE BEEN CONTENT TO FRAME US.
I HOPE IT STAYS ABOUT US.
WHAT ARE YOU SAYING, FRANK?
THAT THEY MIGHT START PUTTING OTHER PEOPLE AT RISK?

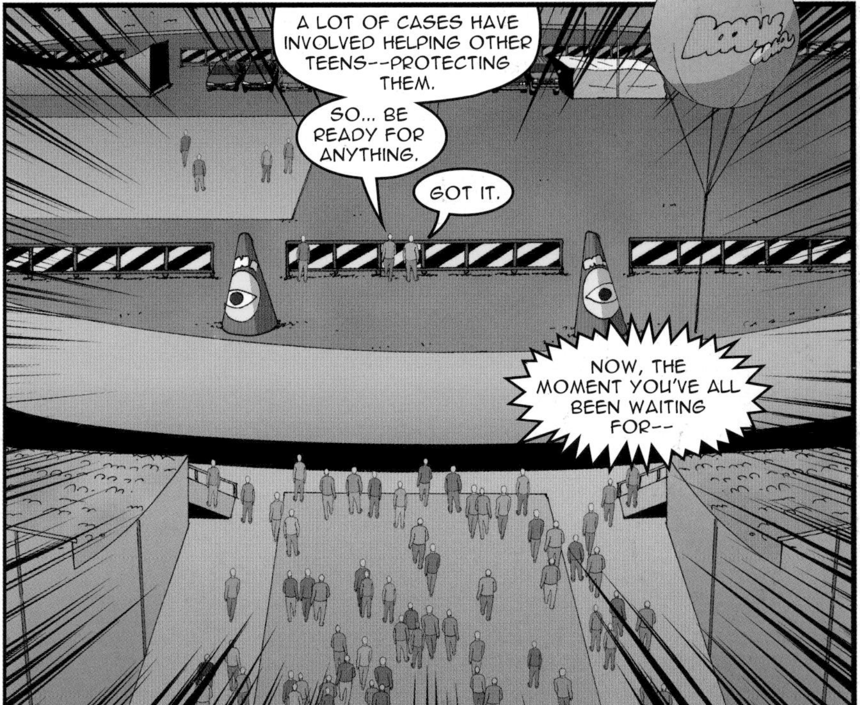
A LOT OF CASES HAVE INVOLVED HELPING OTHER TEENS--PROTECTING THEM.
SO... BE READY FOR ANYTHING.
GOT IT.
NOW, THE MOMENT YOU'VE ALL BEEN WAITING FOR--

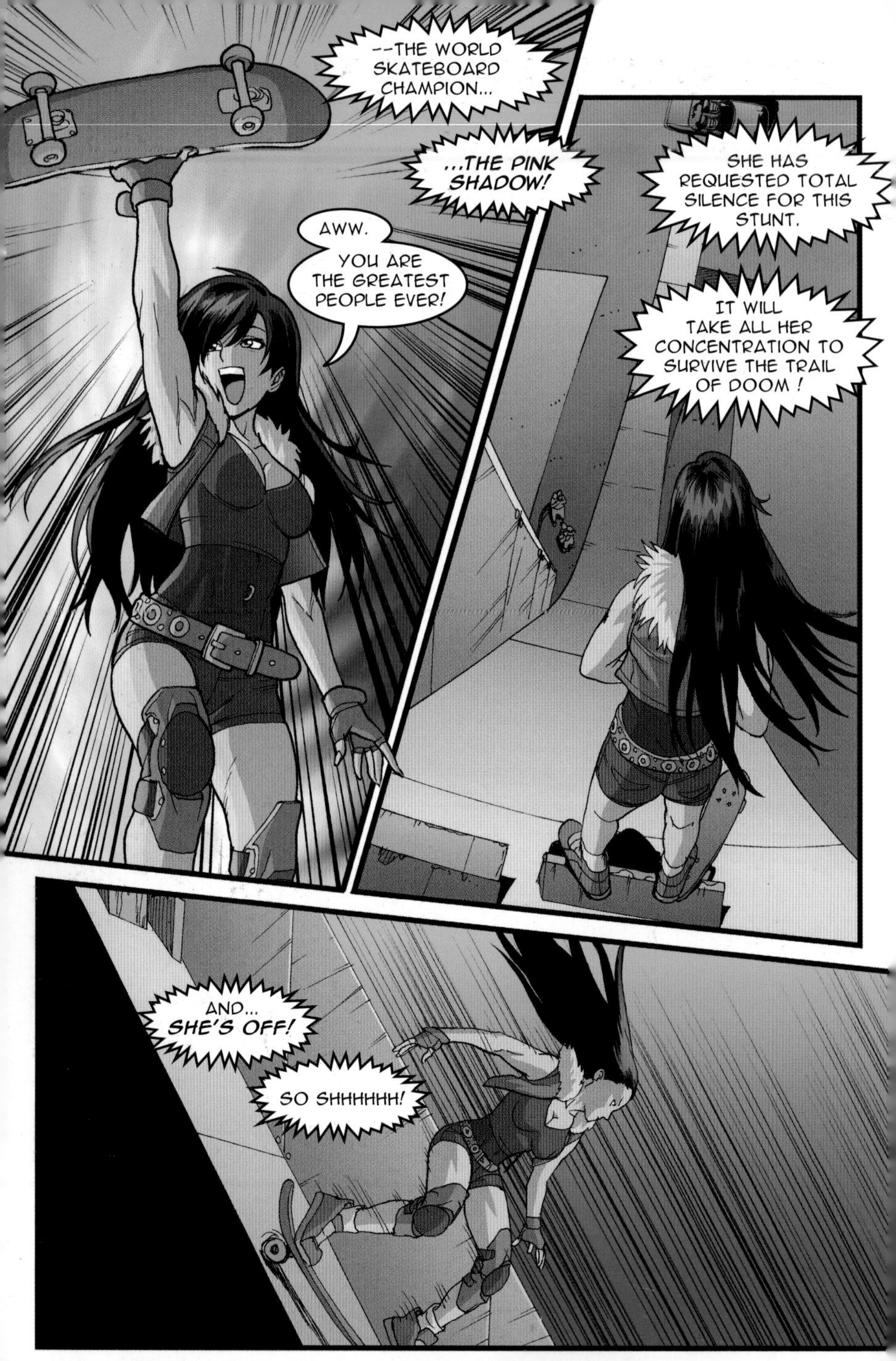
--THE WORLD SKATEBOARD CHAMPION...
...THE PINK SHADOW!
AWW.
YOU ARE THE GREATEST PEOPLE EVER!
SHE HAS REQUESTED TOTAL SILENCE FOR THIS STUNT.
IT WILL TAKE ALL HER CONCENTRATION TO SURVIVE THE TRAIL OF DOOM !
AND... SHE'S OFF!
SO SHHHHHH!

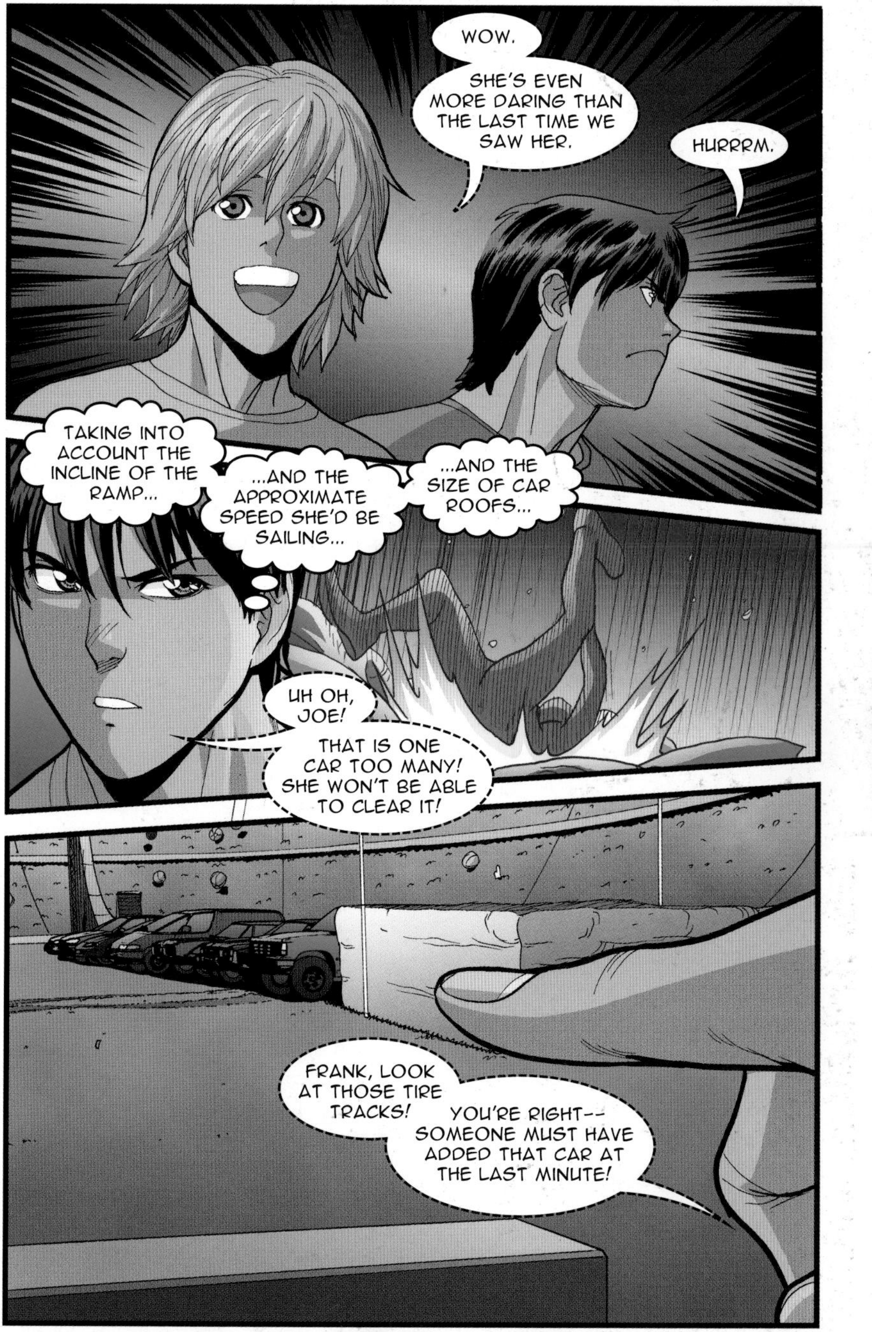
WOW.
SHE'S EVEN MORE DARING THAN THE LAST TIME WE SAW HER.
HURRRM.
TAKING INTO ACCOUNT THE INCLINE OF THE RAMP...
...AND THE APPROXIMATE SPEED SHE'D BE SAILING...
...AND THE SIZE OF CAR ROOFS...
UH OH, JOE!
THAT IS ONE CAR TOO MANY! SHE WON'T BE ABLE TO CLEAR IT!
FRANK, LOOK AT THOSE TIRE TRACKS!
YOU'RE RIGHT-- SOMEONE MUST HAVE ADDED THAT CAR AT THE LAST MINUTE!

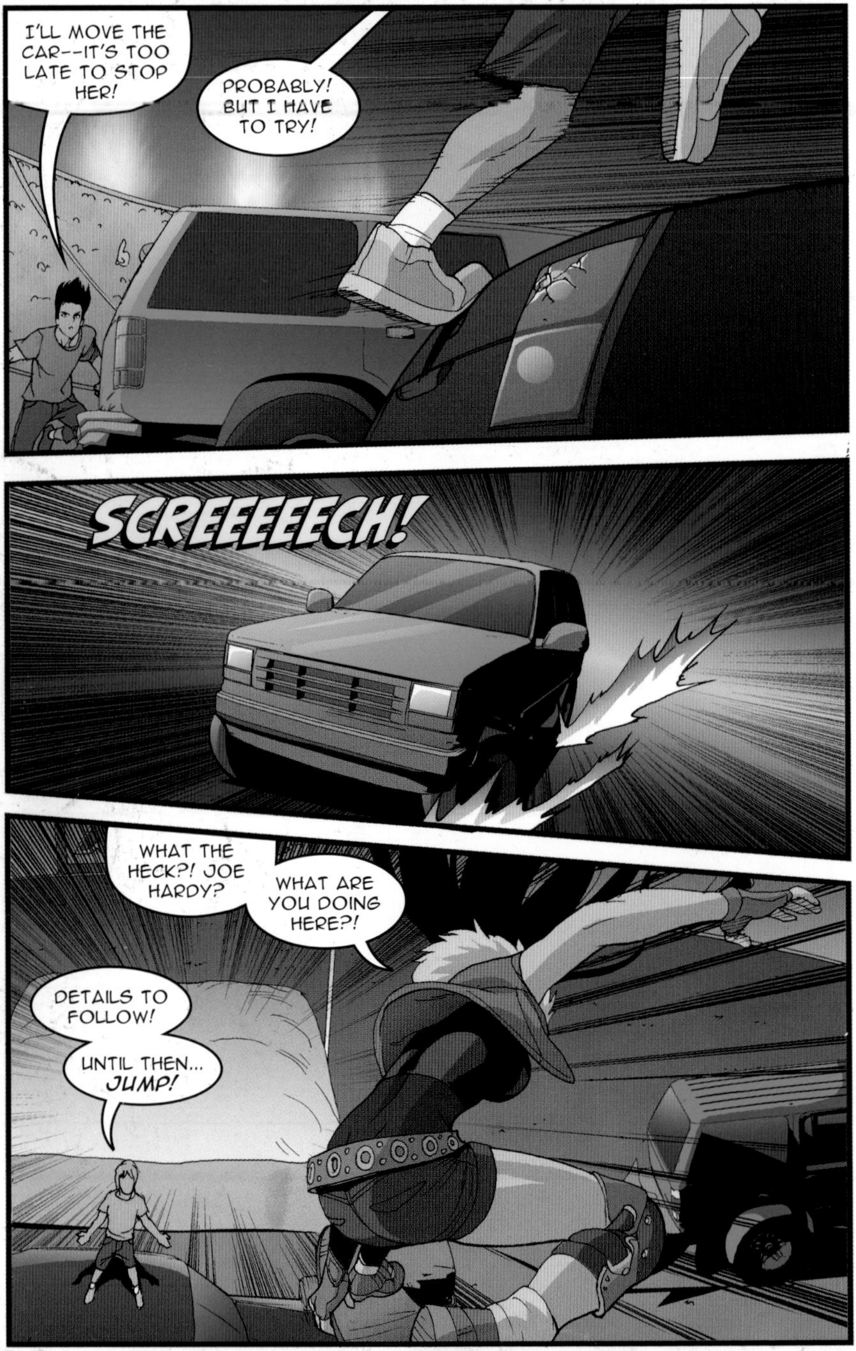
I'LL MOVE THE CAR--IT'S TOO LATE TO STOP HER!
PROBABLY! BUT I HAVE TO TRY!
SCREEEEEECH!
WHAT THE HECK?! JOE HARDY?
WHAT ARE YOU DOING HERE?!
DETAILS TO FOLLOW!
UNTIL THEN... JUMP!

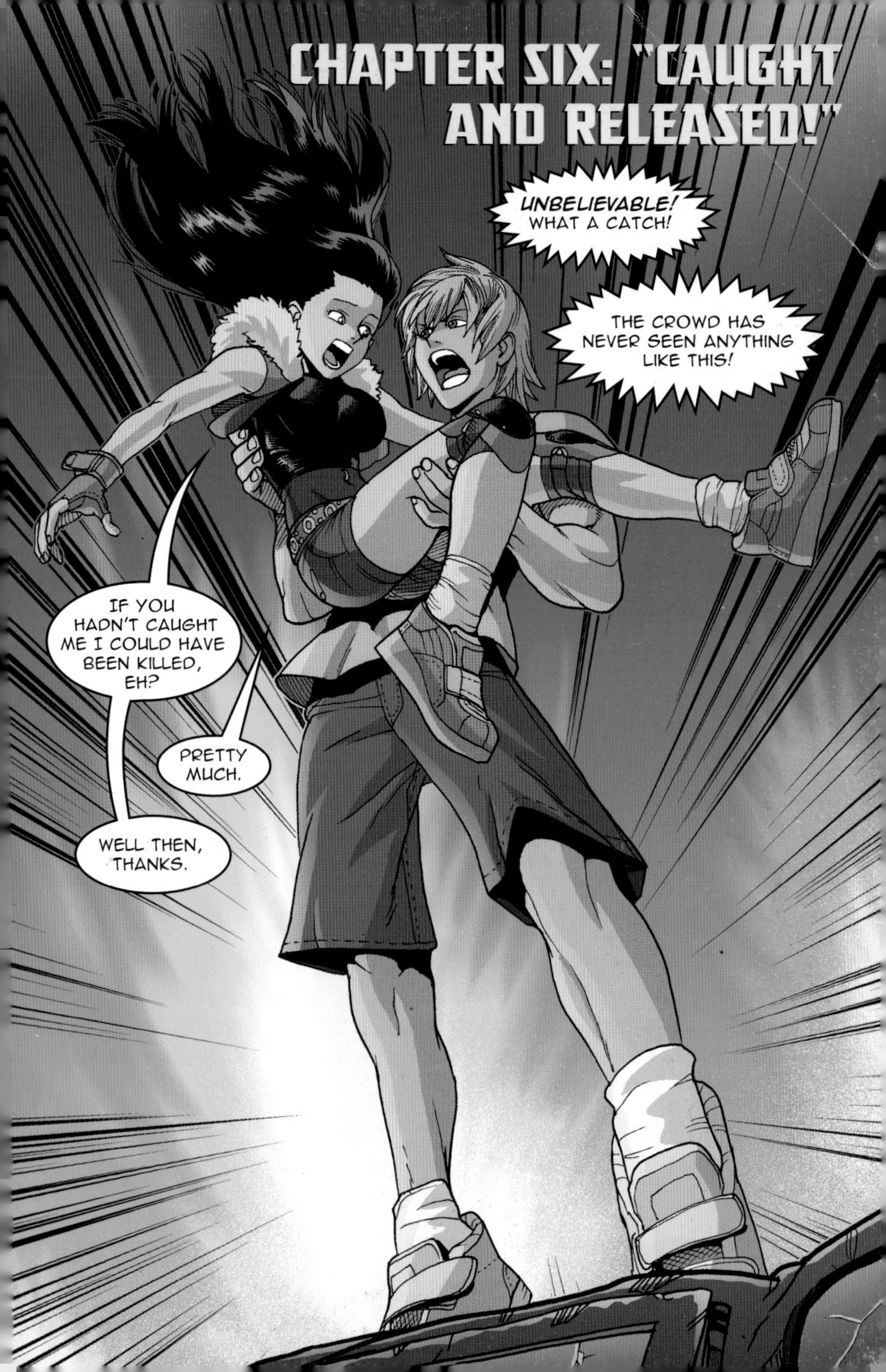
CHAPTER SIX: "CAUGHT AND RELEASED!"
UNBELIEVABLE! WHAT A CATCH!
THE CROWD HAS NEVER SEEN ANYTHING LIKE THIS!
IF YOU HADN'T CAUGHT ME I COULD HAVE BEEN KILLED, EH?
PRETTY MUCH.
WELL THEN, THANKS.

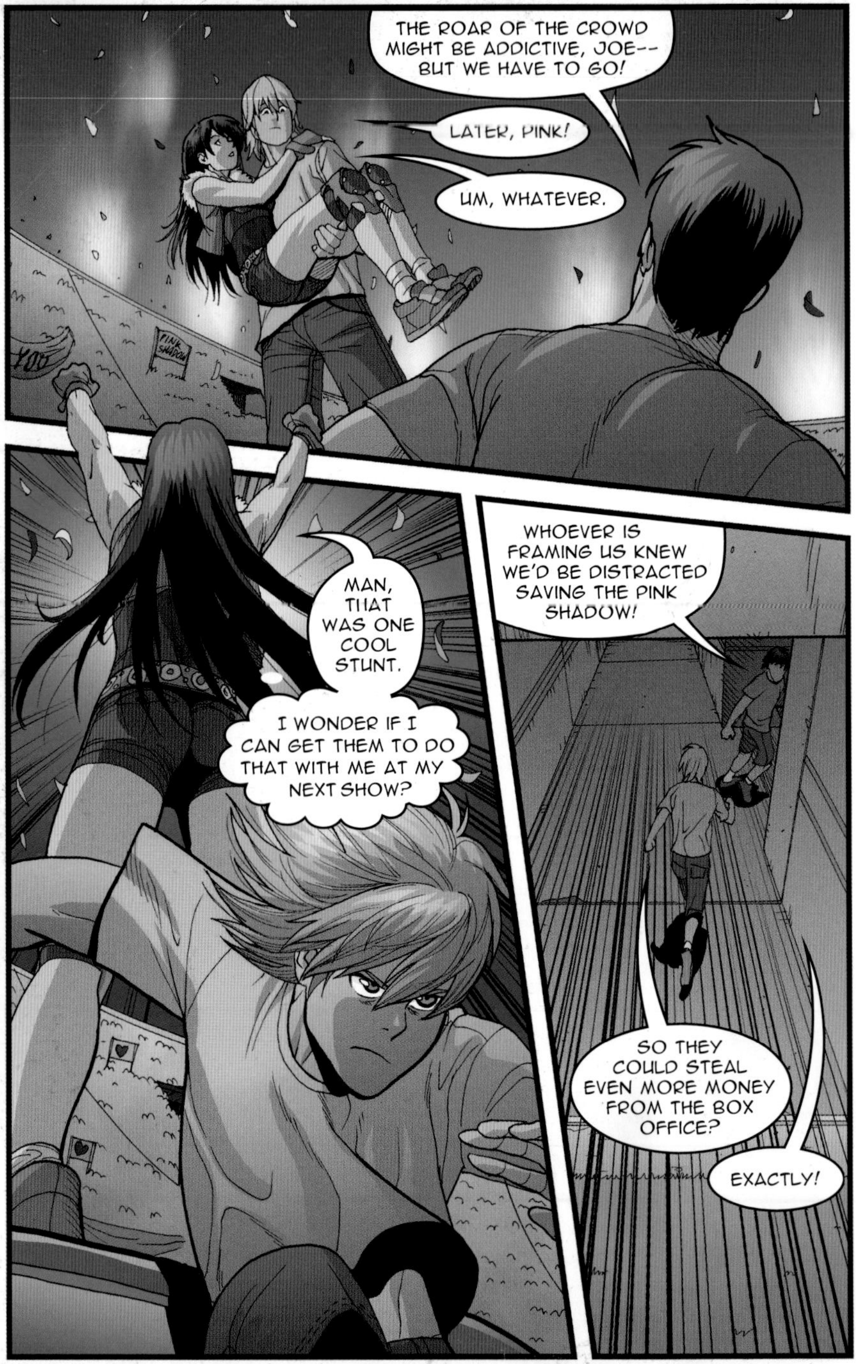
THE ROAR OF THE CROWD MIGHT BE ADDICTIVE, JOE-- BUT WE HAVE TO GO!
LATER, PINK!
UM, WHATEVER.
PINK SHADOW
MAN, THAT WAS ONE COOL STUNT.
I WONDER IF I CAN GET THEM TO DO THAT WITH ME AT MY NEXT SHOW?
WHOEVER IS FRAMING US KNEW WE'D BE DISTRACTED SAVING THE PINK SHADOW!
SO THEY COULD STEAL EVEN MORE MONEY FROM THE BOX OFFICE?
EXACTLY!

CHAPTER SEVEN: "A NUMBERS GAME!"

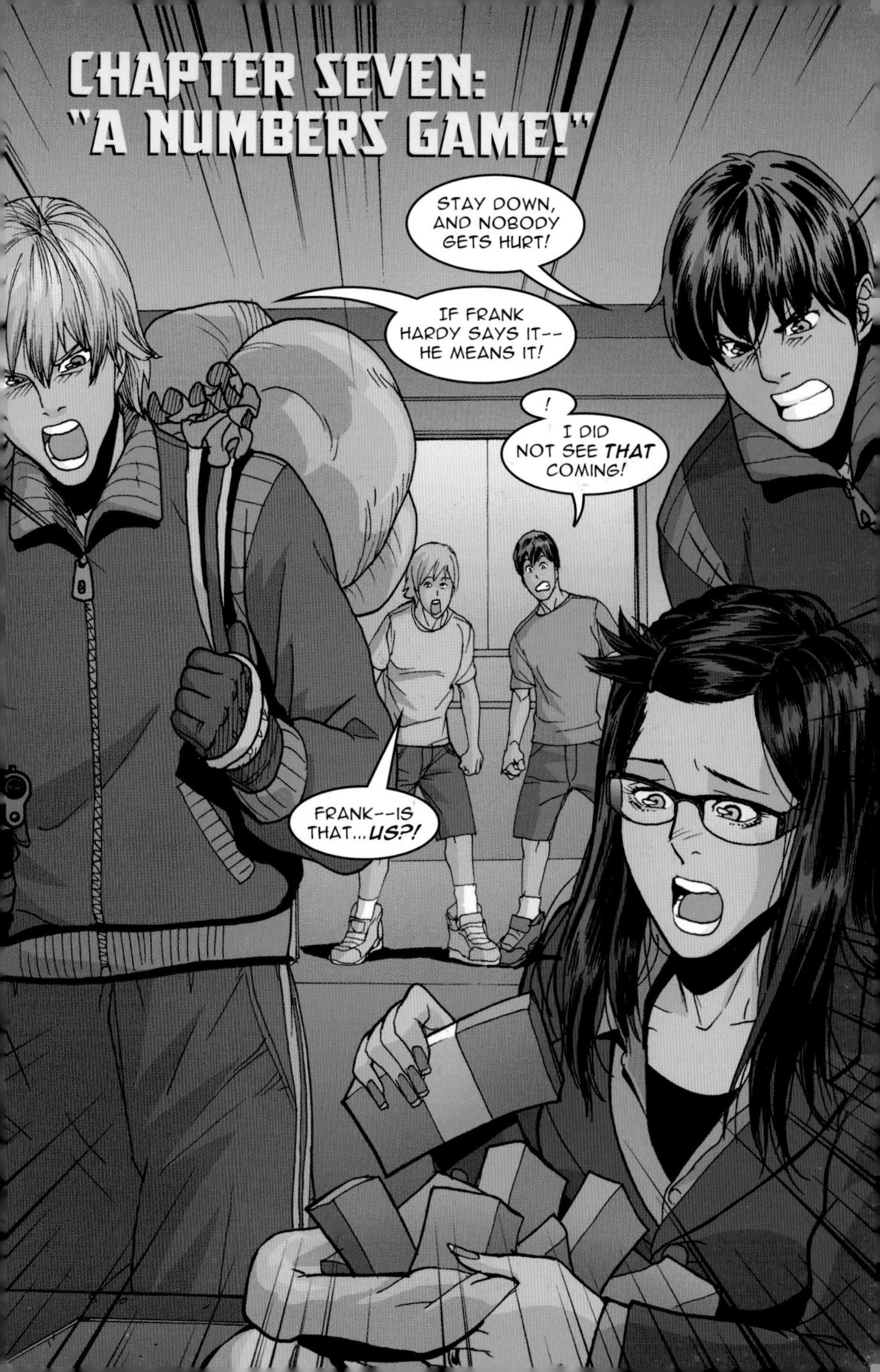
STAY DOWN, AND NOBODY GETS HURT!
IF FRANK HARDY SAYS IT-- HE MEANS IT!
!
I DID NOT SEE *THAT* COMING!
FRANK--IS THAT...*US?!*

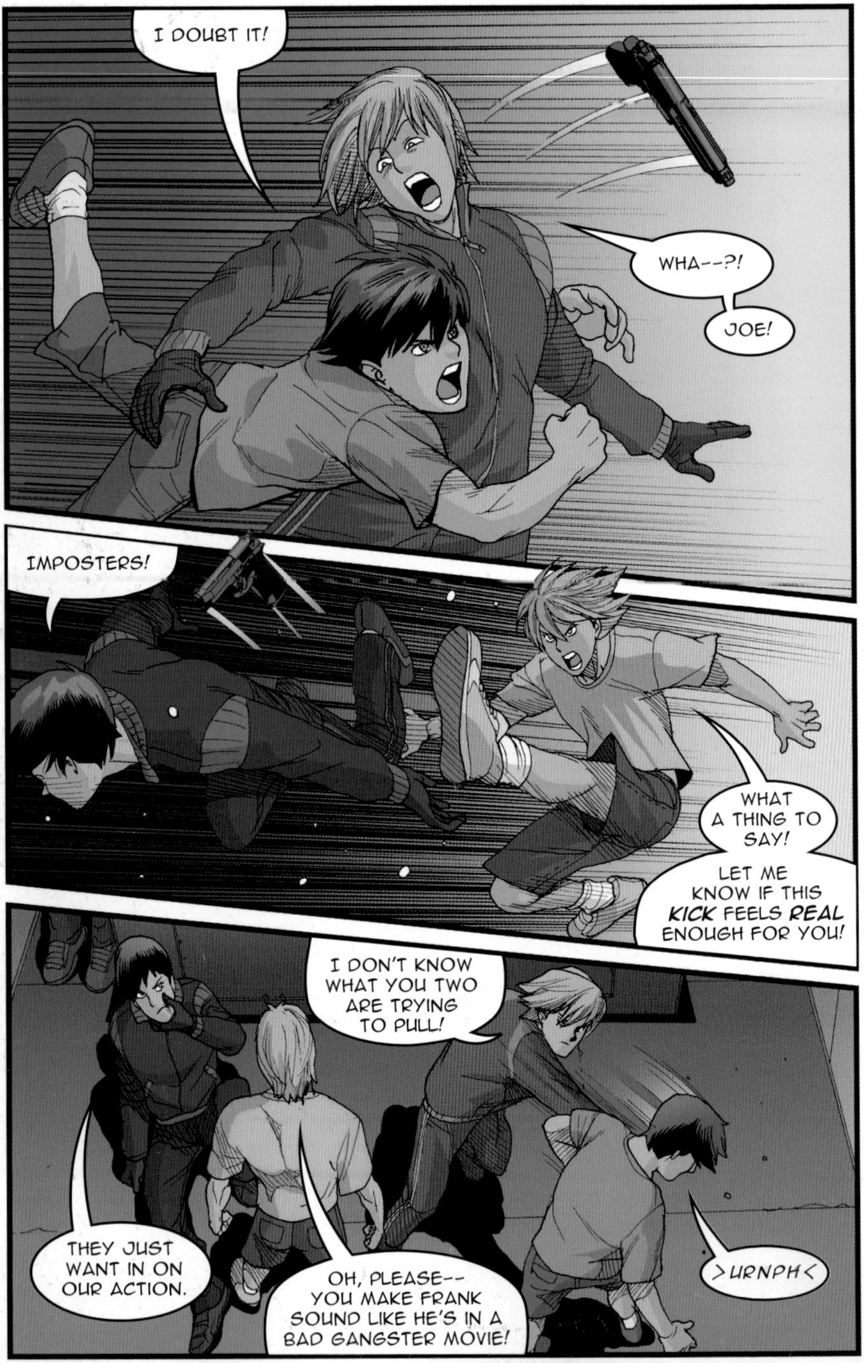
I DOUBT IT!
WHA--?!
JOE!
IMPOSTERS!
WHAT A THING TO SAY!
LET ME KNOW IF THIS KICK FEELS REAL ENOUGH FOR YOU!
I DON'T KNOW WHAT YOU TWO ARE TRYING TO PULL!
THEY JUST WANT IN ON OUR ACTION.
OH, PLEASE-- YOU MAKE FRANK SOUND LIKE HE'S IN A BAD GANGSTER MOVIE!
>URNPH<

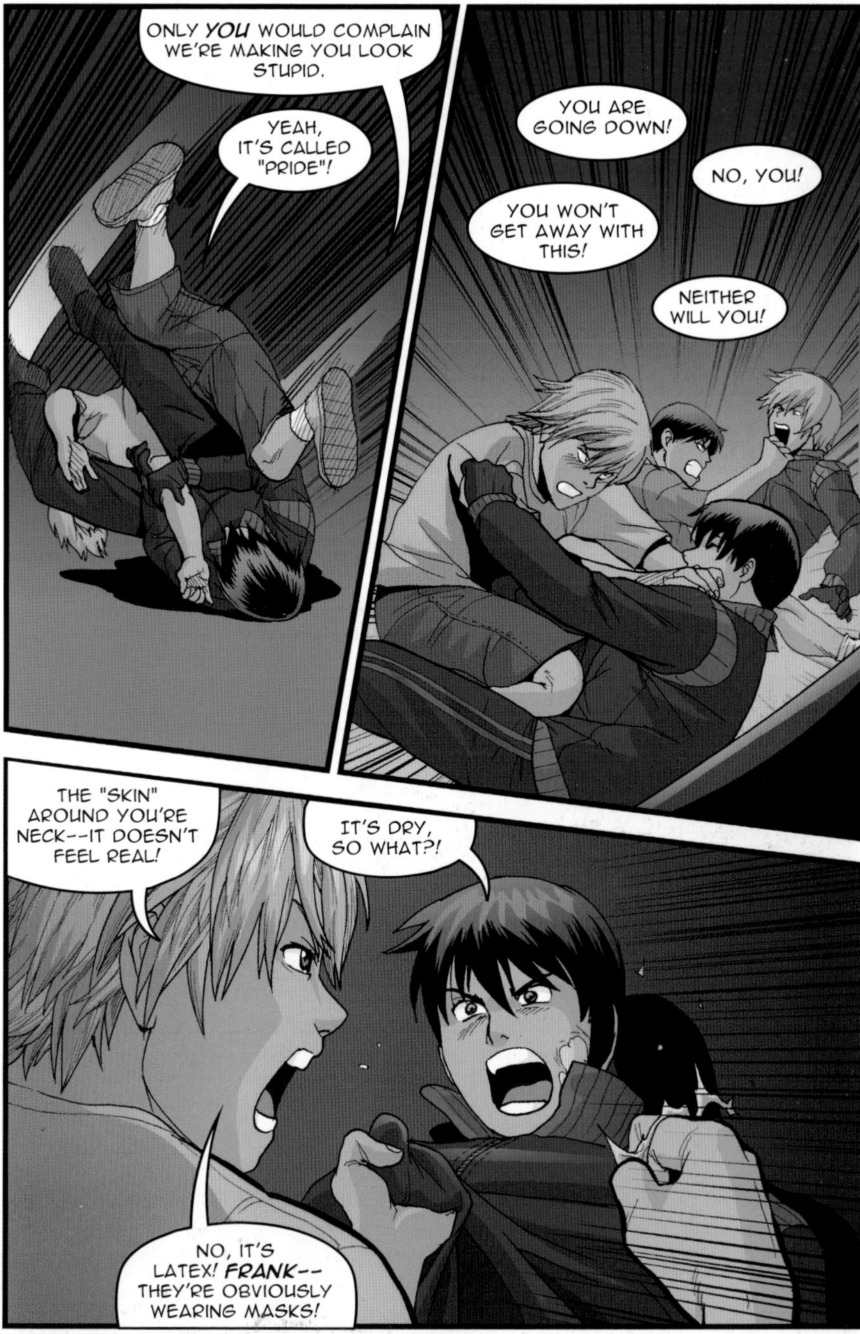
ONLY *YOU* WOULD COMPLAIN WE'RE MAKING YOU LOOK STUPID.
YEAH, IT'S CALLED "PRIDE"!
YOU ARE GOING DOWN!
NO, YOU!
YOU WON'T GET AWAY WITH THIS!
NEITHER WILL YOU!
THE "SKIN" AROUND YOU'RE NECK--IT DOESN'T FEEL REAL!
IT'S DRY, SO WHAT?!
NO, IT'S LATEX! ***FRANK***-- THEY'RE OBVIOUSLY WEARING MASKS!

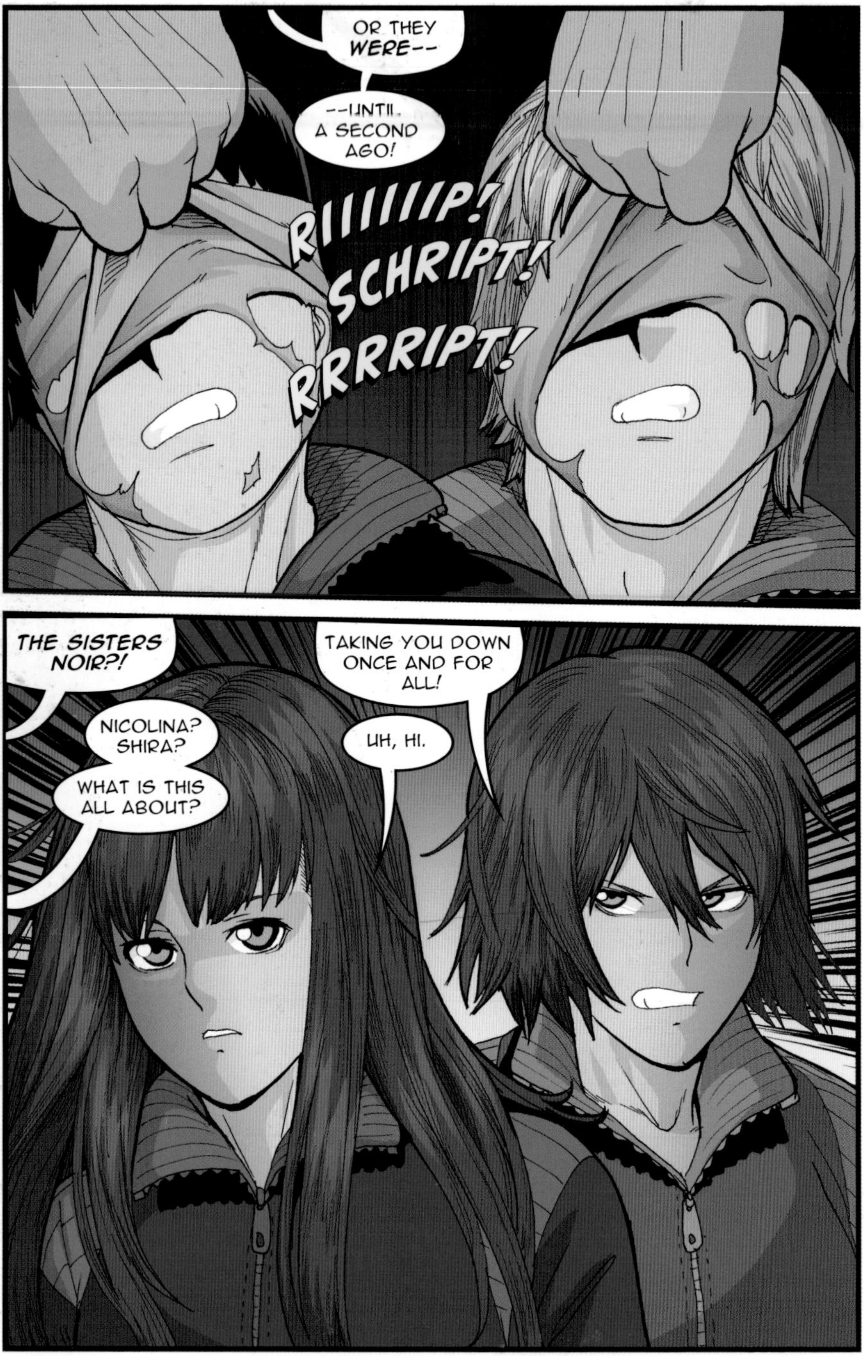
OR THEY WERE--
--UNTIL A SECOND AGO!
RIIIIIIP!
SCHRIPT!
RRRRIPT!
THE SISTERS NOIR?!
NICOLINA? SHIRA?
WHAT IS THIS ALL ABOUT?
TAKING YOU DOWN ONCE AND FOR ALL!
UH, HI.

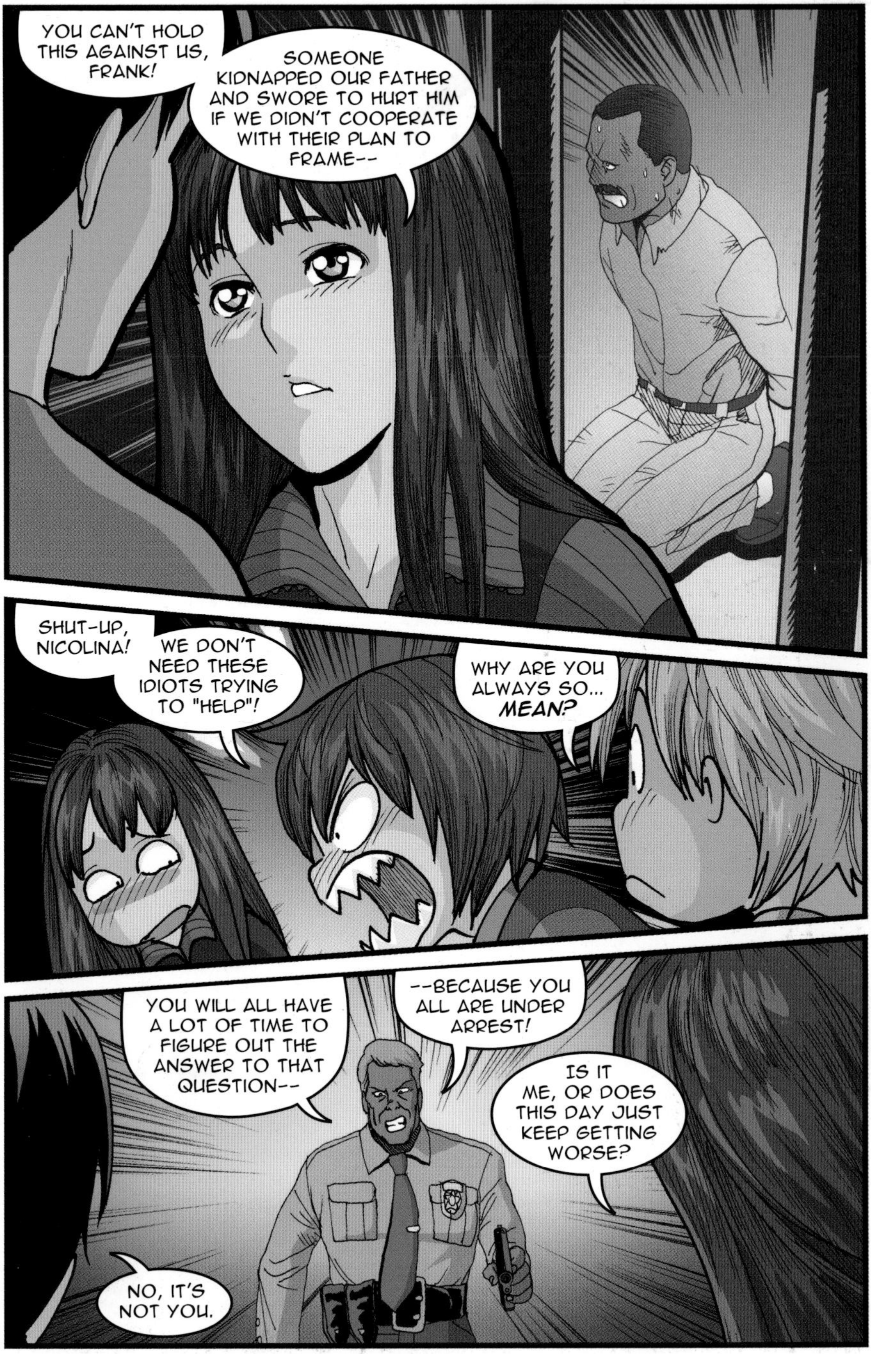

YOU CAN'T HOLD THIS AGAINST US, FRANK!
SOMEONE KIDNAPPED OUR FATHER AND SWORE TO HURT HIM IF WE DIDN'T COOPERATE WITH THEIR PLAN TO FRAME--
SHUT-UP, NICOLINA!
WE DON'T NEED THESE IDIOTS TRYING TO "HELP"!
WHY ARE YOU ALWAYS SO... *MEAN?*
YOU WILL ALL HAVE A LOT OF TIME TO FIGURE OUT THE ANSWER TO THAT QUESTION--
--BECAUSE YOU ALL ARE UNDER ARREST!
IS IT ME, OR DOES THIS DAY JUST KEEP GETTING WORSE?
NO, IT'S NOT YOU.

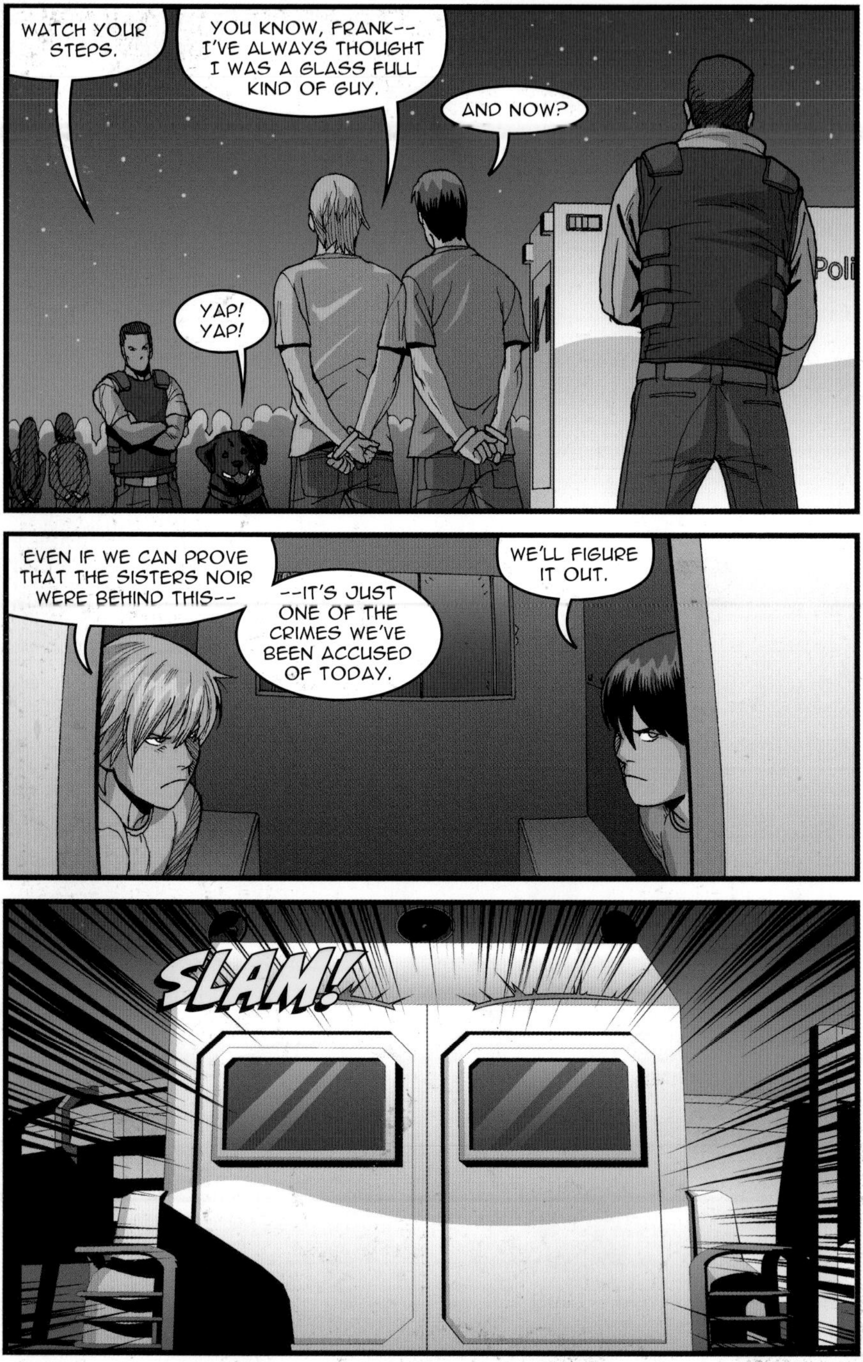
WATCH YOUR STEPS.
YOU KNOW, FRANK-- I'VE ALWAYS THOUGHT I WAS A GLASS FULL KIND OF GUY.
AND NOW?
YAP! YAP!
EVEN IF WE CAN PROVE THAT THE SISTERS NOIR WERE BEHIND THIS--
--IT'S JUST ONE OF THE CRIMES WE'VE BEEN ACCUSED OF TODAY.
WE'LL FIGURE IT OUT.
SLAM!

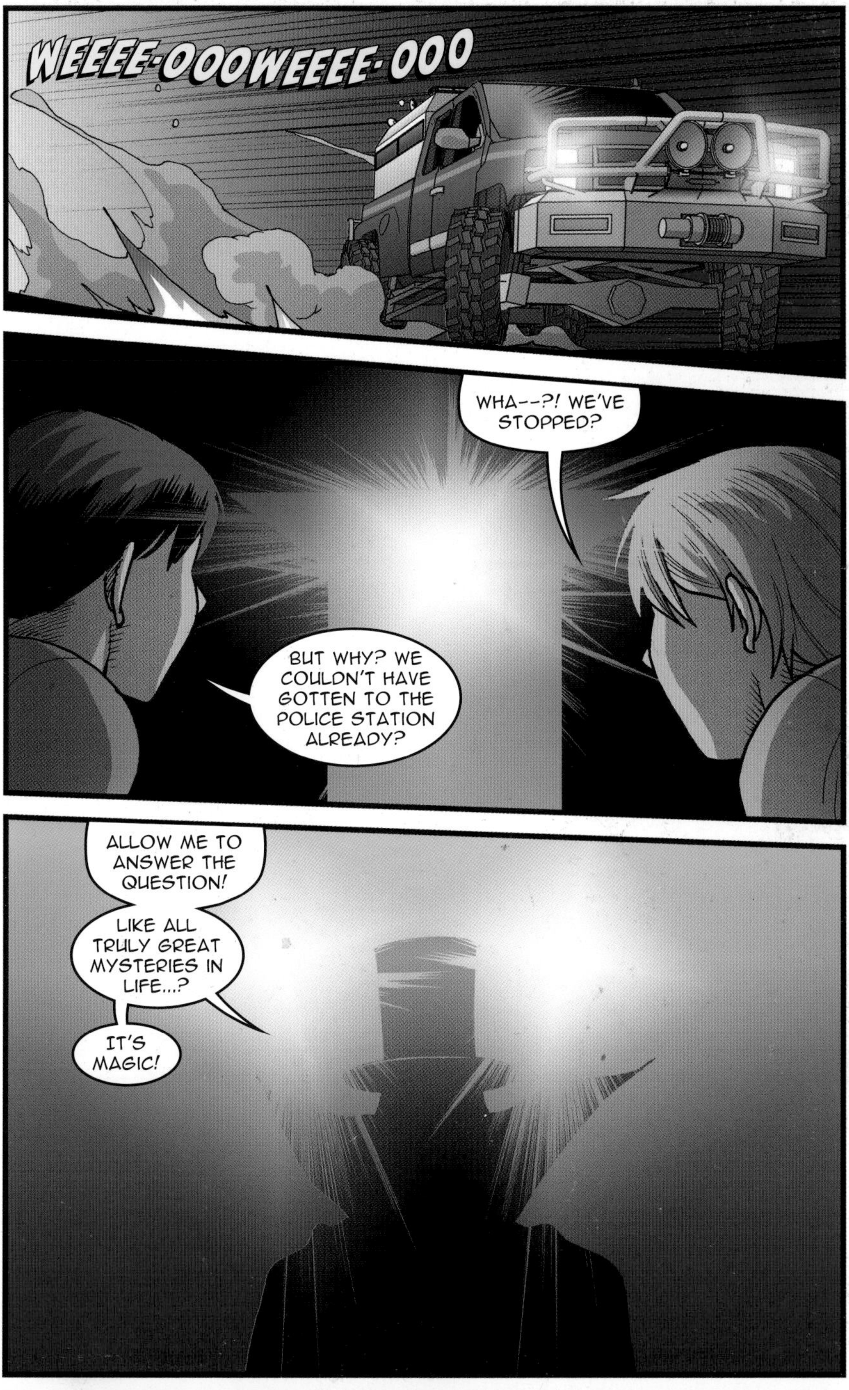
WEEEE-OOOWEEEE-OOO
WHA--?! WE'VE STOPPED?
BUT WHY? WE COULDN'T HAVE GOTTEN TO THE POLICE STATION ALREADY?
ALLOW ME TO ANSWER THE QUESTION!
LIKE ALL TRULY GREAT MYSTERIES IN LIFE...?
IT'S MAGIC!

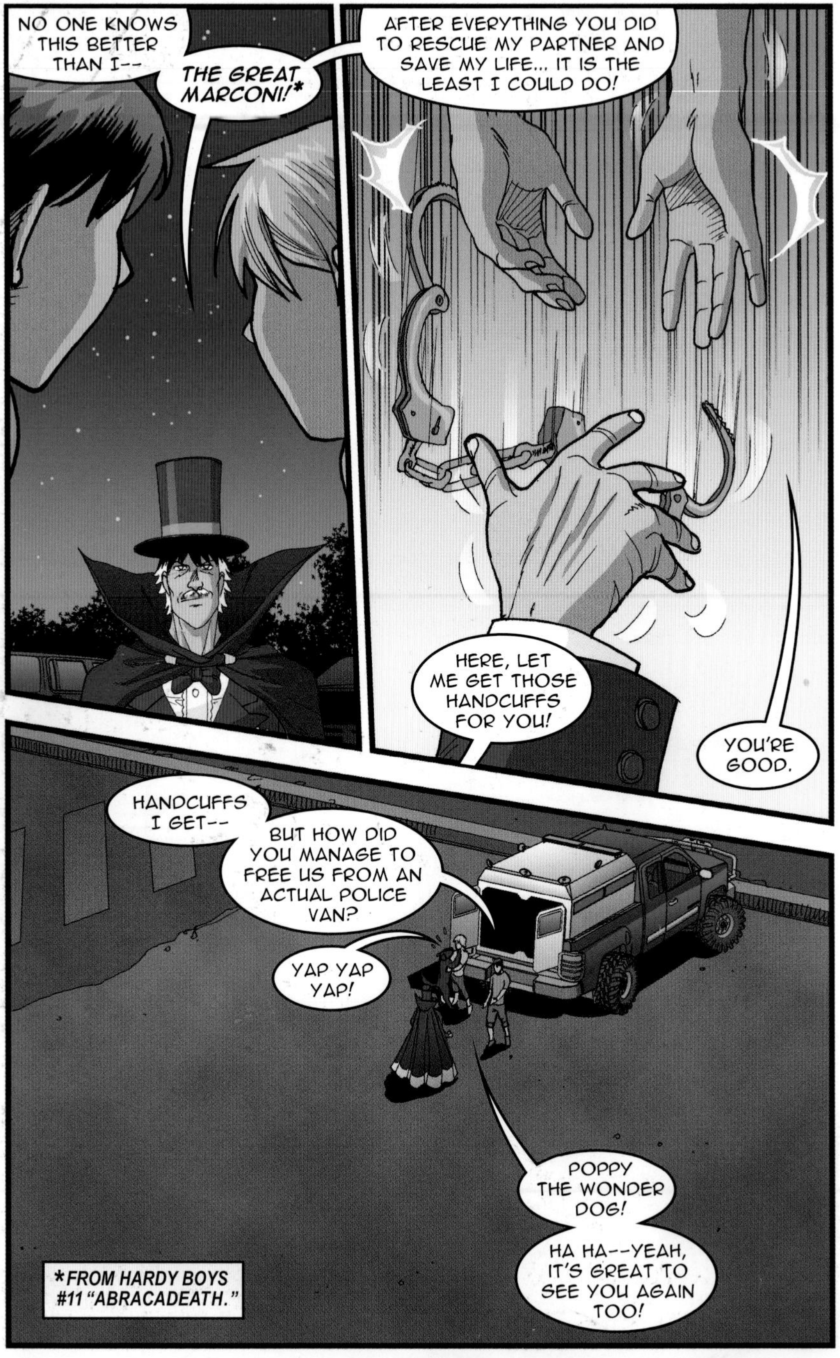
NO ONE KNOWS THIS BETTER THAN I--
THE GREAT MARCONI!*
AFTER EVERYTHING YOU DID TO RESCUE MY PARTNER AND SAVE MY LIFE... IT IS THE LEAST I COULD DO!
HERE, LET ME GET THOSE HANDCUFFS FOR YOU!
YOU'RE GOOD.
HANDCUFFS I GET--
BUT HOW DID YOU MANAGE TO FREE US FROM AN ACTUAL POLICE VAN?
YAP YAP YAP!
POPPY THE WONDER DOG!
HA HA--YEAH, IT'S GREAT TO SEE YOU AGAIN TOO!
*FROM HARDY BOYS #11 "ABRACADEATH."

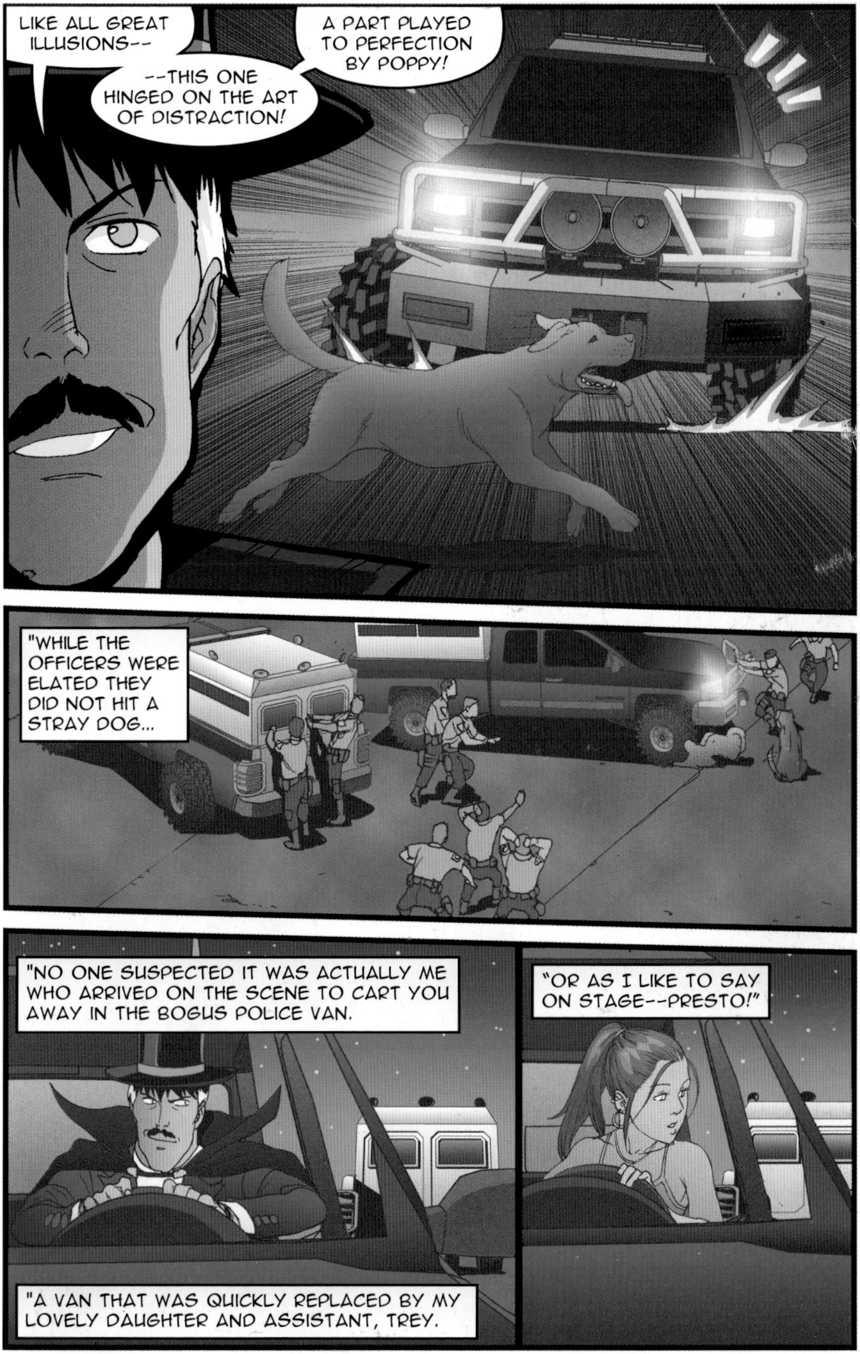
LIKE ALL GREAT ILLUSIONS--
--THIS ONE HINGED ON THE ART OF DISTRACTION!
A PART PLAYED TO PERFECTION BY POPPY!
"WHILE THE OFFICERS WERE ELATED THEY DID NOT HIT A STRAY DOG...
"NO ONE SUSPECTED IT WAS ACTUALLY ME WHO ARRIVED ON THE SCENE TO CART YOU AWAY IN THE BOGUS POLICE VAN.
"A VAN THAT WAS QUICKLY REPLACED BY MY LOVELY DAUGHTER AND ASSISTANT, TREY.
"OR AS I LIKE TO SAY ON STAGE--PRESTO!"

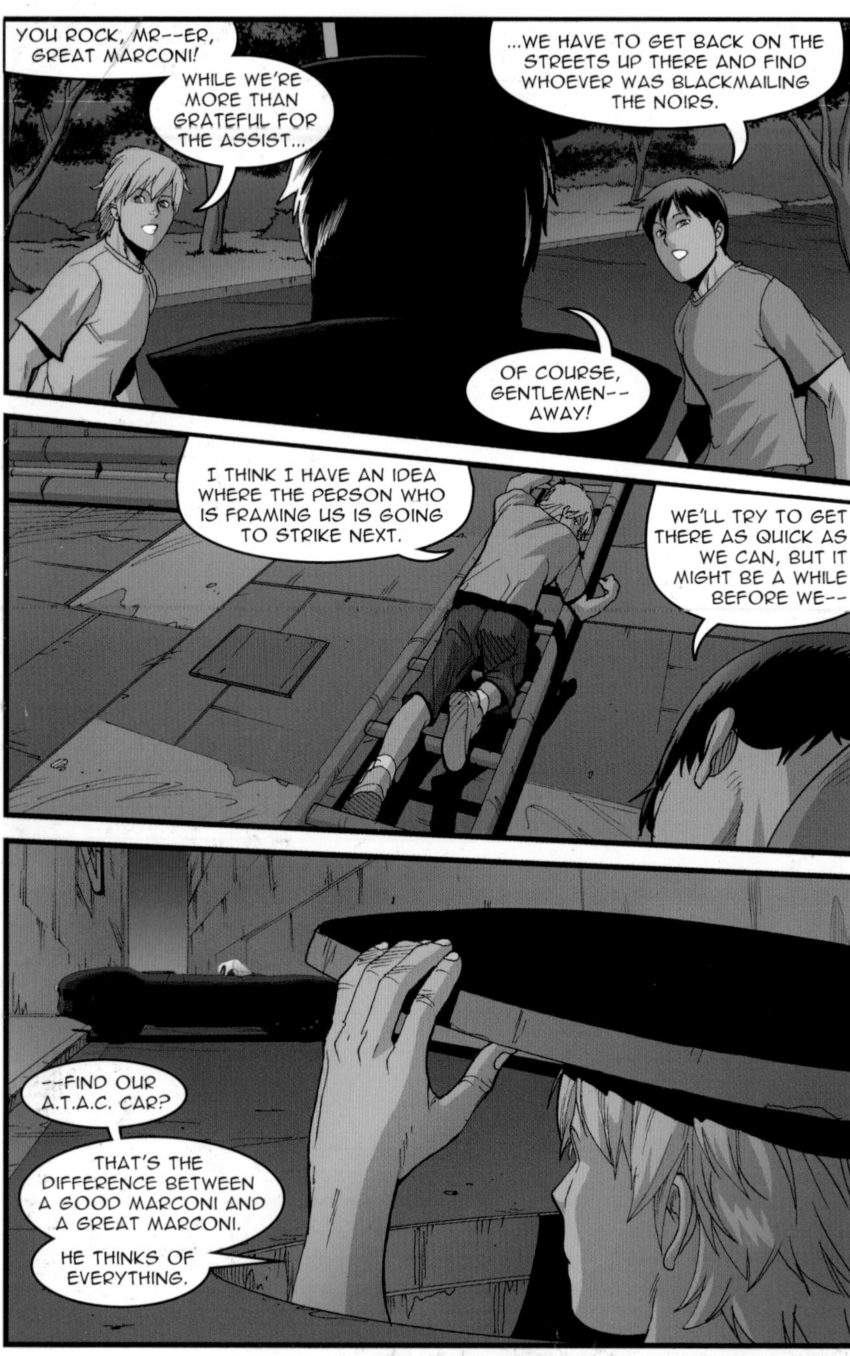
YOU ROCK, MR--ER, GREAT MARCONI!
WHILE WE'RE MORE THAN GRATEFUL FOR THE ASSIST...
...WE HAVE TO GET BACK ON THE STREETS UP THERE AND FIND WHOEVER WAS BLACKMAILING THE NOIRS.
OF COURSE, GENTLEMEN--AWAY!
I THINK I HAVE AN IDEA WHERE THE PERSON WHO IS FRAMING US IS GOING TO STRIKE NEXT.
WE'LL TRY TO GET THERE AS QUICK AS WE CAN, BUT IT MIGHT BE A WHILE BEFORE WE--
--FIND OUR A.T.A.C. CAR?
THAT'S THE DIFFERENCE BETWEEN A GOOD MARCONI AND A GREAT MARCONI.
HE THINKS OF EVERYTHING.

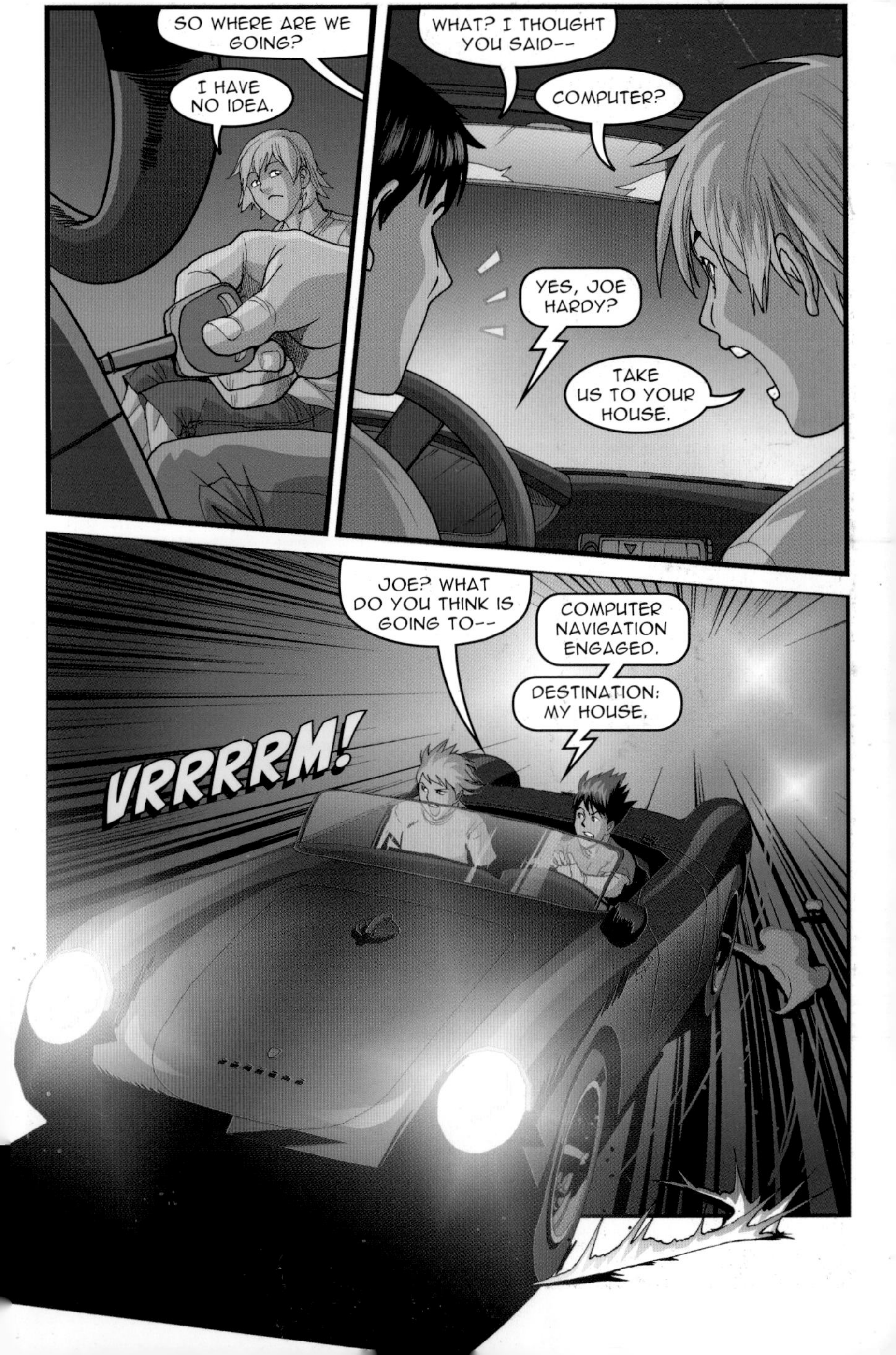
SO WHERE ARE WE GOING?
I HAVE NO IDEA.
WHAT? I THOUGHT YOU SAID--
COMPUTER?
YES, JOE HARDY?
TAKE US TO YOUR HOUSE.
JOE? WHAT DO YOU THINK IS GOING TO--
COMPUTER NAVIGATION ENGAGED.
DESTINATION: MY HOUSE.
VRRRRM!

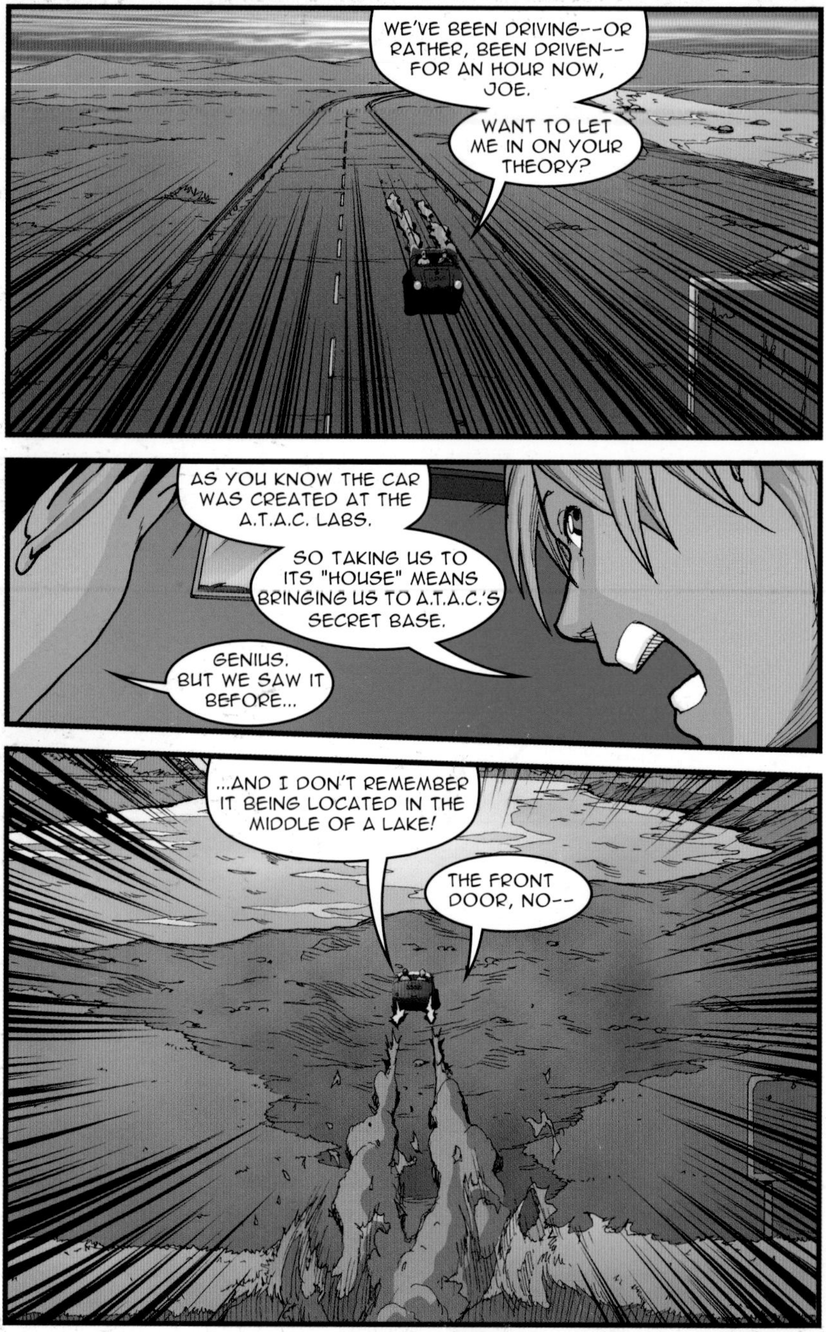
WE'VE BEEN DRIVING--OR RATHER, BEEN DRIVEN--FOR AN HOUR NOW, JOE.
WANT TO LET ME IN ON YOUR THEORY?
AS YOU KNOW THE CAR WAS CREATED AT THE A.T.A.C. LABS.
SO TAKING US TO ITS "HOUSE" MEANS BRINGING US TO A.T.A.C.'S SECRET BASE.
GENIUS. BUT WE SAW IT BEFORE...
...AND I DON'T REMEMBER IT BEING LOCATED IN THE MIDDLE OF A LAKE!
THE FRONT DOOR, NO--

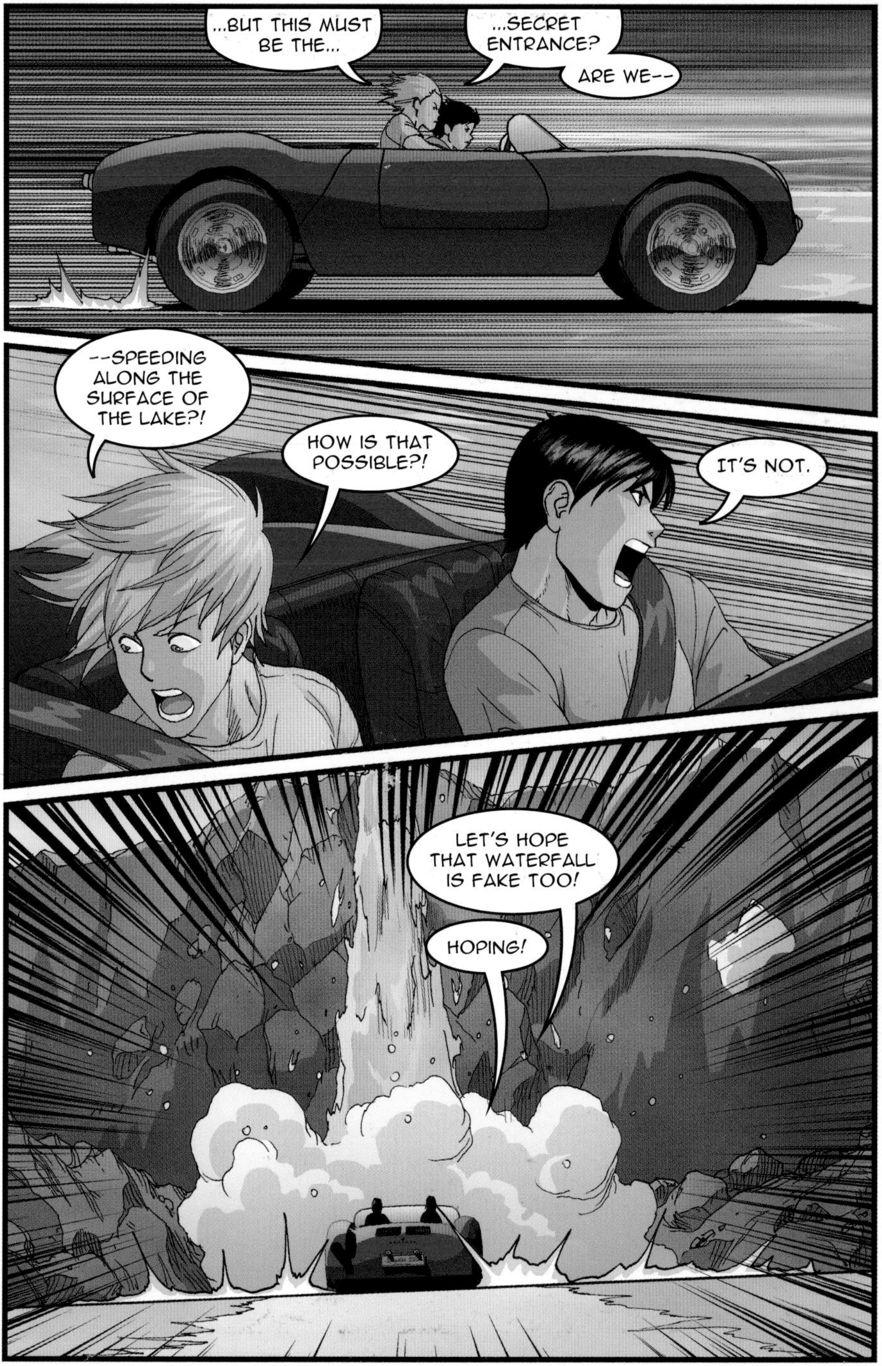
...BUT THIS MUST BE THE...
...SECRET ENTRANCE?
ARE WE--
--SPEEDING ALONG THE SURFACE OF THE LAKE?!
HOW IS THAT POSSIBLE?!
IT'S NOT.
LET'S HOPE THAT WATERFALL IS FAKE TOO!
HOPING!

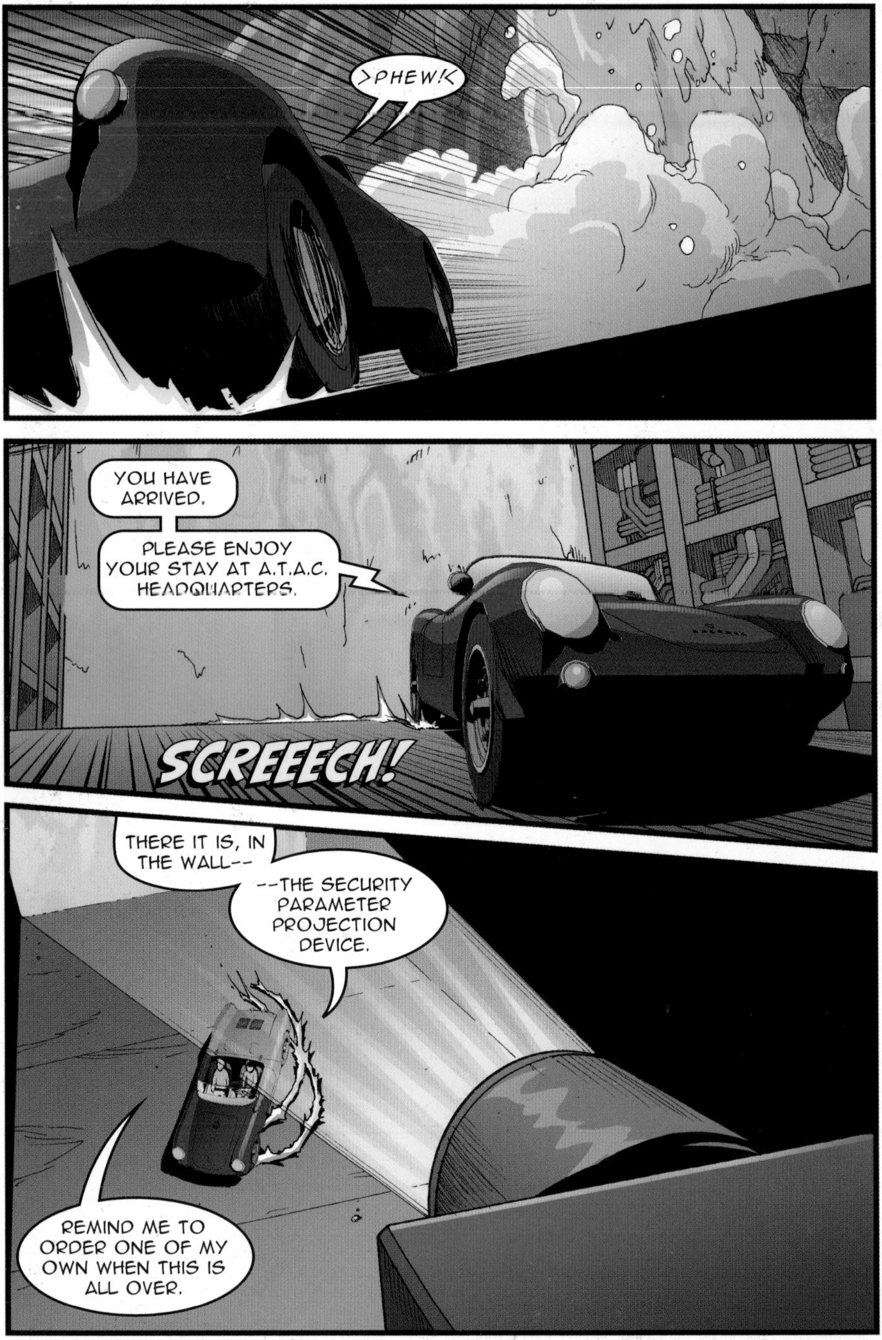
>PHEW!<
YOU HAVE ARRIVED.
PLEASE ENJOY YOUR STAY AT A.T.A.C. HEADQUARTERS.
SCREEECH!
THERE IT IS, IN THE WALL--
--THE SECURITY PARAMETER PROJECTION DEVICE.
REMIND ME TO ORDER ONE OF MY OWN WHEN THIS IS ALL OVER.

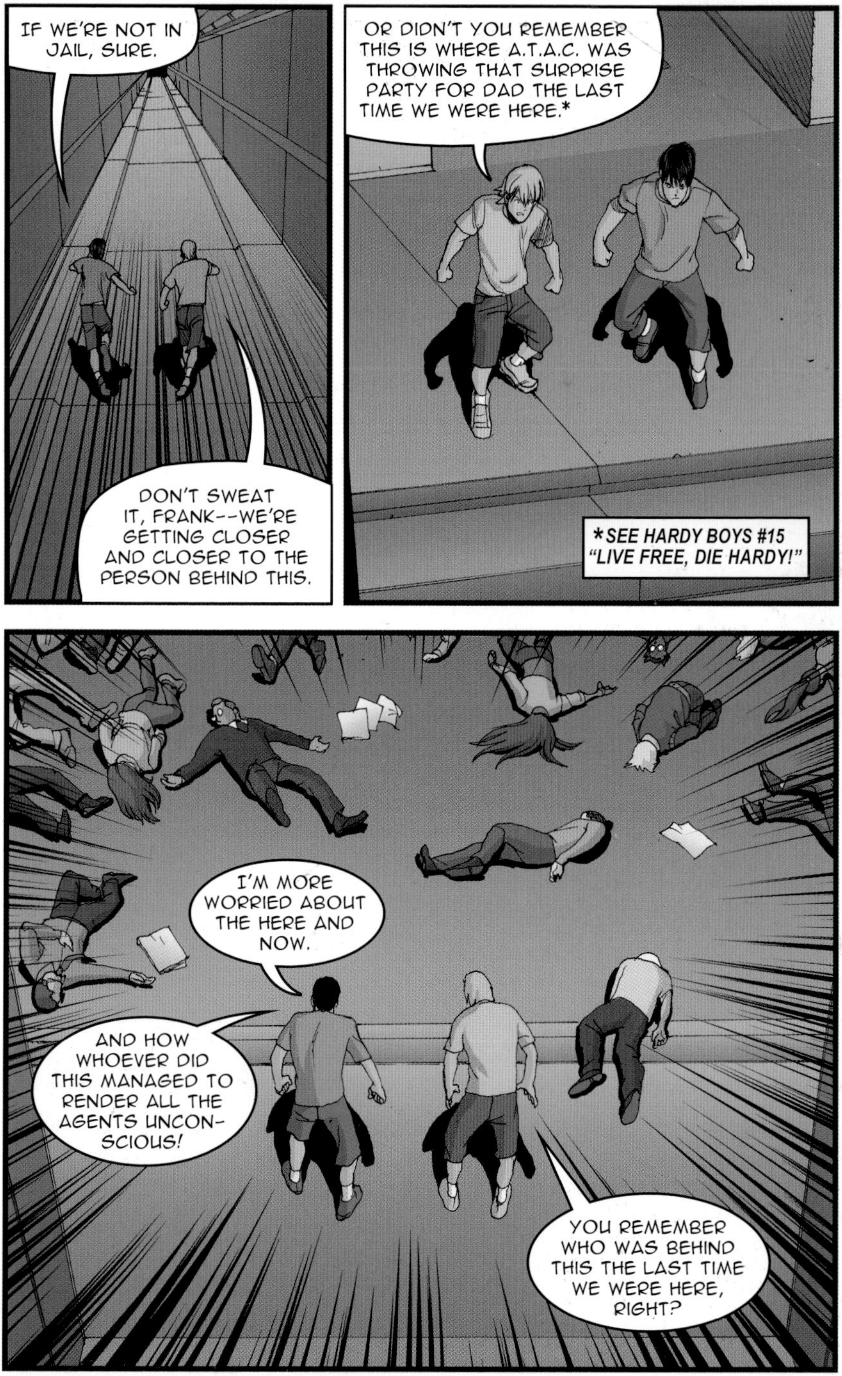
IF WE'RE NOT IN JAIL, SURE.
DON'T SWEAT IT, FRANK--WE'RE GETTING CLOSER AND CLOSER TO THE PERSON BEHIND THIS.
OR DIDN'T YOU REMEMBER THIS IS WHERE A.T.A.C. WAS THROWING THAT SURPRISE PARTY FOR DAD THE LAST TIME WE WERE HERE.*
*SEE HARDY BOYS #15 "LIVE FREE, DIE HARDY!"
I'M MORE WORRIED ABOUT THE HERE AND NOW.
AND HOW WHOEVER DID THIS MANAGED TO RENDER ALL THE AGENTS UNCON-SCIOUS!
YOU REMEMBER WHO WAS BEHIND THIS THE LAST TIME WE WERE HERE, RIGHT?

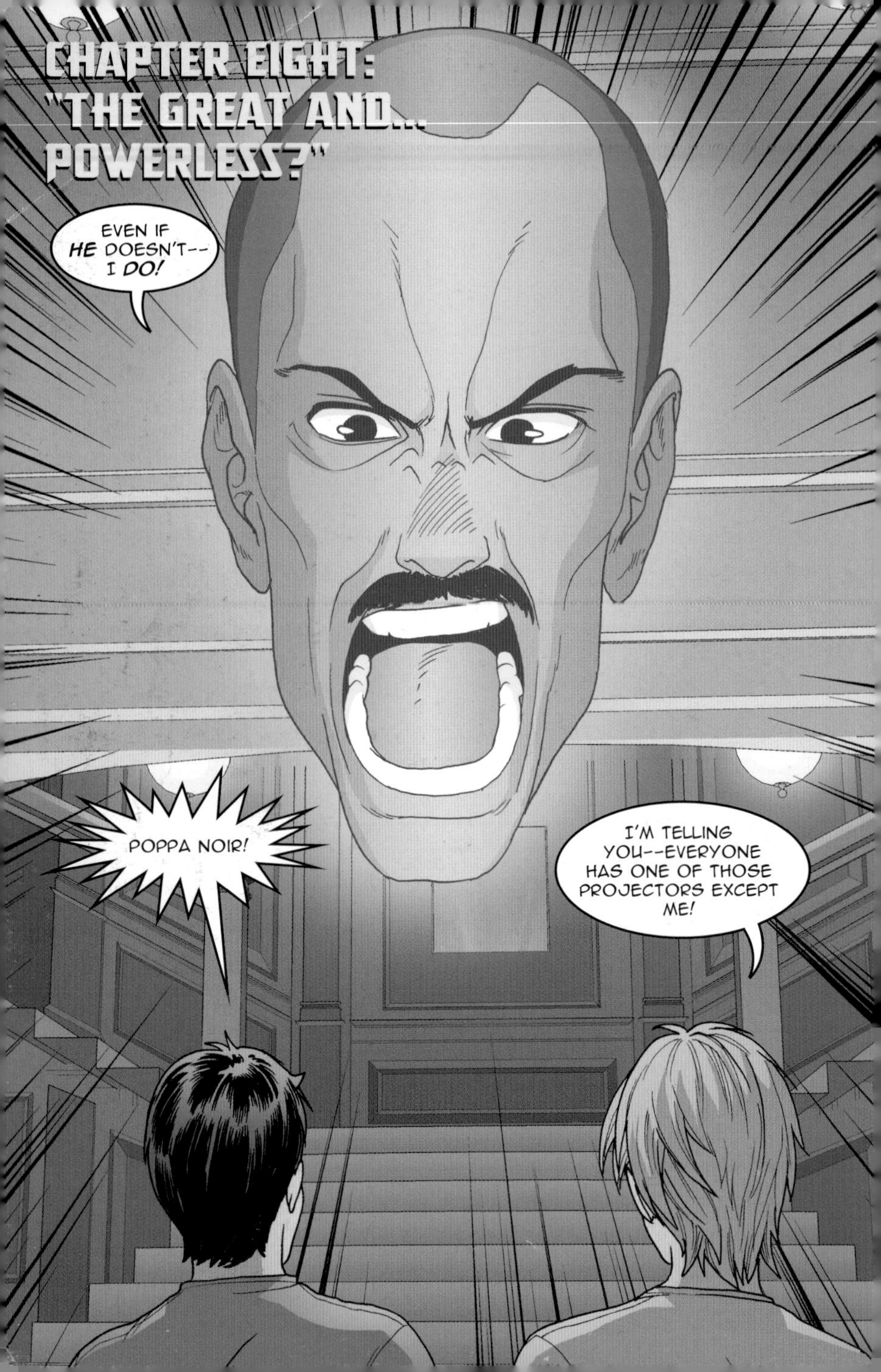
CHAPTER EIGHT:
"THE GREAT AND... POWERLESS?"
EVEN IF HE DOESN'T-- I DO!
POPPA NOIR!
I'M TELLING YOU--EVERYONE HAS ONE OF THOSE PROJECTORS EXCEPT ME!

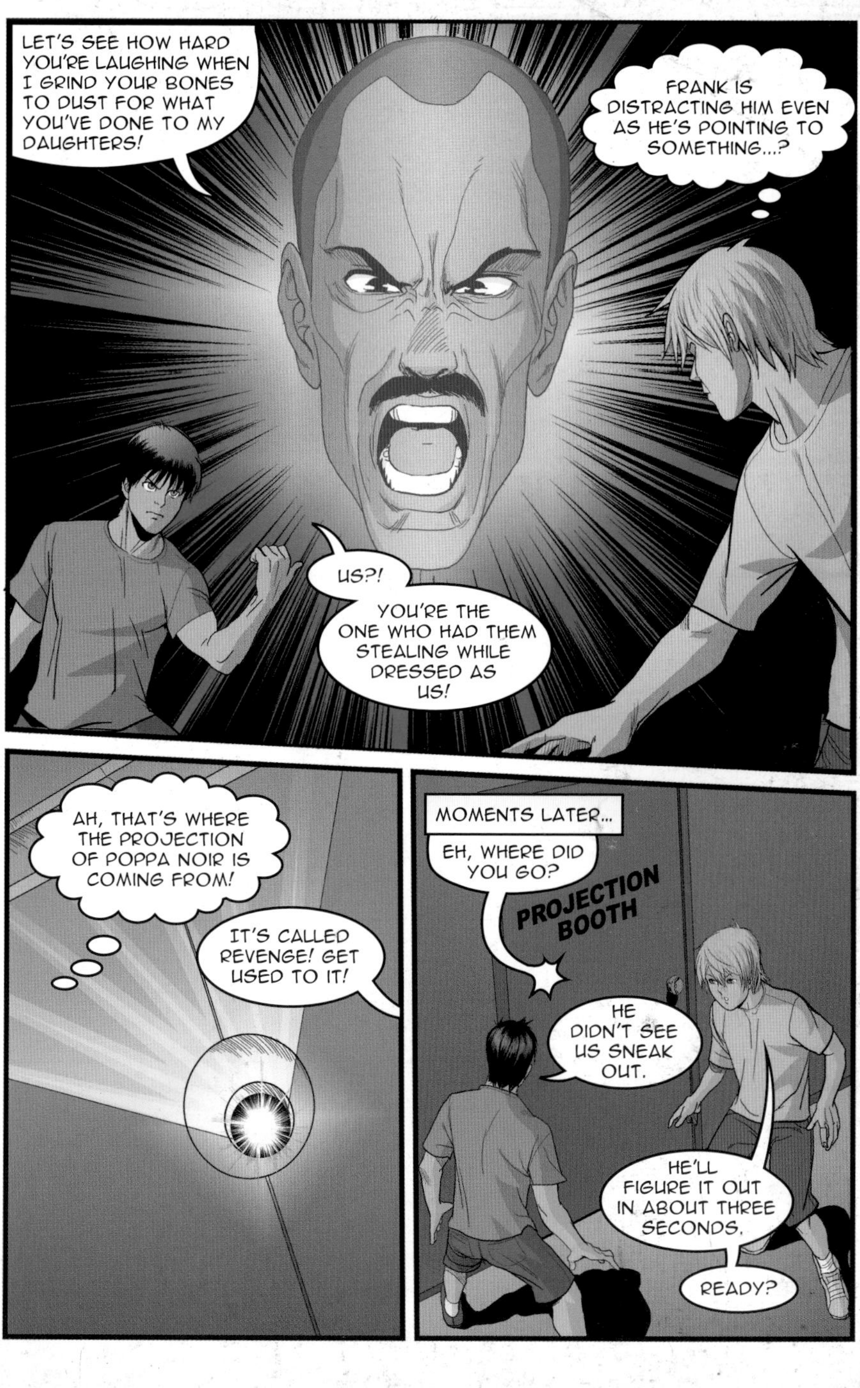
LET'S SEE HOW HARD YOU'RE LAUGHING WHEN I GRIND YOUR BONES TO DUST FOR WHAT YOU'VE DONE TO MY DAUGHTERS!
FRANK IS DISTRACTING HIM EVEN AS HE'S POINTING TO SOMETHING...?
US?!
YOU'RE THE ONE WHO HAD THEM STEALING WHILE DRESSED AS US!
AH, THAT'S WHERE THE PROJECTION OF POPPA NOIR IS COMING FROM!
IT'S CALLED REVENGE! GET USED TO IT!
MOMENTS LATER...
EH, WHERE DID YOU GO?
PROJECTION BOOTH
HE DIDN'T SEE US SNEAK OUT.
HE'LL FIGURE IT OUT IN ABOUT THREE SECONDS.
READY?

CHAPTER NINE:

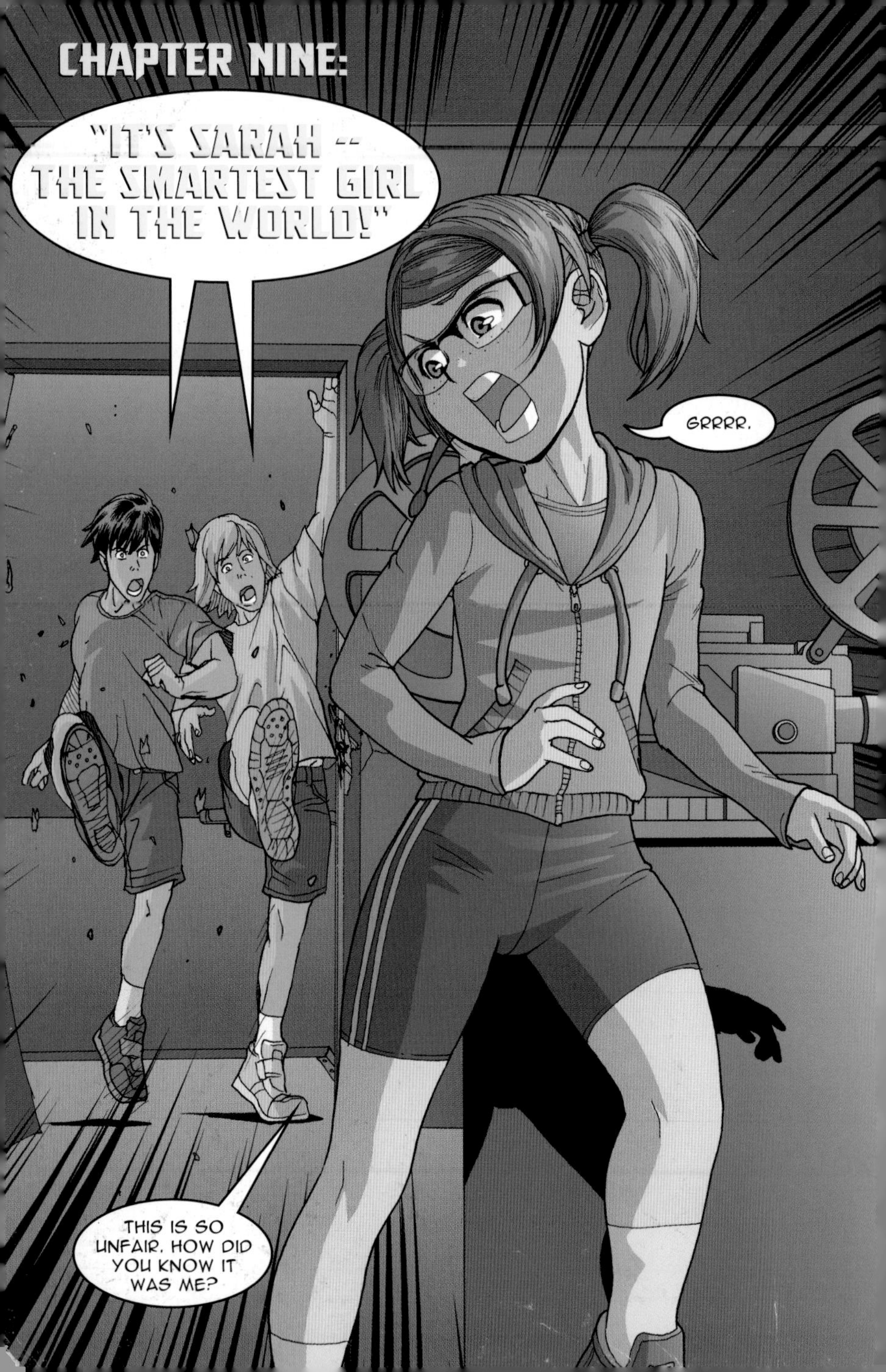

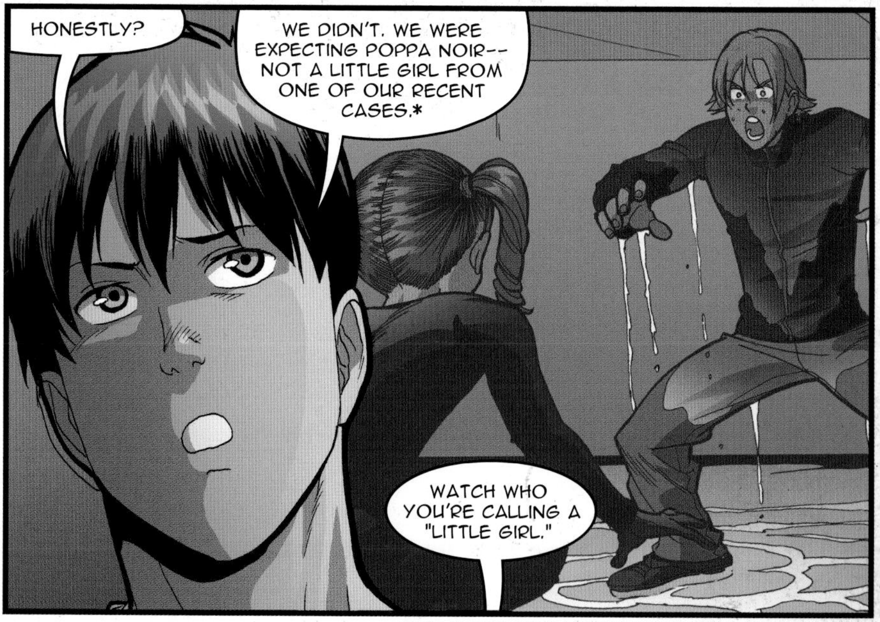
HONESTLY?
WE DIDN'T. WE WERE EXPECTING POPPA NOIR-- NOT A LITTLE GIRL FROM ONE OF OUR RECENT CASES.*
WATCH WHO YOU'RE CALLING A "LITTLE GIRL."

**SEE HARDY BOYS #14 "HALEY DANIELLE'S TOP EIGHT"*

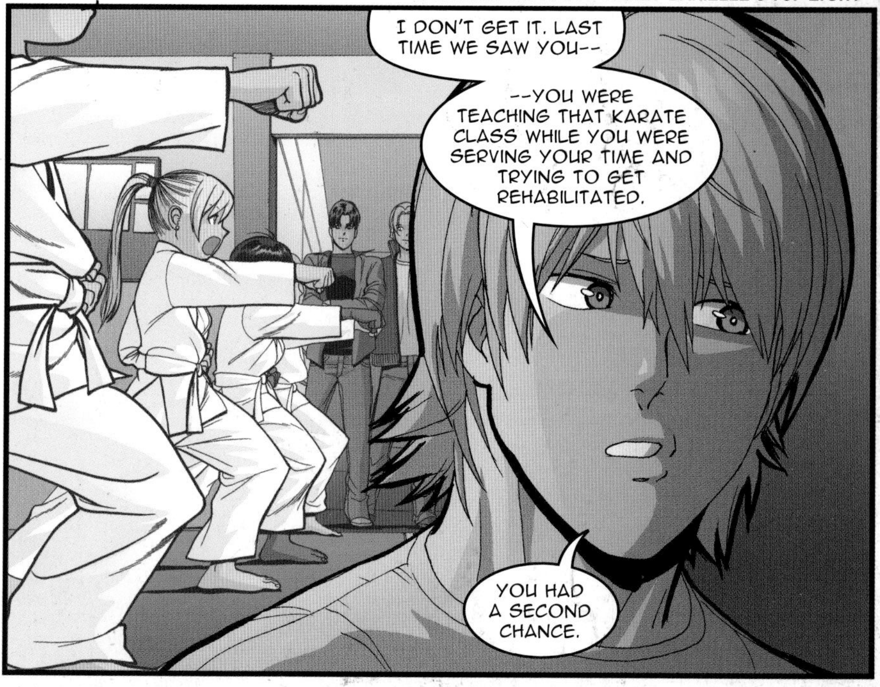
I DON'T GET IT. LAST TIME WE SAW YOU--
--YOU WERE TEACHING THAT KARATE CLASS WHILE YOU WERE SERVING YOUR TIME AND TRYING TO GET REHABILITATED.
YOU HAD A SECOND CHANCE.

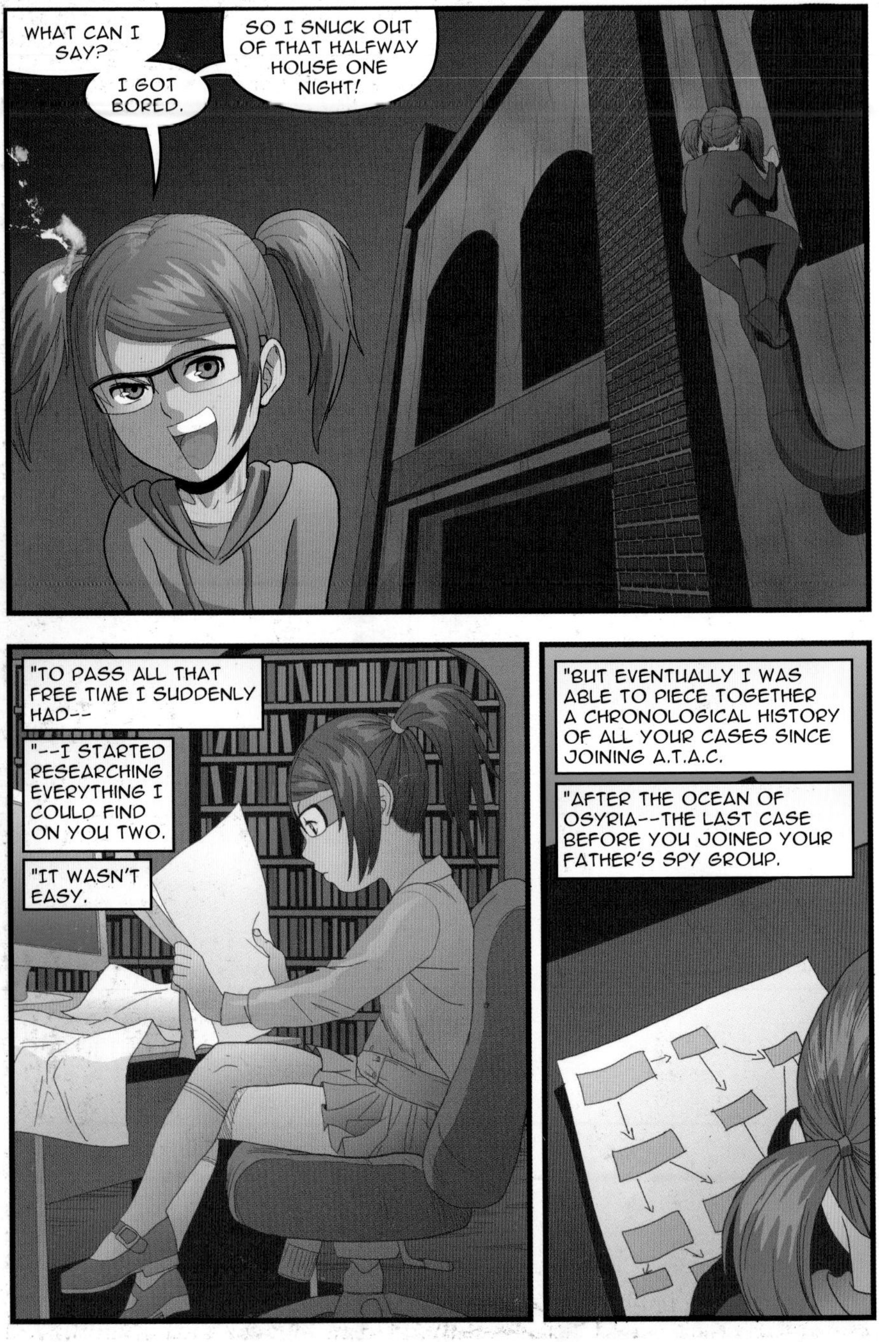

WHAT CAN I SAY?
I GOT BORED.
SO I SNUCK OUT OF THAT HALFWAY HOUSE ONE NIGHT!
"TO PASS ALL THAT FREE TIME I SUDDENLY HAD--
"--I STARTED RESEARCHING EVERYTHING I COULD FIND ON YOU TWO.
"IT WASN'T EASY.
"BUT EVENTUALLY I WAS ABLE TO PIECE TOGETHER A CHRONOLOGICAL HISTORY OF ALL YOUR CASES SINCE JOINING A.T.A.C.
"AFTER THE OCEAN OF OSYRIA--THE LAST CASE BEFORE YOU JOINED YOUR FATHER'S SPY GROUP.

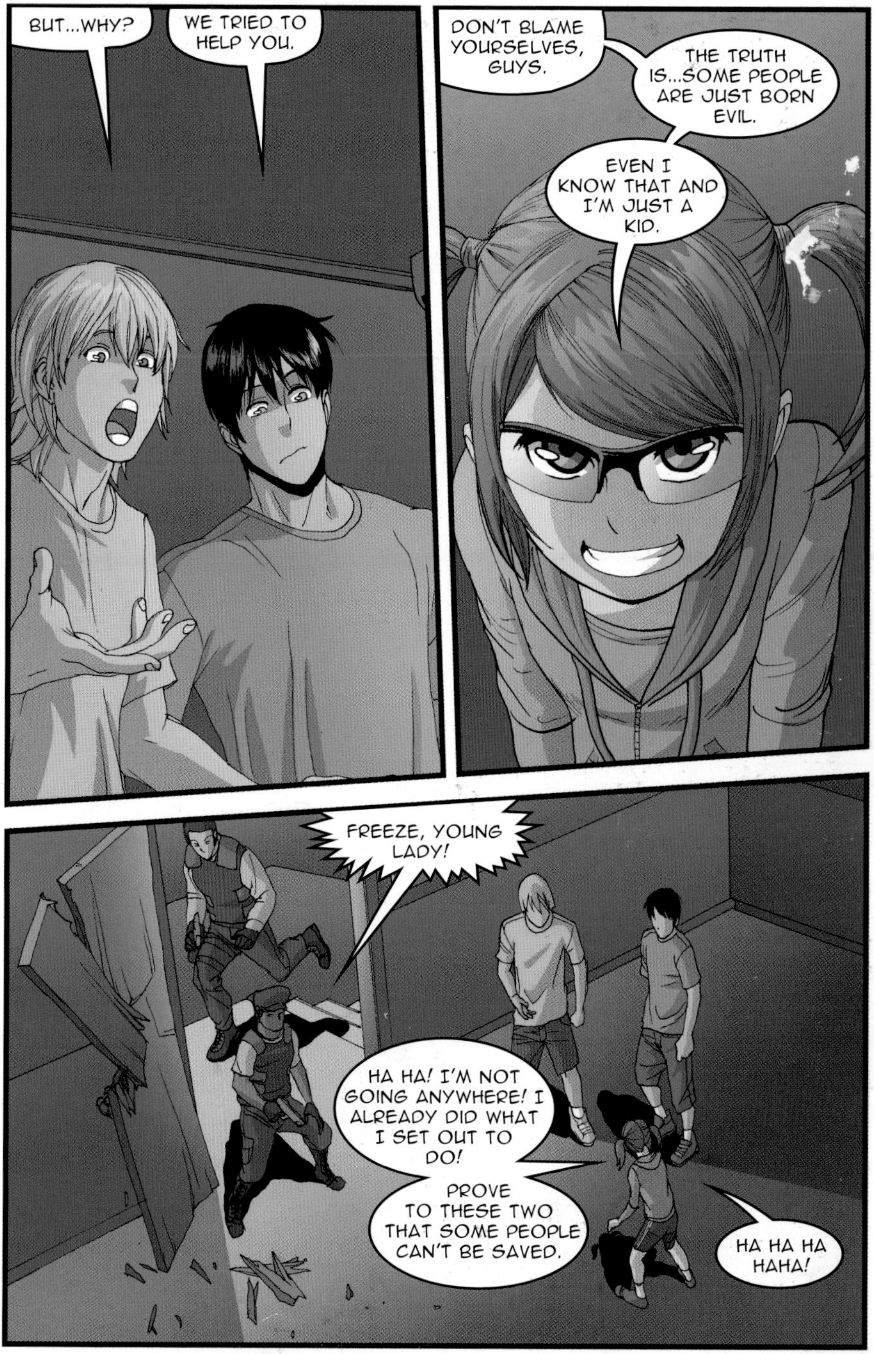
BUT...WHY?
WE TRIED TO HELP YOU.
DON'T BLAME YOURSELVES, GUYS.
THE TRUTH IS...SOME PEOPLE ARE JUST BORN EVIL.
EVEN I KNOW THAT AND I'M JUST A KID.
FREEZE, YOUNG LADY!
HA HA! I'M NOT GOING ANYWHERE! I ALREADY DID WHAT I SET OUT TO DO!
PROVE TO THESE TWO THAT SOME PEOPLE CAN'T BE SAVED.
HA HA HA HAHA!

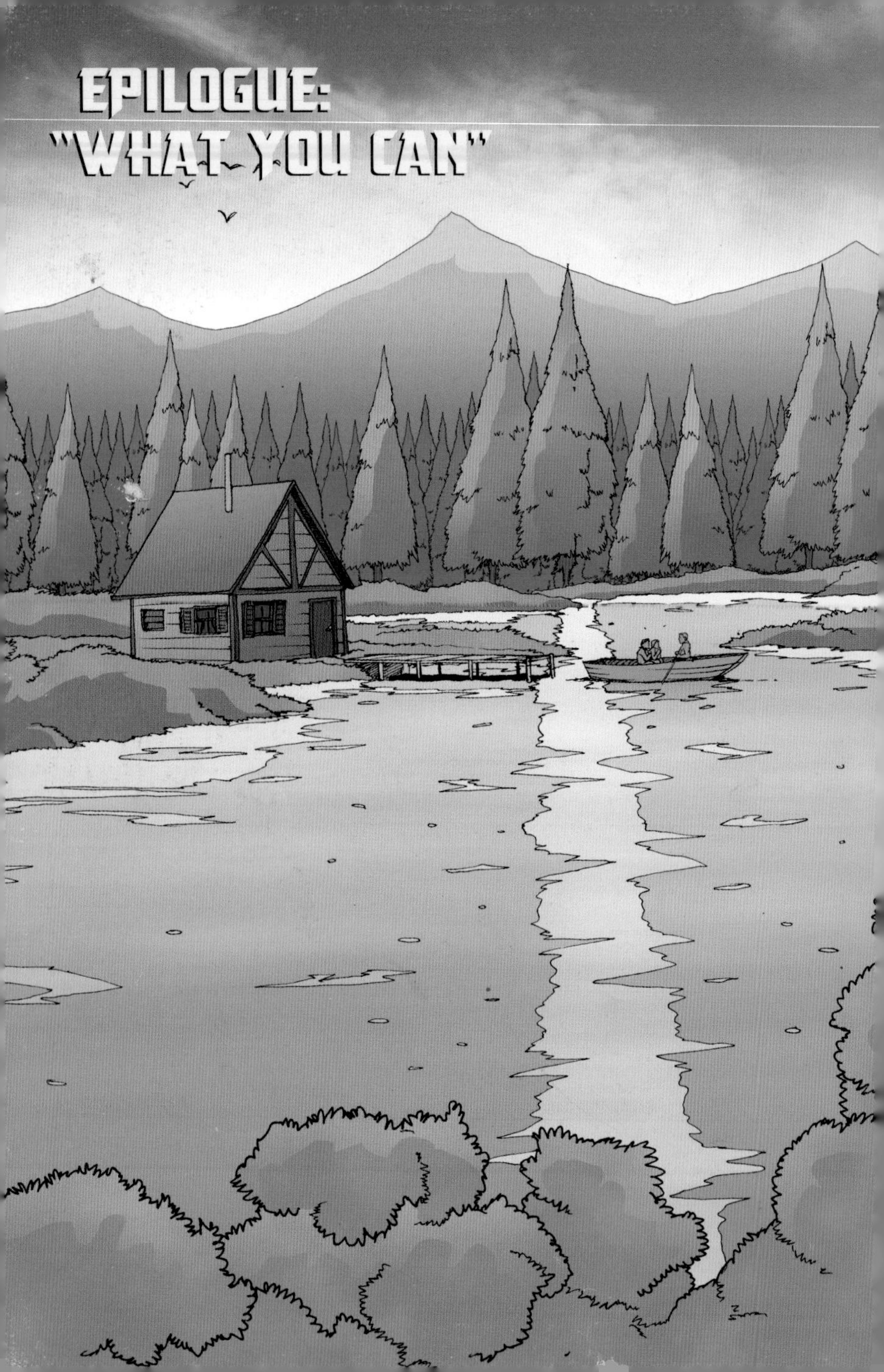
EPILOGUE:
"WHAT YOU CAN"

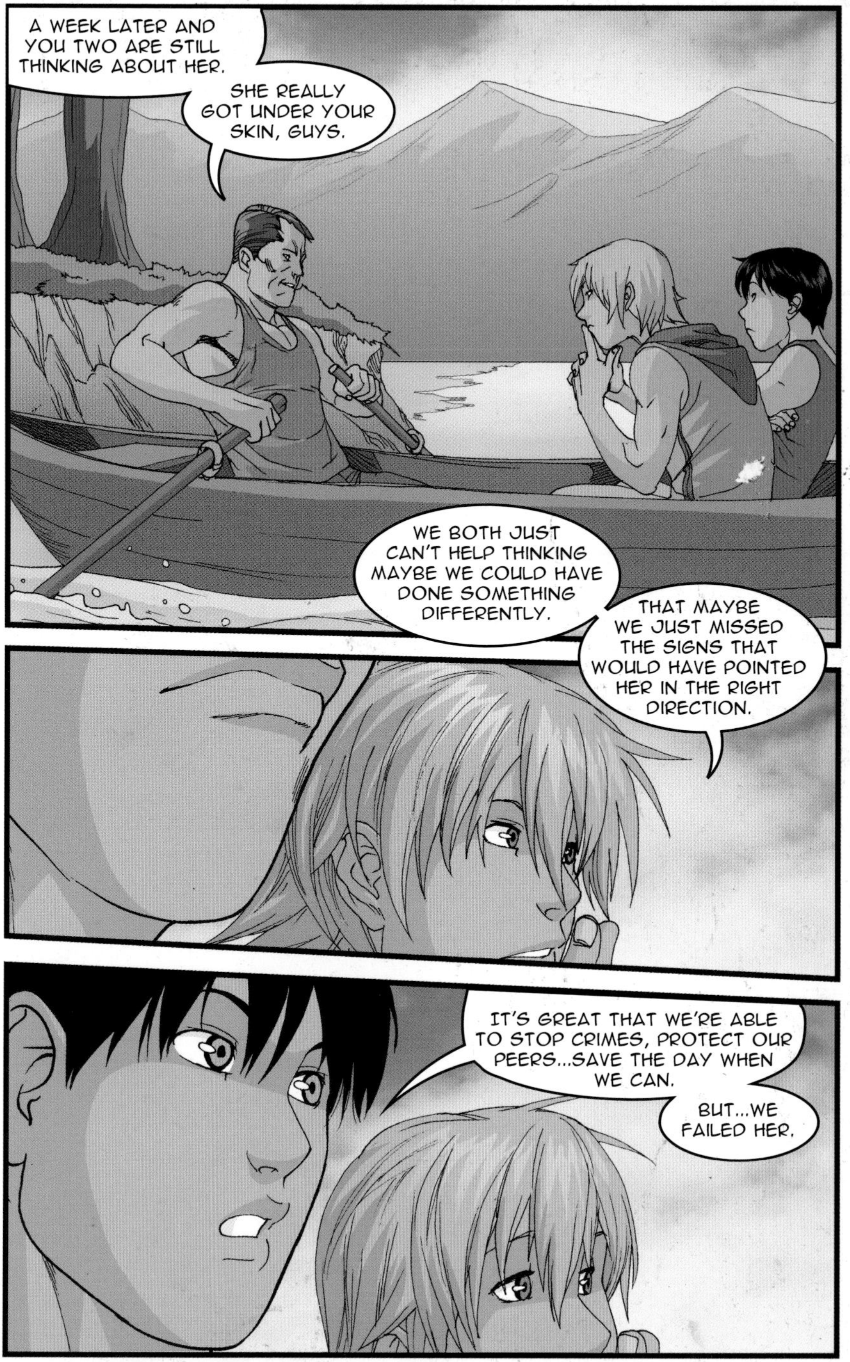
A WEEK LATER AND YOU TWO ARE STILL THINKING ABOUT HER.
SHE REALLY GOT UNDER YOUR SKIN, GUYS.
WE BOTH JUST CAN'T HELP THINKING MAYBE WE COULD HAVE DONE SOMETHING DIFFERENTLY.
THAT MAYBE WE JUST MISSED THE SIGNS THAT WOULD HAVE POINTED HER IN THE RIGHT DIRECTION.
IT'S GREAT THAT WE'RE ABLE TO STOP CRIMES, PROTECT OUR PEERS...SAVE THE DAY WHEN WE CAN.
BUT...WE FAILED HER.

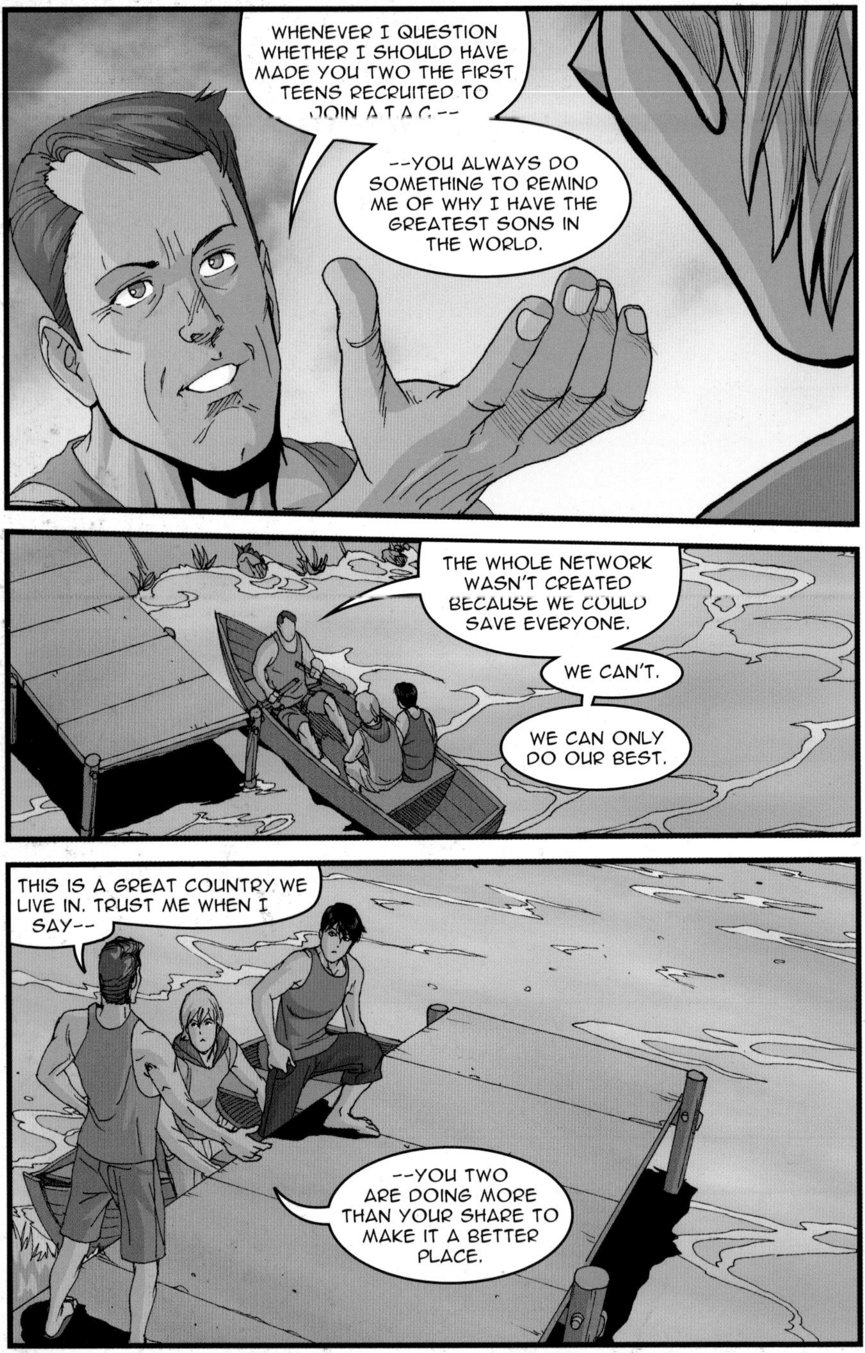
WHENEVER I QUESTION WHETHER I SHOULD HAVE MADE YOU TWO THE FIRST TEENS RECRUITED TO JOIN A.T.A.C.--
--YOU ALWAYS DO SOMETHING TO REMIND ME OF WHY I HAVE THE GREATEST SONS IN THE WORLD.
THE WHOLE NETWORK WASN'T CREATED BECAUSE WE COULD SAVE EVERYONE.
WE CAN'T.
WE CAN ONLY DO OUR BEST.
THIS IS A GREAT COUNTRY WE LIVE IN. TRUST ME WHEN I SAY--
--YOU TWO ARE DOING MORE THAN YOUR SHARE TO MAKE IT A BETTER PLACE.

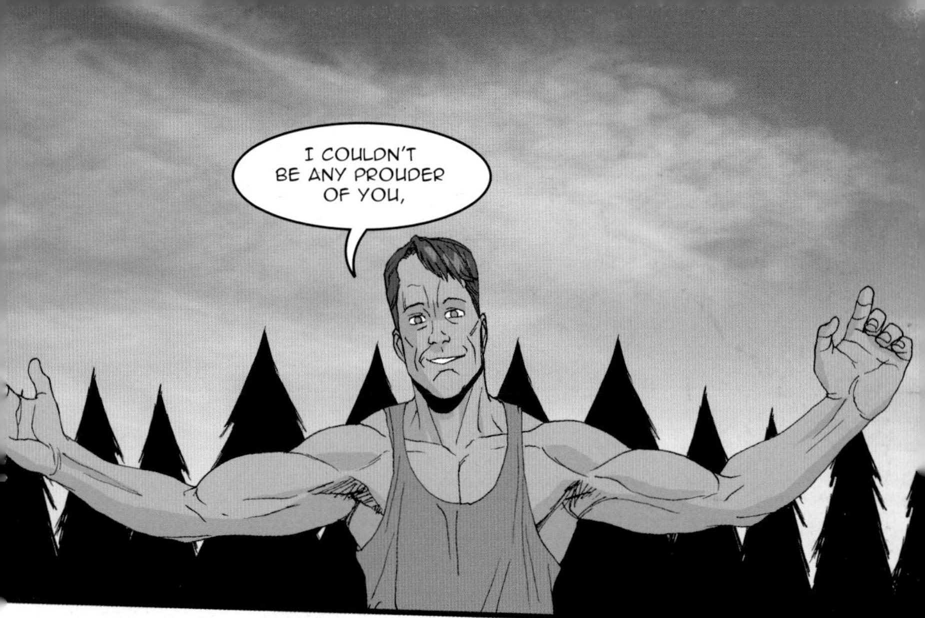
I COULDN'T
BE ANY PROUDER
OF YOU,

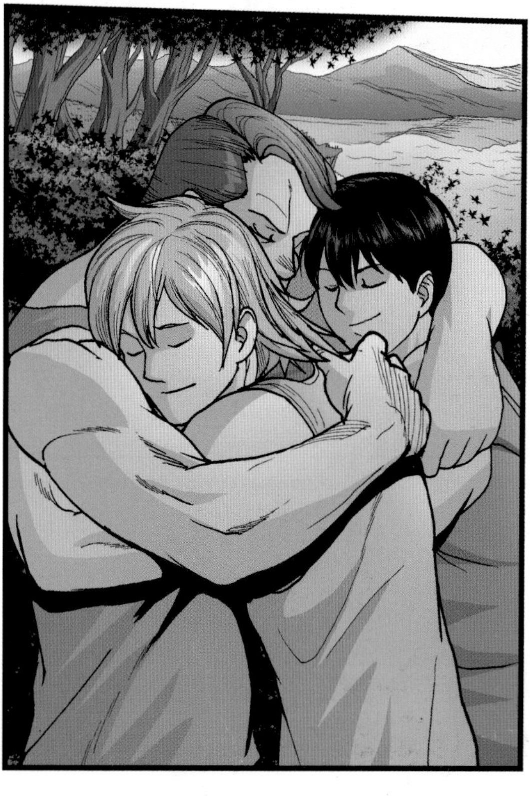

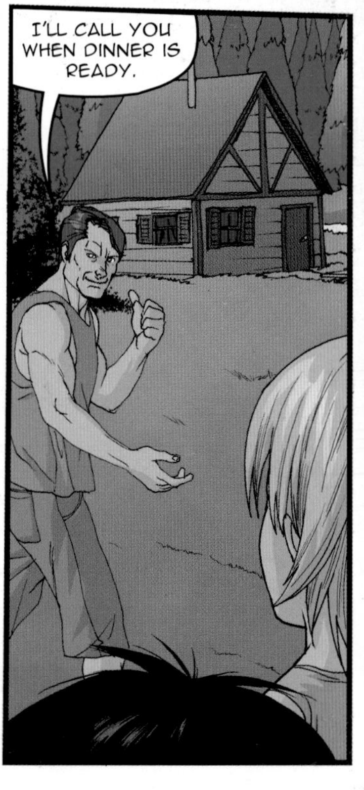
I'LL CALL YOU
WHEN DINNER IS
READY.

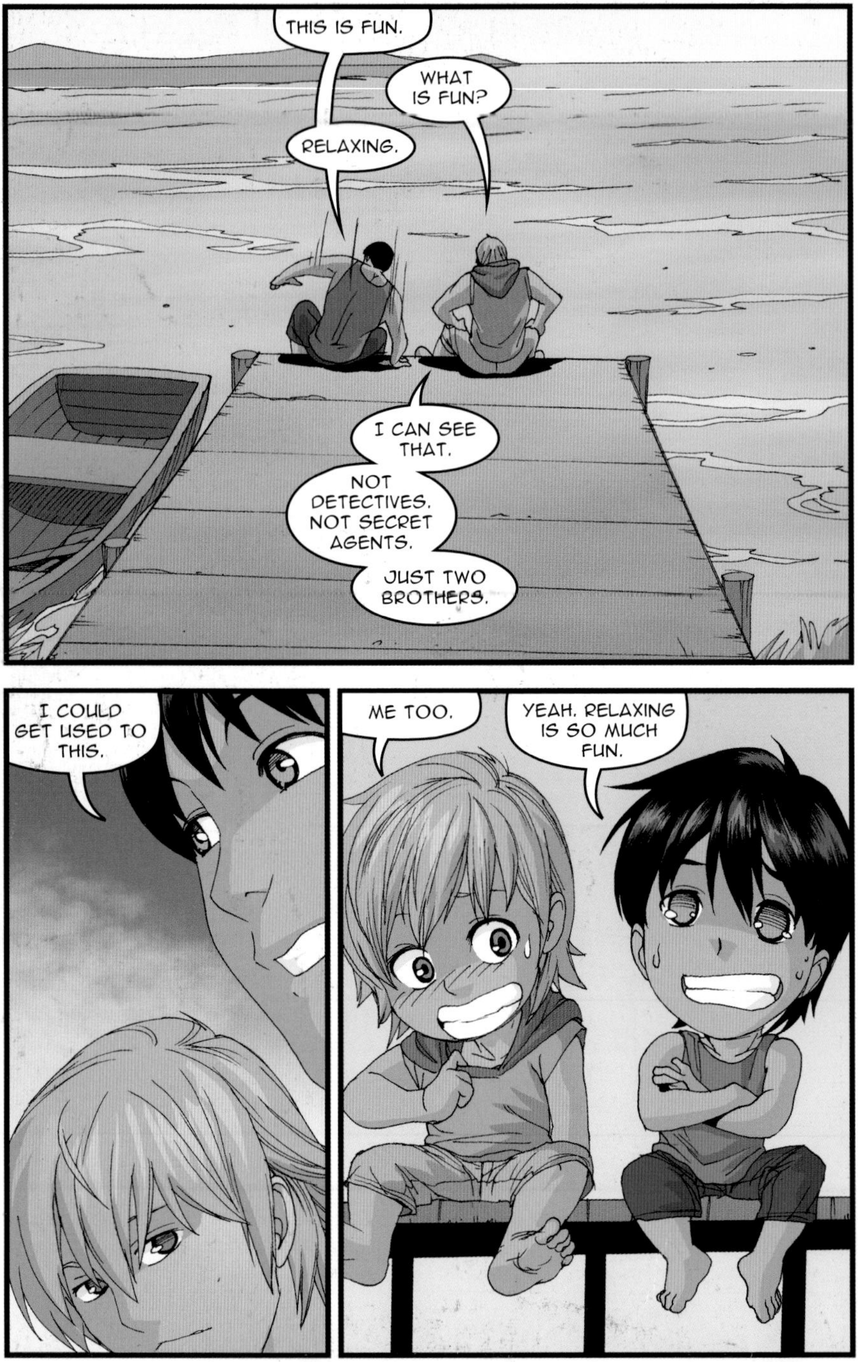
THIS IS FUN.
WHAT IS FUN?
RELAXING.
I CAN SEE THAT.
NOT DETECTIVES. NOT SECRET AGENTS.
JUST TWO BROTHERS.
I COULD GET USED TO THIS.
ME TOO.
YEAH. RELAXING IS SO MUCH FUN.

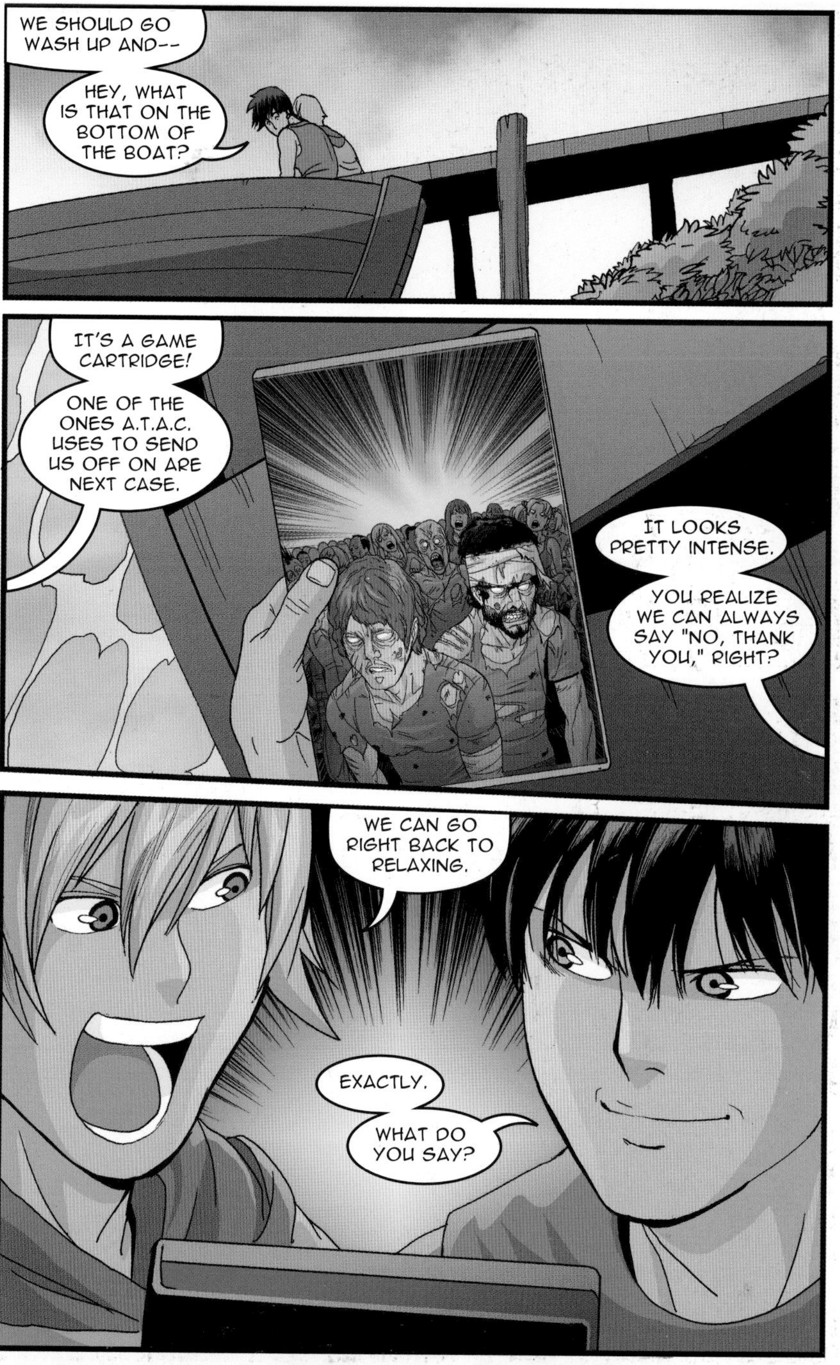
WE SHOULD GO WASH UP AND--
HEY, WHAT IS THAT ON THE BOTTOM OF THE BOAT?
IT'S A GAME CARTRIDGE!
ONE OF THE ONES A.T.A.C. USES TO SEND US OFF ON ARE NEXT CASE.
IT LOOKS PRETTY INTENSE.
YOU REALIZE WE CAN ALWAYS SAY "NO, THANK YOU," RIGHT?
WE CAN GO RIGHT BACK TO RELAXING.
EXACTLY.
WHAT DO YOU SAY?

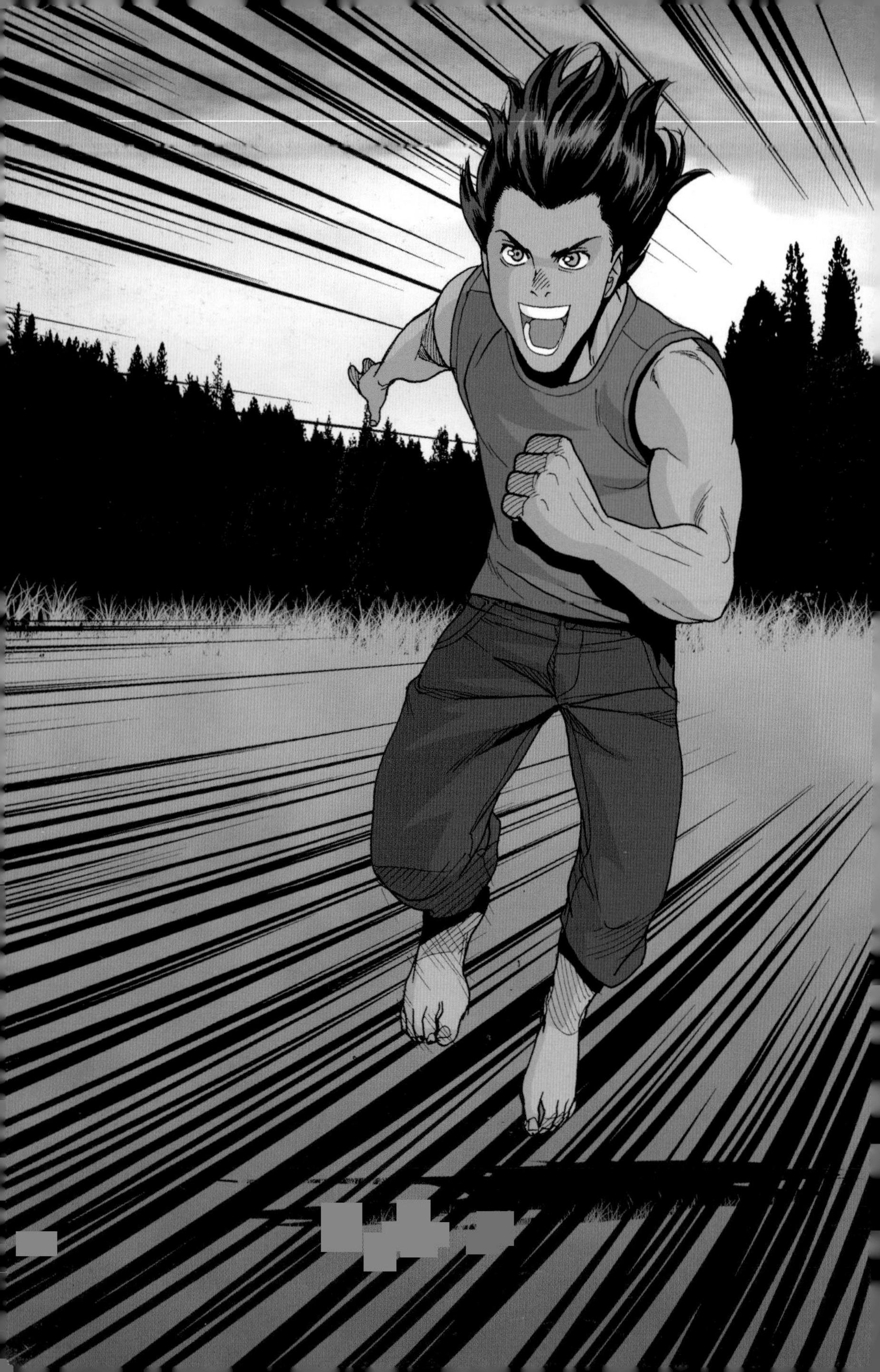

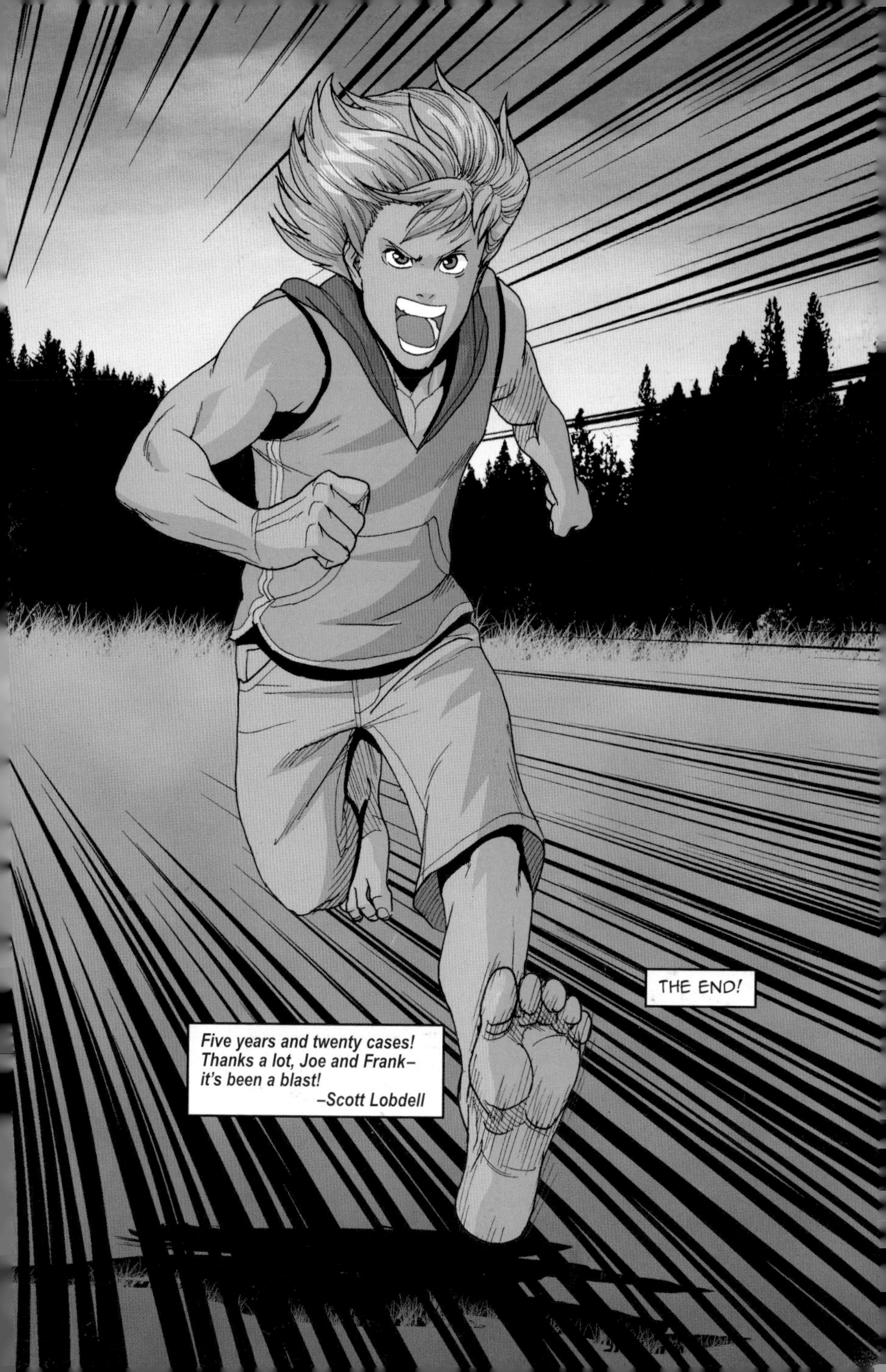
THE END!
Five years and twenty cases! Thanks a lot, Joe and Frank– it's been a blast!
–Scott Lobdell

WATCH OUT FOR PAPERCUTZ

We've got good news and bad news for fans of our NANCY DREW and HARDY BOYS graphic novel series. The bad news is that NANCY DREW #21 "High School Musical Mystery Part Two: The Lost Verse" and HARDY BOYS #20 "Deadly Strategy" are the final volumes in each series.

The good news is that Papercutz is proud to announce two new graphic novel series: NANCY DREW THE NEW CASE FILES and THE HARDY BOYS THE NEW CASE FILES.

Confused? Don't be. We decided that after five years of bringing you the best teenage sleuths in our traditional pocket-sized graphic novel format, it was time for an upgrade. The new graphic novel series will be bigger and better than ever. First, we'll be super-sizing our format, jumping up from our current 5" x 7 ½" format to the larger 6" x 9" size, popularized by our CLASSICS ILLUSTRATED and GERONIMO STILTON graphic novels. If you've loved the action-packed pages by Paulo Henrique (with colorist Laurie E. Smith) in HARDY BOYS or the delightfully-designed, anime-like art of Sho Murase in NANCY DREW, you'll love 'em even more at the new size. And it goes without saying that there will be less eye-strain for those of you who scrutinize every little detail on every page.

But that's not all! We know that in the recent Recession, many families have had to cut back on spending, and buying graphic novels can be tough to justify no matter how much you enjoy 'em. That's why the new HARDY BOYS and NANCY DREW graphic novels will be bargain-priced at only $6.99 each. (And of course, don't forget that many Papercutz graphic novels are available at your local library. There's a deal that can't be beat!)

One more bit of good news and bad news. The bad news is that after writing each and every one of the twenty HARDY BOYS graphic novels, our good friend Scott Lobdell is calling it quits. He has so many movie, TV, and publishing projects in the works right now, that something had to give, and unfortunately that something turned out to be THE HARDY BOYS. Let me take this opportunity to thank Scott for not only doing such a great job putting Frank and Joe through their paces in such a dynamic style, but to also thank him for being such a great friend. Time after time, Scott has been there for me when I needed him. Our relationship is a lot like Frank and Joe's, brothers through thick and thin (even though I already have a brother, and Scott has three brothers and three sisters!). While I'm sure we'll all miss Scott's scripts on THE HARDY BOYS, know that Scott's already cooking up ideas for future all-new original Papercutz graphic novel series.

As for the good news…? One of greatest comicbook writers of all time has agreed to write the upcoming HARDY BOYS THE NEW CASE FILES. Just as he was able to step in as writer on *The Amazing Spider-Man* after Stan Lee left, and not miss a beat, but also script such classics as "The Night Gwen Stacy Died," and even create the controversial Punisher, he's now ready to reach new heights of greatness with THE HARDY BOYS. Yes, I'm talking about none other than Gerry Conway! Back when I was Marvel's *Spider-Man* editor, Gerry wrote both *Web of Spider-Man* and *Spectacular Spider-Man*, and created the man called Tombstone, a truly terrifying super-villain. After years of writing such top TV series as *Hercules: The Legendary Journeys* and *Law & Order: Criminal Intent*, Gerry has just recently returned to writing comics, starting with *The Last Days of Animal Man* at DC Comics, and we're super-excited to have him writing THE HARDY BOYS!

On the following pages, we're offering advance peeks at the premiere volumes of both THE HARDY BOYS THE NEW CASE FILES #1 "Crawling with Zombies" and NANCY DREW THE NEW CASE FILES #1 "Vampire Slayer." Now some of you may be shocked to see such super-natural creatures as zombies and vampires entering the relatively realistic world of The Hardy Boys and Nancy Drew. Well, not everything is what it appears to be at first—or is it? Can you determine from the few preview pages provided whether these creatures are real or not? The answers will be revealed in September and October when these two new series debut at your favorite booksellers! So until then, happy sleuthing!

Thanks,

JIM

Special Preview of NANCY DREW THE NEW CASE FILES #1 – "Vampire Slayer"!

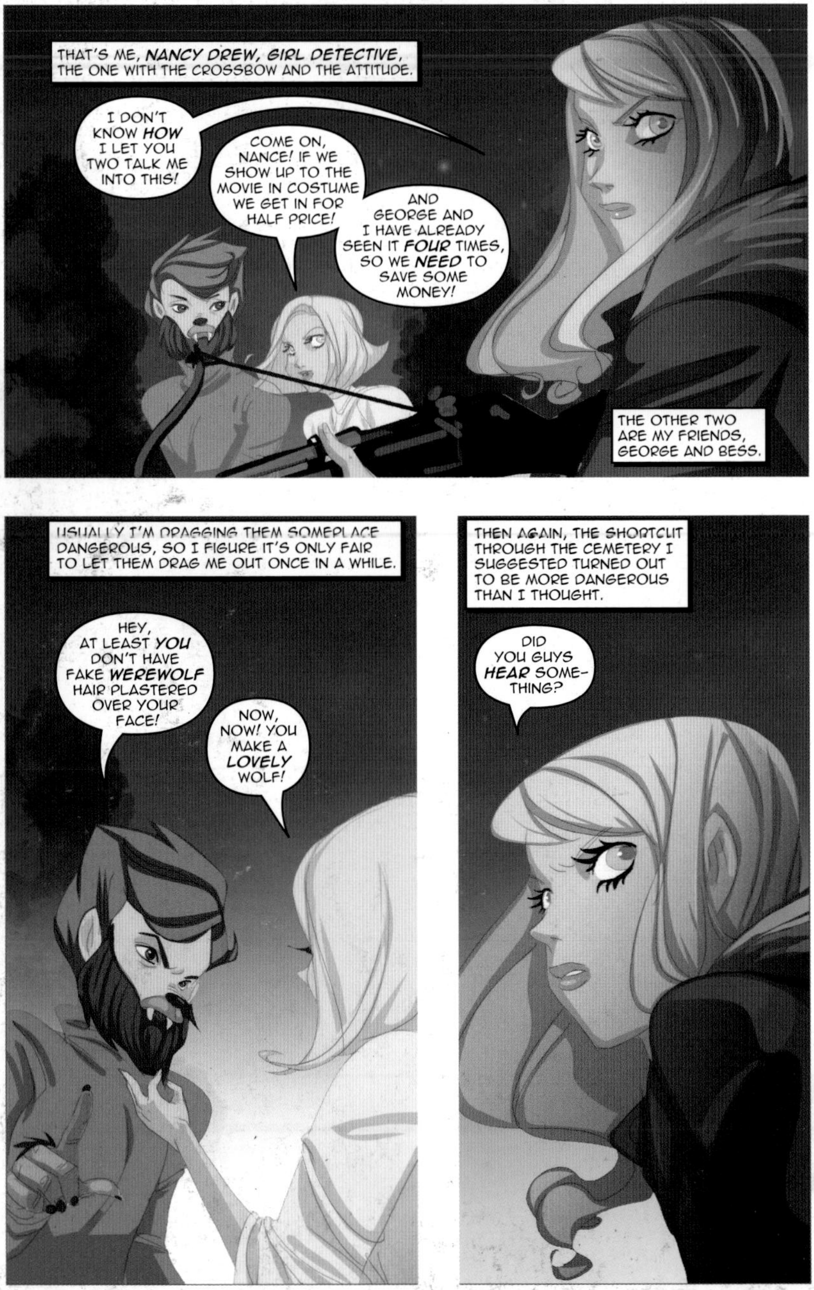
THAT'S ME, NANCY DREW, GIRL DETECTIVE, THE ONE WITH THE CROSSBOW AND THE ATTITUDE.
I DON'T KNOW HOW I LET YOU TWO TALK ME INTO THIS!
COME ON, NANCE! IF WE SHOW UP TO THE MOVIE IN COSTUME WE GET IN FOR HALF PRICE!
AND GEORGE AND I HAVE ALREADY SEEN IT FOUR TIMES, SO WE NEED TO SAVE SOME MONEY!
THE OTHER TWO ARE MY FRIENDS, GEORGE AND BESS.
USUALLY I'M DRAGGING THEM SOMEPLACE DANGEROUS, SO I FIGURE IT'S ONLY FAIR TO LET THEM DRAG ME OUT ONCE IN A WHILE.
HEY, AT LEAST YOU DON'T HAVE FAKE WEREWOLF HAIR PLASTERED OVER YOUR FACE!
NOW, NOW! YOU MAKE A LOVELY WOLF!
THEN AGAIN, THE SHORTCUT THROUGH THE CEMETERY I SUGGESTED TURNED OUT TO BE MORE DANGEROUS THAN I THOUGHT.
DID YOU GUYS HEAR SOME-THING?

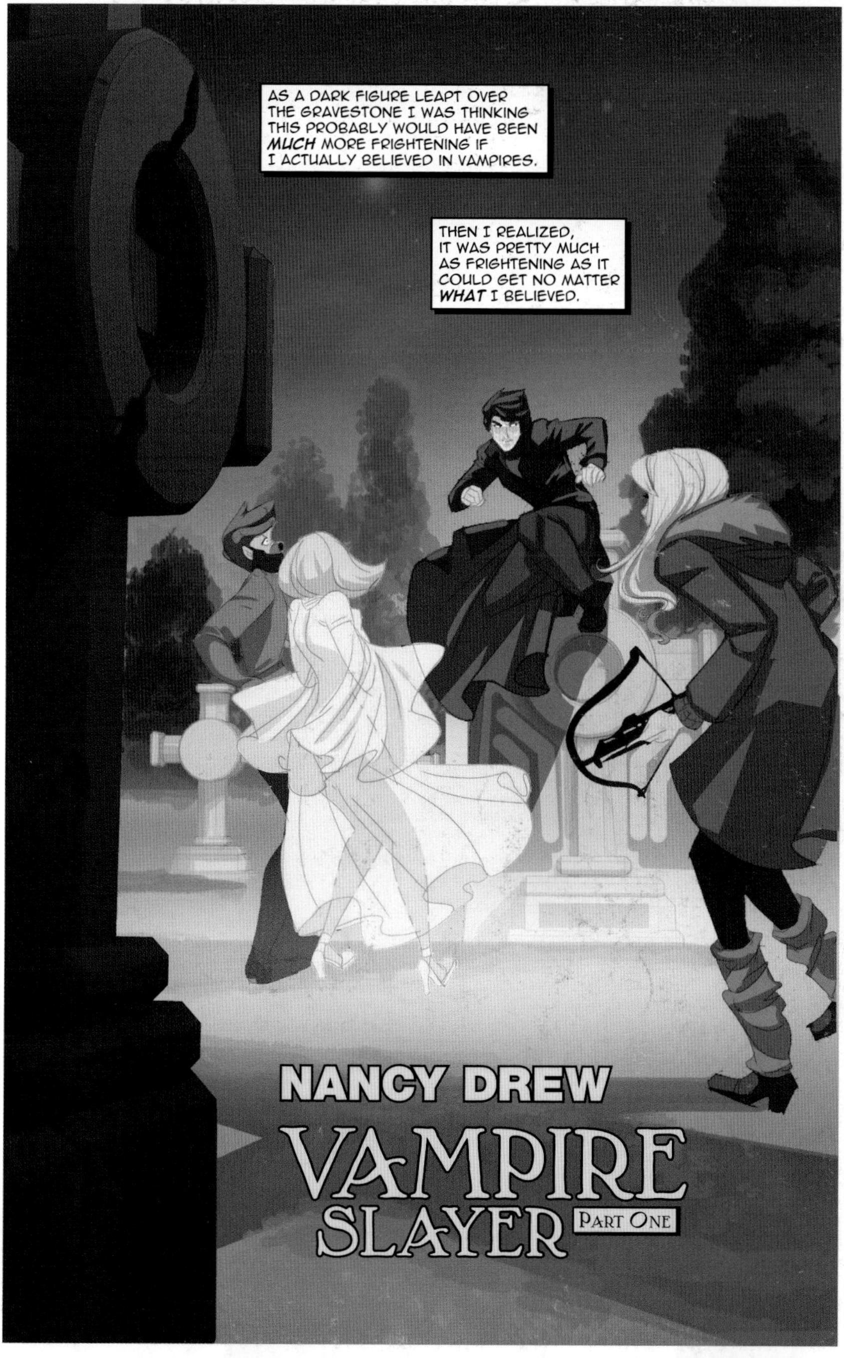
AS A DARK FIGURE LEAPT OVER THE GRAVESTONE I WAS THINKING THIS PROBABLY WOULD HAVE BEEN *MUCH* MORE FRIGHTENING IF I ACTUALLY BELIEVED IN VAMPIRES.
THEN I REALIZED, IT WAS PRETTY MUCH AS FRIGHTENING AS IT COULD GET NO MATTER *WHAT* I BELIEVED.
NANCY DREW
VAMPIRE SLAYER
PART ONE

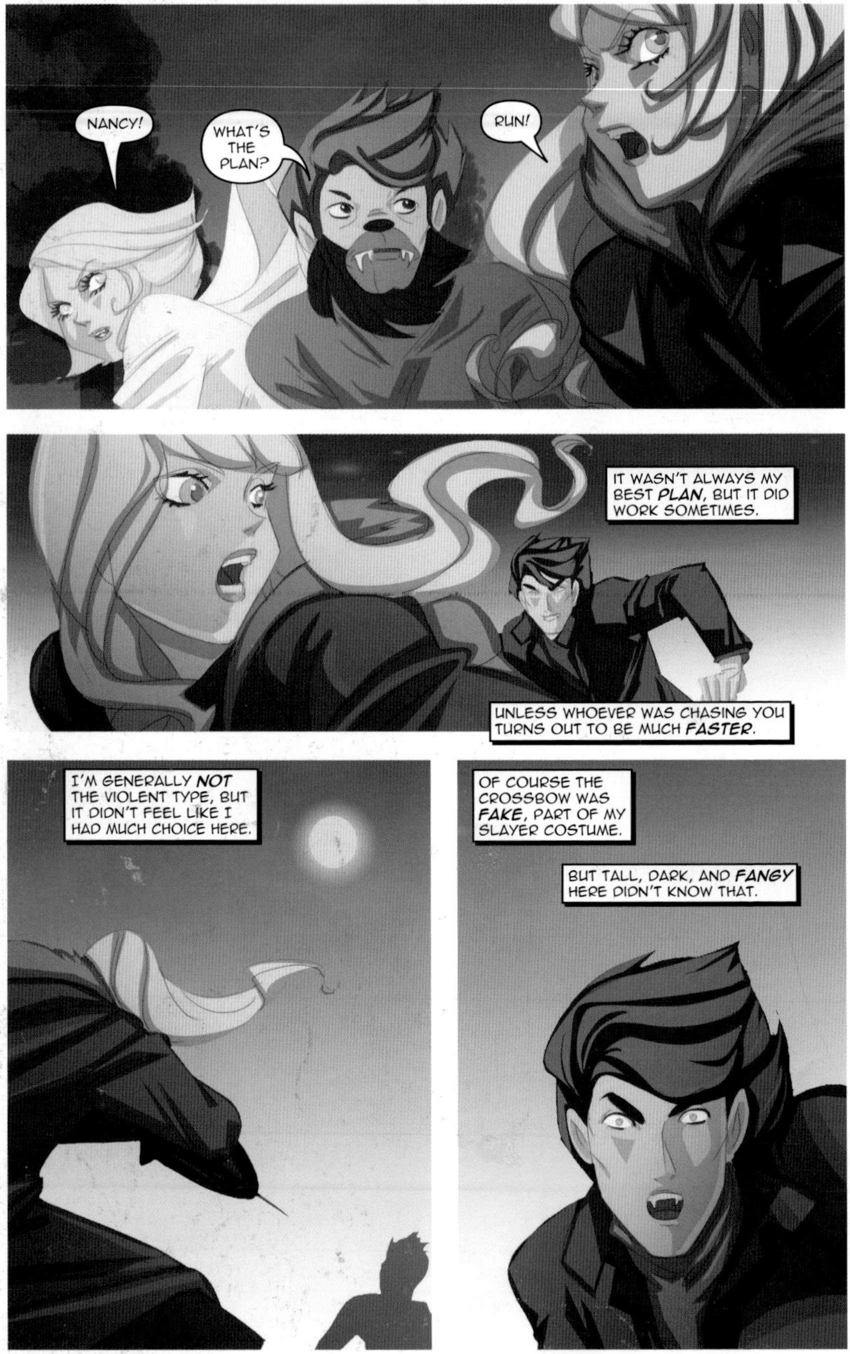

NANCY!
WHAT'S THE PLAN?
RUN!
IT WASN'T ALWAYS MY BEST PLAN, BUT IT DID WORK SOMETIMES.
UNLESS WHOEVER WAS CHASING YOU TURNS OUT TO BE MUCH FASTER.
I'M GENERALLY NOT THE VIOLENT TYPE, BUT IT DIDN'T FEEL LIKE I HAD MUCH CHOICE HERE.
OF COURSE THE CROSSBOW WAS FAKE, PART OF MY SLAYER COSTUME.
BUT TALL, DARK, AND FANGY HERE DIDN'T KNOW THAT.

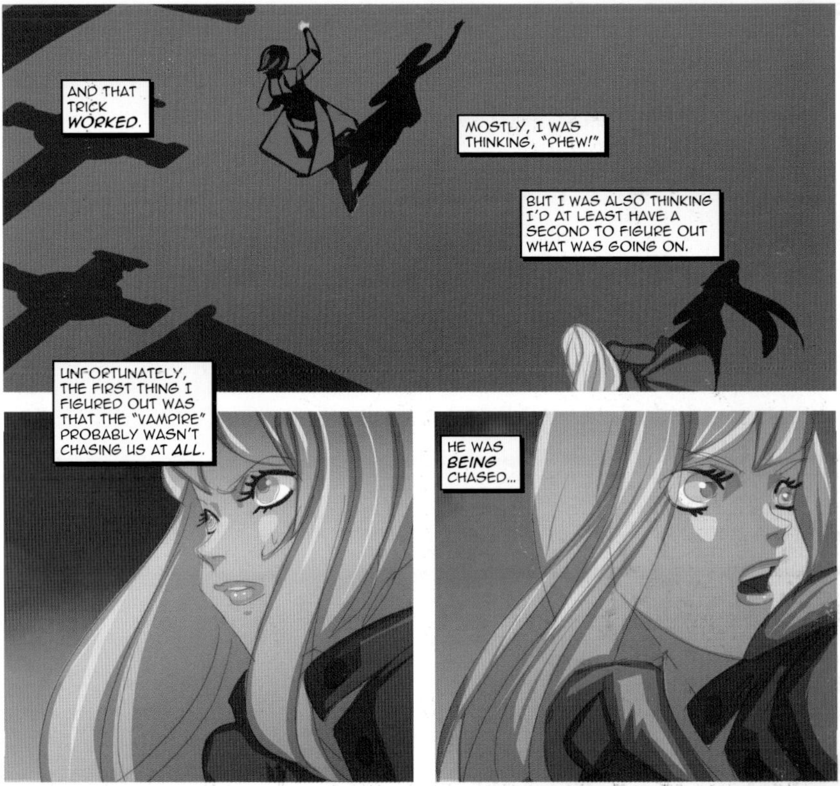
AND THAT TRICK *WORKED*.
MOSTLY, I WAS THINKING, "PHEW!"
BUT I WAS ALSO THINKING I'D AT LEAST HAVE A SECOND TO FIGURE OUT WHAT WAS GOING ON.
UNFORTUNATELY, THE FIRST THING I FIGURED OUT WAS THAT THE "VAMPIRE" PROBABLY WASN'T CHASING US AT *ALL*.
HE WAS *BEING* CHASED...

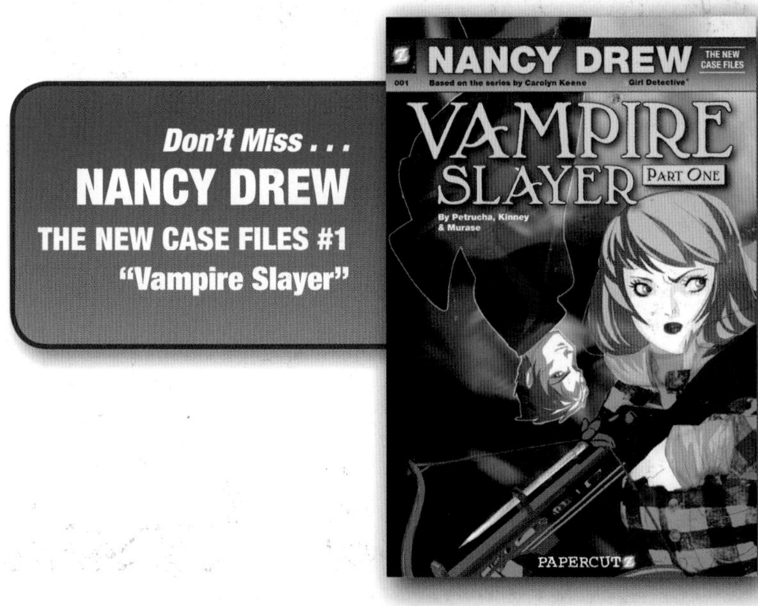
NANCY DREW
THE NEW CASE FILES
001
Based on the series by Carolyn Keene
Girl Detective
VAMPIRE SLAYER
PART ONE
By Petrucha, Kinney & Murase
PAPERCUTZ

Recover Royal Treasure on the Rails in Europe in

THE HARDY BOYS®
TREASURE ON THE TRACKS

NEARLY A CENTURY AGO, the Russian Royal Family attempted to flee from Russia with their treasure to avoid the impending Revolution, planning to return the following year by train. But the family disappeared, and no one can account for the missing Romanov treasure—until now. Journey on the Royal Express to track down the lost clues and secrets of the Royal Romanov Family in the great cities of Europe!

Order online at www.HerInteractive.com or call 1-800-461-8787. Also in stores!

EVERYONE
E
Mild Violence
ESRB CONTENT RATING   www.esrb.org

NINTENDO DS.

HeR INTERACTIVE   SEGA

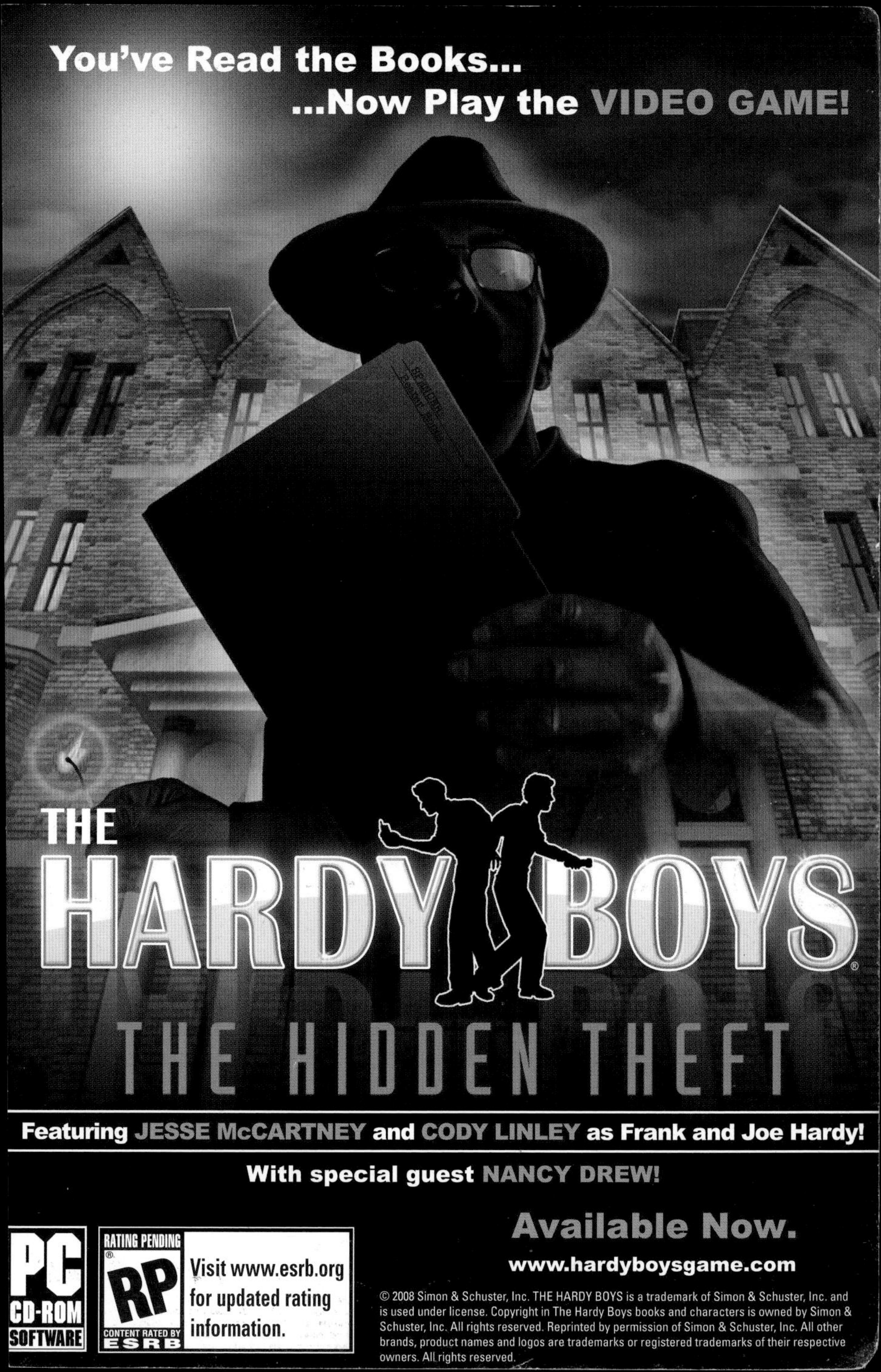

You've Read the Books...
...Now Play the VIDEO GAME!
THE
HARDY BOYS®
THE HIDDEN THEFT
Featuring JESSE McCARTNEY and CODY LINLEY as Frank and Joe Hardy!
With special guest NANCY DREW!
Available Now.
www.hardyboysgame.com
PC
CD-ROM
SOFTWARE
RATING PENDING
RP
CONTENT RATED BY
ESRB
Visit www.esrb.org for updated rating information.
© 2008 Simon & Schuster, Inc. THE HARDY BOYS is a trademark of Simon & Schuster, Inc. and is used under license. Copyright in The Hardy Boys books and characters is owned by Simon & Schuster, Inc. All rights reserved. Reprinted by permission of Simon & Schuster, Inc. All other brands, product names and logos are trademarks or registered trademarks of their respective owners. All rights reserved.

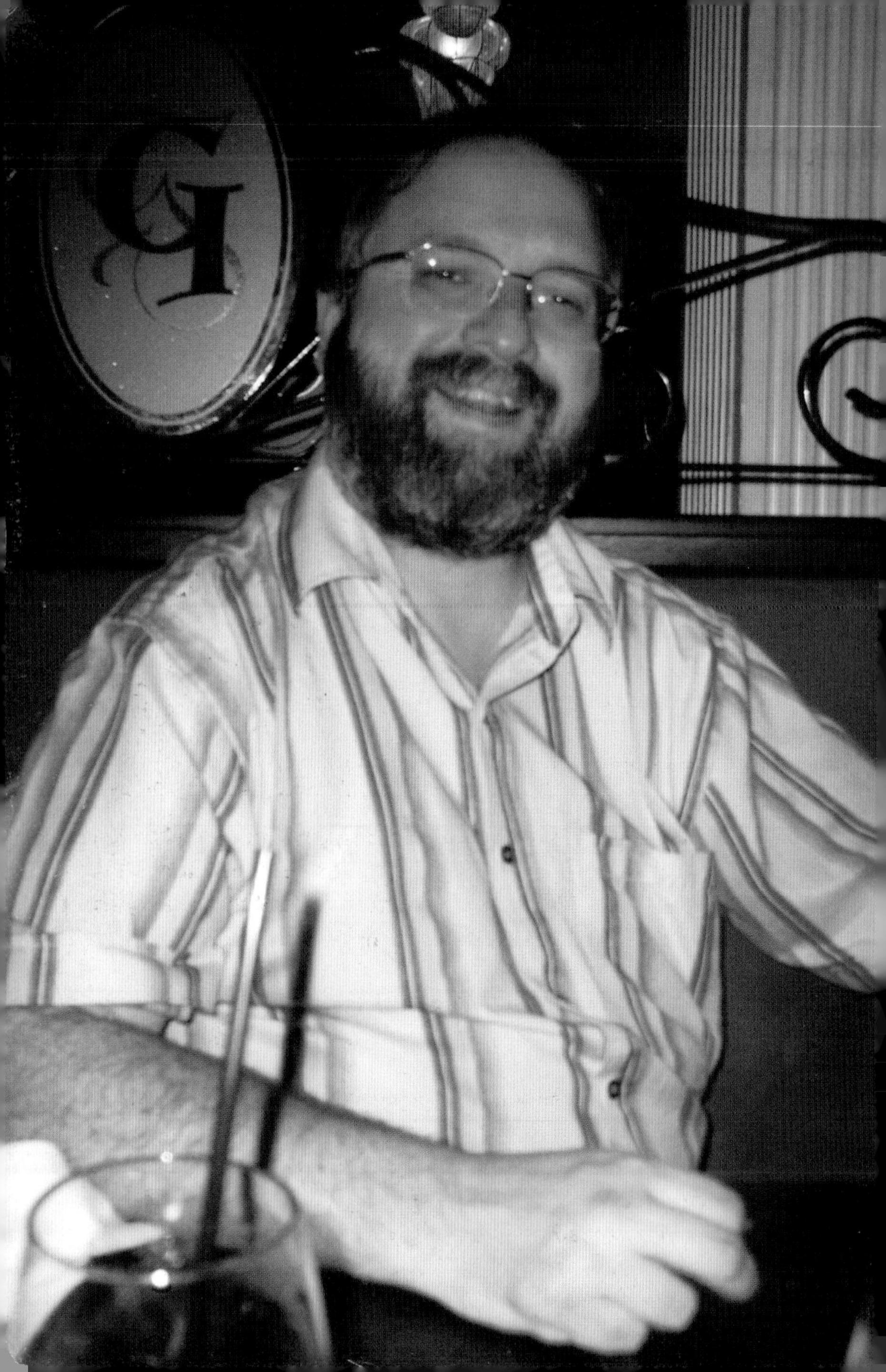

MEET BIONICLE ® GRAPHIC NOVELS WRITER
GREG FARSHTEY!

─── A **PAPERCUT** Profile ───

We emailed a bunch of questions to the brilliant brain behind the BIONICLE graphic novels, to better get to know this talented writer. Here are the fun-filled, insightful results…

PAPERCUTZ:
When and where were you born?

GREG FARSHTEY: I was born in 1965 in Mount Kisco, NY.

P: What were your favorite toys?

GREG: Mego action figures, and when I was older, LEGO bricks (LEGO bricks didn't come to the US until I was 9). I had a ton of action figures and used to make up stories with them that lasted for months

P: At what age did you start to read?

GREG: I was reading pretty young. I was reading

ALL-NEW! ALL-OUT AWESOME ACTION!
FULL-COLOR GRAPHIC NOVEL
BIONICLE
#8: LEGENDS OF BARA MAGNA
GREG FARSHTEY · CHRISTIAN ZANIER · STUART SAYGER
PAPERCUTZ   LEGO

BIONICLE is © 2010 The LEGO Group

Shakespeare for fun when I was in first grade, I remember. Plus I learned a lot of vocabulary from comicbooks.

P: What did you read when you were a young boy?

GREG: Comics, especially Batman, Encyclopedia Brown books. The Great Brain books, Sherlock Holmes, and history books.

P: When did you start to write?

GREG: I think the first writing I did was in fourth grade, but I didn't really get serious about it until high school.

P: Who were your favorite writers and artists?

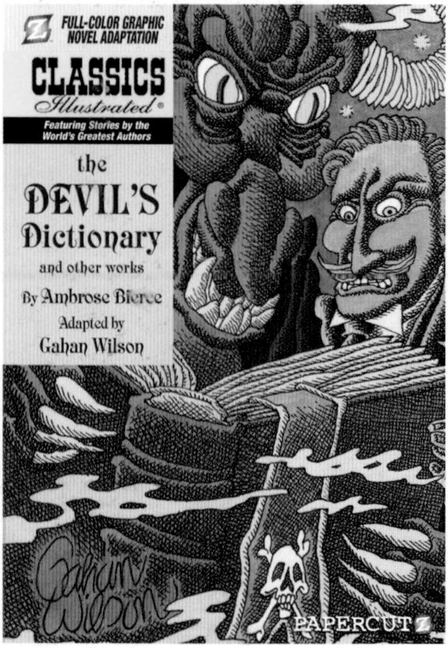
FULL-COLOR GRAPHIC NOVEL ADAPTATION
CLASSICS Illustrated
Featuring Stories by the World's Greatest Authors
the DEVIL'S Dictionary
and other works
By Ambrose Bierce
Adapted by Gahan Wilson
Gahan Wilson
PAPERCUTZ

GREG: My favorite writers are Ambrose Bierce, Jeffery Deaver, Raymond Chandler, and most recently, Christopher Fowler. I don't really have favorite artists, though I loved Gene Colan's comicbook work.

P: Did you take any special courses in school to become a writer?

GREG: No. I don't really believe you can teach someone to write. I think you can teach them to read, and to read things that will, in the long run, improve their writing. But I think a lot of writing is instinctive, you can do it or you can't.

P: What was your first published writing?

GREG: I self-published an underground paper in high school, and in college I had a short story published in a literary magazine. The first creative writing I was paid for was a humor column called Town Crier in the first paper I worked at.

P: How did you wind up working on BIONICLE?

GREG: I was hired at the LEGO Company in 2000 as the Club writer, to work on the LEGO Magazine. They were just getting ready to launch BIONICLE then. I knew they were going to do a comic, but figured I was too new to get to do it. I wrote a couple pages just for fun and showed them to my boss. Turned out they needed the first script right away, so I got the chance to do it.

P: Why was the BIONICLE concept ever called "The Bone-Heads of Voodoo Island"?

GREG: Well, I wasn't working on the BIONICLE line at that time, but I suspect that was a combination of placeholder name and code name. Toy and game companies often use code names for projects, just in case the competition gets wind of what you're doing before you release. I once worked on a very, very serious science fiction game whose code name was "Dogs in Space."

P: Did you know when you started writing the BIONICLE stories how sprawling an epic it would become?

GREG: Not really. When I first started working on BIONICLE, the story was largely being dictated to me and I was just adapting it to comics. It really wasn't until the novels started that the universe started to expand.

P: How do you write a BIONICLE story-- what are your working methods?

GREG: Basically, I write it like I do any other fiction -- I let the characters do the heavy lifting. If you create a character the right way, he/she/it becomes like a real person in some ways -- you know what they do and don't like, what they would and wouldn't do, the same way you know that about a friend. Then it becomes easy to know how they would react in a given situation, how they would get along with others or not get along, what would anger them or frighten them. The trick is to not force your character to do something he wouldn't normally do, because at that moment, it becomes impossible to predict his actions and your story grinds to a halt.

P: Which story, in any of the books, comics, or DVDs is your favorite?

GREG: BIONICLE Adventures 10: Time Trap. It's the "smallest" story I have written, in that it really only focuses on two characters, Makuta and

Vakama. It was also the story in which I rebooted Makuta and turned him from a super villain who always lost to a really complex character who sometimes ALLOWED himself to lose to throw off his opponents.

P: Do you have a favorite BIONICLE character?

GREG: Makuta Teridax and Kopaka. I also like a Dark Hunter named Lariska a lot and the Glatorian named Kiina.

P: Which is your favorite BIONICLE toy? And why?

GREG: I'm not sure I have a favorite set. I tend to like the bigger, more elaborate ones, like the Skopio, because I like longer builds.

P: Do you have a favorite experience meeting BIONICLE fans?

GREG: Yes. I met a young boy named Evan back in 2003, who was a huge BIONICLE fan and had Asperger syndrome. I became close friends with him and his family and we exchanged birthday gifts for years. I am still friends with his Mom and have gotten to see him grow up in photos.

P: What's the best way for BIONICLE fans to contact you?

GREG: Most BIONICLE fans send me questions through a website called BZPower.com, where I am on under the screen name GregF. So that is probably the easiest way to get in touch.

P: Thanks so much, Greg! And keep up the great work!

Special Preview of THE HARDY BOYS THE NEW CASE FILES #1 – "Crawling with Zombies"!

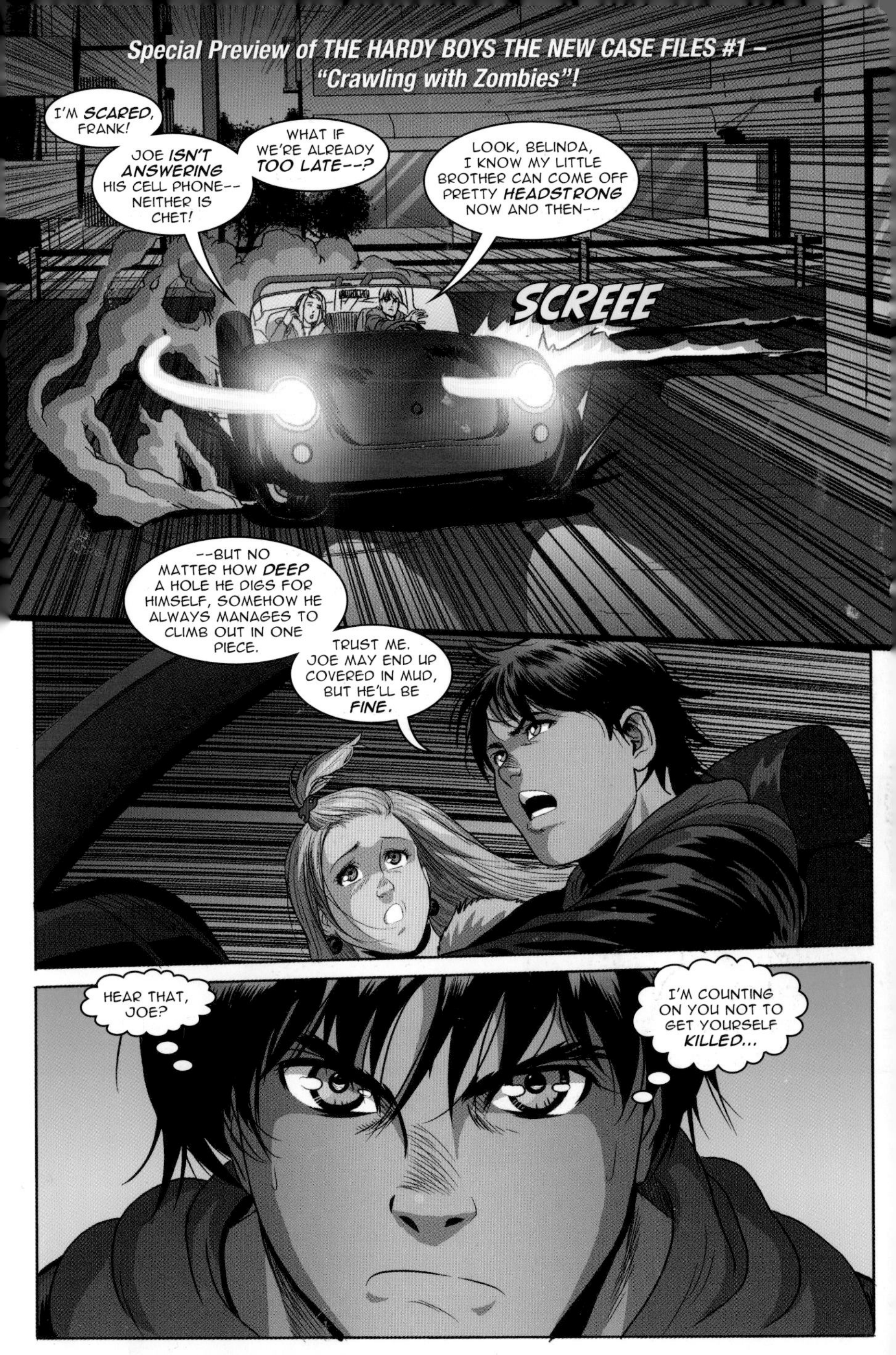
I'M SCARED, FRANK!
JOE ISN'T ANSWERING HIS CELL PHONE-- NEITHER IS CHET!
WHAT IF WE'RE ALREADY TOO LATE--?
LOOK, BELINDA, I KNOW MY LITTLE BROTHER CAN COME OFF PRETTY HEADSTRONG NOW AND THEN--
SCREEE
--BUT NO MATTER HOW DEEP A HOLE HE DIGS FOR HIMSELF, SOMEHOW HE ALWAYS MANAGES TO CLIMB OUT IN ONE PIECE.
TRUST ME. JOE MAY END UP COVERED IN MUD, BUT HE'LL BE FINE.
HEAR THAT, JOE?
I'M COUNTING ON YOU NOT TO GET YOURSELF KILLED...

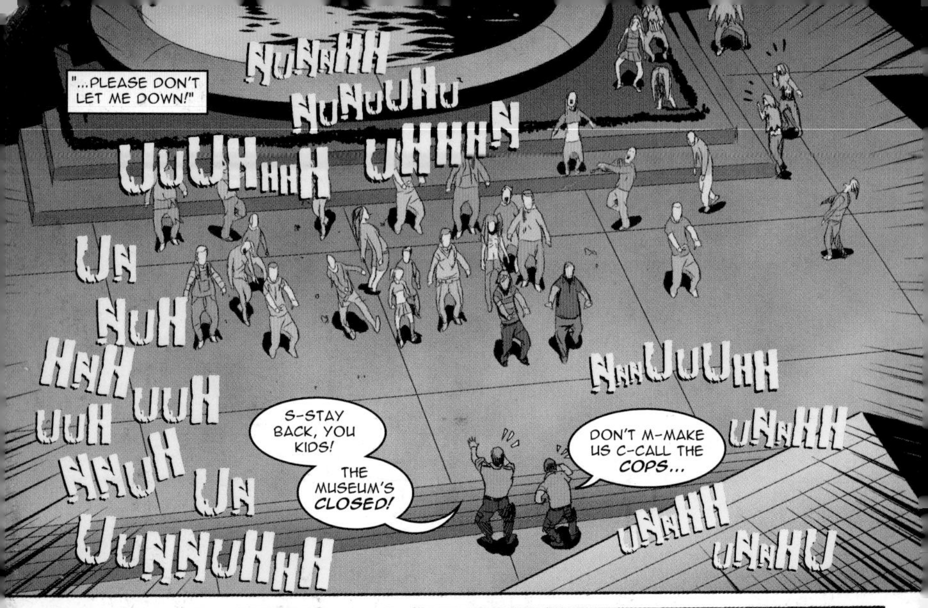
"...PLEASE DON'T LET ME DOWN!"
NUNAHH
NUNUUHU
UUUHHHH UHHHN
UN
NUH
HNH
UUH UUH
NNUH
UN
UUNNUHHH
NNNUUUHH
S-STAY BACK, YOU KIDS!
THE MUSEUM'S CLOSED!
DON'T M-MAKE US C-CALL THE COPS...
UNAHH
UNAHH
UNAHU

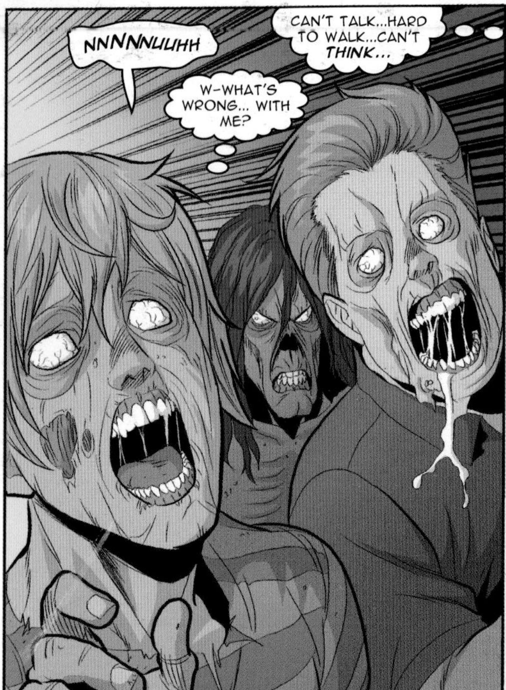
NNNNNUUHH
CAN'T TALK...HARD TO WALK...CAN'T THINK...
W-WHAT'S WRONG... WITH ME?

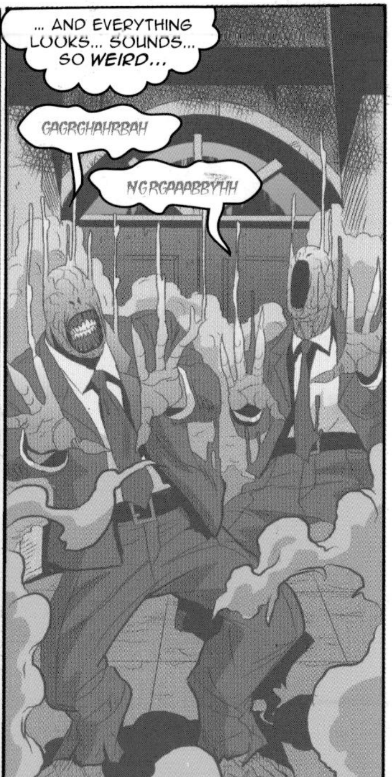
... AND EVERYTHING LOOKS... SOUNDS... SO WEIRD...
GAGRGHAHRBAH
NGRGAAABBYHH

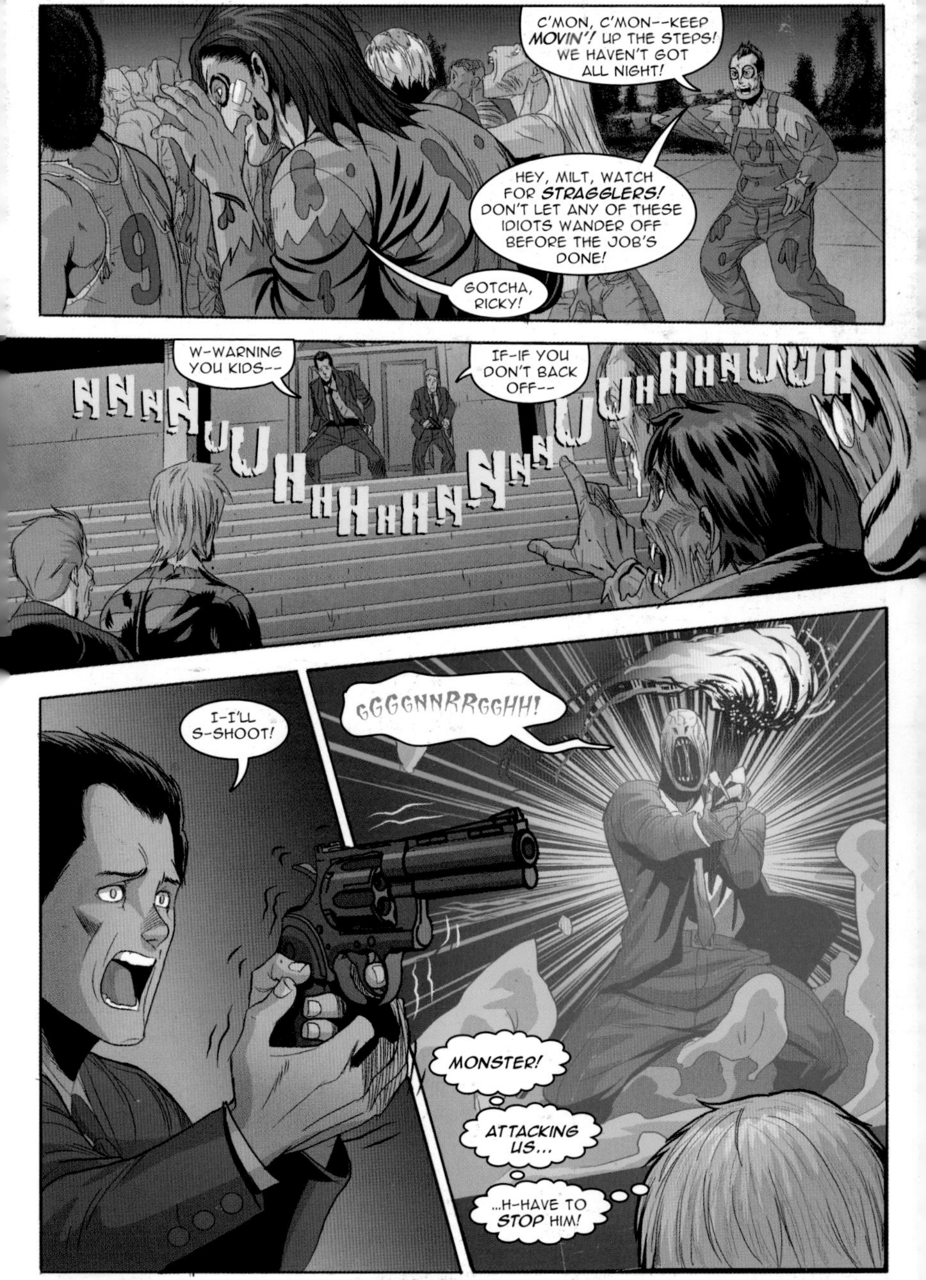
C'MON, C'MON--KEEP MOVIN'! UP THE STEPS! WE HAVEN'T GOT ALL NIGHT!
HEY, MILT, WATCH FOR STRAGGLERS! DON'T LET ANY OF THESE IDIOTS WANDER OFF BEFORE THE JOB'S DONE!
GOTCHA, RICKY!
W-WARNING YOU KIDS--
IF-IF YOU DON'T BACK OFF--
NNNNUUHHHHHNNNUUHHHUUH
I-I'LL S-SHOOT!
GGGGNNRRGGHH!
MONSTER!
ATTACKING US...
...H-HAVE TO STOP HIM!

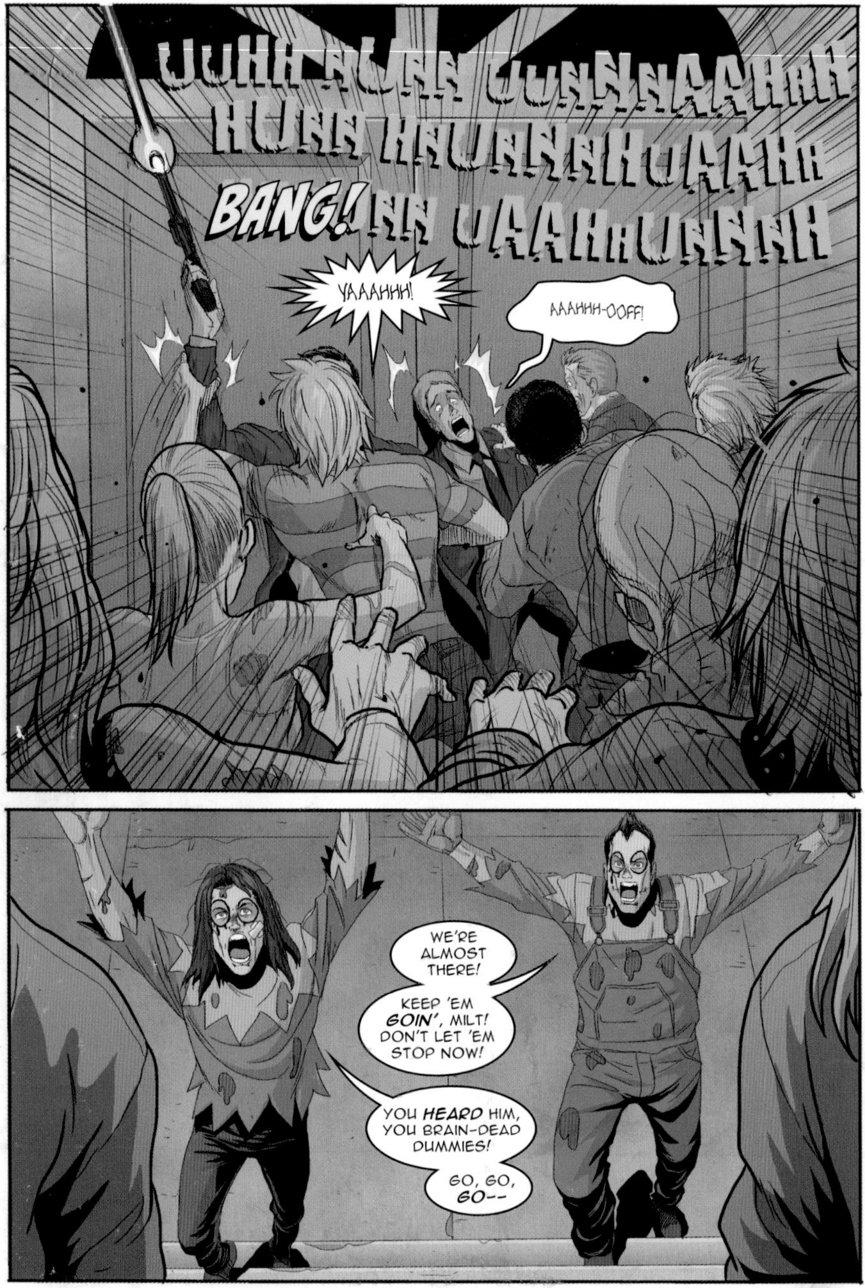
UUHH HUNN UUNNNAAAHHH
HUNN HHUNNNHUAAHHH
BANG!
NN UAAHHUNNNH
YAAAHHH!
AAAHHH-OOFF!
WE'RE ALMOST THERE!
KEEP 'EM GOIN', MILT! DON'T LET 'EM STOP NOW!
YOU HEARD HIM, YOU BRAIN-DEAD DUMMIES!
GO, GO, GO--

Don't Miss THE HARDY BOYS THE NEW CASE FILES #1 - "Crawling with Zombies"!